Endlessly Courted, Finally Loved

SCANDALOUS SEASONS
SS
THE SERIES

USA Today Bestseller

CHRISTI CALDWELL©

Endlessly Courted, Finally Loved

The Scandalous Seasons Series

For more information about the author:
www.christicaldwellauthor.com
christicaldwellauthor@gmail.com
Twitter: @ChristiCaldwell
Or on Facebook at: Christi Caldwell Author

For first glimpse at covers, excerpts, and free bonus material, be sure to sign up for my monthly newsletter!

Printed in the USA.

Cover Design and Interior Format
© The Killion Group, Inc.

OTHER TITLES BY
CHRISTI CALDWELL

ALL THE DUKE'S SINS

Along Came a Lady

Desperately Seeking a Duchess

ALL THE DUKE'S SIN'S PREQUEL SERIES

It Had to Be the Duke

One for My Baron

SCANDALOUS AFFAIRS

A Groom of Her Own

Taming of the Beast

My Fair Marchioness

It Happened One Winter

Loved and Found

HEART OF A DUKE

In Need of a Duke—Prequel Novella

For Love of the Duke

More than a Duke

The Love of a Rogue

Loved by a Duke

To Love a Lord

The Heart of a Scoundrel

To Wed His Christmas Lady

To Trust a Rogue

The Lure of a Rake

To Woo a Widow

To Redeem a Rake

One Winter with a Baron

To Enchant a Wicked Duke

Beguiled by a Baron

To Tempt a Scoundrel

To Hold a Lady's Secret
To Catch a Viscount
Defying the Duke
To Marry Her Marquess
The Devil and the Debutante
Devil by Daylight
My Heart Forever

THE HEART OF A SCANDAL

In Need of a Knight—Prequel Novella
Schooling the Duke
A Lady's Guide to a Gentleman's Heart
A Matchmaker for a Marquess
His Duchess for a Day
Five Days with a Duke

LORDS OF HONOR

Seduced by a Lady's Heart
Captivated by a Lady's Charm
Rescued by a Lady's Love
Tempted by a Lady's Smile
Courting Poppy Tidemore

SCANDALOUS SEASONS

Forever Betrothed, Never the Bride
Never Courted, Suddenly Wed
Always Proper, Suddenly Scandalous
Always a Rogue, Forever Her Love
A Marquess for Christmas
Once a Wallflower, at Last His Love
Endlessly Courted, Finally Loved
Once a Rake, Suddenly a Suitor
Once Upon a Betrothal

SINFUL BRIDES

The Rogue's Wager
The Scoundrel's Honor
The Lady's Guard
The Heiress's Deception

THE WICKED WALLFLOWERS

The Hellion
The Vixen
The Governess
The Bluestocking
The Spitfire

THE THEODOSIA SWORD

Only For His Lady
Only For Her Honor
Only For Their Love

DANBY

A Season of Hope
Winning a Lady's Heart

THE BRETHREN

The Spy Who Seduced Her
The Lady Who Loved Him
The Rogue Who Rescued Her
The Minx Who Met Her Match
The Spinster Who Saved a Scoundrel

LOST LORDS OF LONDON

In Bed with the Earl
In the Dark with the Duke
Undressed with the Marquess

BRETHREN OF THE LORDS

My Lady of Deception
Her Duke of Secrets

THE READ FAMILY SAGA

A Winter Wish

MEMOIR: NON-FICTION

Uninterrupted Joy

DANBY

A Season of Hope

Winning a Lady's Heart

THE BRETHREN

The Spy Who Seduced Her

The Lady Who Loved Him

The Rogue Who Rescued Her

The Minx Who Met Her Match

The Spinster Who Saved A Scoundrel

LOST LORDS OF LONDON

In Bed with the Earl

BRETHREN OF THE LORDS

My Lady of Deception

Her Duke of Secrets

REGENCY DUETS

Rogues Rush In: Tessa Dare and Christi Caldwell

Yuletide Wishes: Grace Burrowes and Christi Caldwell

Her Christmas Rogue

STANDALONE

Fighting for His Lady

MEMOIR: NON-FICTION

Uninterrupted Joy

PROLOGUE

My dearest Hamish,

For so long, I watched my family and those around me all find love and their lifelong partner; a person who is a friend, whom they could trust with their deepest secrets, their greatest hopes. I've secretly yearned for those gifts and wondered why I'm continually thrown over. Now, I know why. It was you. It was always you. I was waiting for you.

Come back to me.

With love and longing,
Beatrice

Summer, 1830
Scottish Highlands, Near Dunnottar Castle
Aberdeenshire coastline

EVERYONE KNEW THE ENGLISH DETESTED the Highlands—everything Scottish, really.

The lords and ladies of London flocked to London during the

Season, and retreated to their country seats when summer came, invariably steering clear of the Highlands. Even the landowning lords who held territories in that region of the kingdom went out of their way to avoid the still untamed lands.

That was, everyone *except* Lady Beatrice Dennington.

It was for all those very wonderful reasons, Beatrice loved visiting her family's ancestral seats there. Nay, not all of them.

At that very moment, Lady Beatrice Dennington picked her way along the craggy Scottish countryside. The quiet chittering of the Crested Tits filled the air. That passerine bird's song the only sound in the otherwise morning still.

Slightly out of breath from her long hike, Beatrice didn't slow her stride. As she made the now familiar march, she surveyed the Scottish moorland. The abundant heather now in full bloom lay like a magnificent blanket crafted of a dozen different shades of purple.

The glorious sights were ones she'd never not appreciate.

It was a land so wild and untamed, no doubt the reason puffed up pompous lords and ladies would never and could never appreciate the splendor of Scotland. At first, that was what had brought her here. Sadly, she too had failed to appreciate the majesty of the untamed lands. Before, she'd only come seeking a hiding spot away from it all—the London Seasons, the mocking looks, the pitying ones. The suitors…who weren't really serious suitors.

All of it.

Slowing her steps, Beatrice skimmed her gaze over the land around her, it was as if the Lord had painted a thousand different landscapes in just this one land. The steep hills and fields of heather gave way to winding, wildly overgrown paths that led higher up.

Beatrice eyed the long, narrow trail ahead.

A cool wind gusted; it howled a mournful wail as if warning her away, as it always did on her visits. Undeterred, as she'd been the thirteen other times she'd made the same climb, Beatrice drew her cloak closer.

After all, a lady would, and could, do anything for love.

Beatrice continued her slow march along an uneven stone path that had, some decades or so prior, been filled in and covered with overlong grass. The road grew more winding and narrower, until at last she reached it—the tunnel.

A sane person would have turned away before entering the darkened stone channel. Beatrice continued through. In an instant, the bright afternoon sun was swallowed whole by the stone walls.

She blinked several times, attempting to adjust her eyes to the sudden darkness.

The first time, she had been here, Beatrice had been caught in a deluge, with raging winds and sheets of rain and bolts of lightning, which had made the ghosts that surely haunted these lands a safer daily companion than the elements of the savage summer storm.

The tread of her boots striking the uneven rock flooring, reflected off the walls and returned as an echo. That illusion of footsteps joining hers having been one she'd not noted in her earliest visits—that eerie sense of being followed had nearly sent her running in terror.

Nearly.

The day's light illuminated the winding passage, and Beatrice's breath grew more even, as it invariably did when she'd finished the unnerving trek. Until, at last, she reached the arched end that led out into full sunlight. Bright, blinding light flooded her eyes. Squinting, Beatrice raised a hand and shielded herself from that glare.

Only when she'd grown accustomed to the bright day, once more, did she let her arm fall to her side. Her breath caught, as it always did at the sight.

She suspected a person could search all ends of the earth and never find a place as remote or a view more dramatic or majestic than the one before her.

The ancient keep sat perched upon a cliff, surrounded on three sides by the volatile North Sea. An air of ominousness hovered over the impressive castle that harkened back to ancient days when knights had sparred with swords for the right to possess lands and peoples. The ghosts here had surely driven out all living, breathing men.

It's what made this place so very perfect to her *and* for her.

Reaching inside her cloak pocket, Beatrice collected the neatly folded vellum.

"I'm here," she announced. The thundering sound of the waves striking the rocks below served as the only answering echo. "You're here, too," she called more loudly.

He always was.

She could rely on that constant.

His presence.

After all, loyal, loving sweethearts invariably were steadfast in their devotion. This man was no different.

With but one small, but very important distinction—her sweetheart was a fictitious fellow, crafted of nothing more than her own imagination.

Her lips twitched.

"I'll have you know," she said, as she approached the castle, "it is becoming increasingly difficult for me to steal away. I've begun to attract notice."

It'd been one thing when she'd declared to her brother and his wife, Helena, that she was merely off for a walk. It was quite another when those walks had become part of a daily routine, and often didn't see her return home until the sun had just begun to set.

At last, she reached the keep. "I'll also have you know, it is worth it. *You* are worth it," she corrected.

That familiar silence proved as always, her only answer.

Her mouth quirked in a wry grin. If the pitying people of London could see her now; here, talking to herself, and an invented suitor. But after twelve—*had it truly been twelve? It oftentimes felt like more*—London Seasons, a spinster who found herself in a constant state of courtship from gentlemen who invariably chose other ladies, did what a spinster must.

Beatrice smoothed her hand along the uneven rocks that made up the northernmost wall of the old castle. Until, her fingers collided with a familiar stone, some five or six inches wide.

With the same triumphant thrill she'd felt when she'd first discovered the clever concealment, Beatrice wiggled the rock free.

Bending down, she inspected the two dozen letters written there. They sat inside, undisturbed, in the same neat stack she'd left them yesterday, tied with the same pretty pink bow. Carefully setting aside the brick, she reached inside and removed her notes.

All twenty-two of them.

Sinking onto the earthen floor, Beatrice rested her back against the side of the castle keep, and as she settled herself on the ground, proceeded to sing.

"As I walk'd thro' the meadows
To take the fresh air,
The flowers were blooming and gay;
I heard a fair damsel so sweetly asinging
Her cheeks like the blossom in May..."

Humming the remainder of those lyrics, Beatrice tugged free that ribbon and added her latest—and now, last—note atop the pile.

She stared at the pile of written letters that had never been read and would *never* be read. Years ago, she would have been mournful, maybe even bitter at her existence as the lady gentleman constantly threw over in favor of other ladies. Approaching her thirtieth year, she'd very well come to accept her circumstances.

Beatrice frowned.

Nay, not *accept*. She'd learned to *embrace* her fate and future.

Certainly, she found herself in far better circumstances than most women: she'd a loving family who'd not require her to marry. She'd a fortune in a dowry, built by her brother and sister-in-law—funds which she would someday be free to use as she saw fit.

What more could she ask for?

Certainly not a husband whose only interest in Beatrice stemmed from the power and prestige that came from marrying a duke's sister. No, she was more than content with her life—she was elated. And now, she had something even more. Beatrice's lips curved upwards once more in a pleased smile. She'd a suitor to keep all other suitors away.

Resuming her earlier song, Beatrice tucked the notes back inside their resting place, and gathering up the oddly-shaped stone, she slid it back into place until the letters were once more, hidden.

It was done.

An ominous breeze stole over the castle ruins, the gust of wind producing a mournful wail that mingled with the distant slap of waves against the jagged sea rocks.

Gooseflesh sprung up along Beatrice's arms and her nape prickled.

She drew her cloak closer in a futile attempt to ward off the chill. This wasn't the first time she'd felt the presence of someone near. In the earliest days of her visit, she'd established an uneasy truce with the spirits who haunted the halls of the keep. She'd vowed not to enter their ancestral home. In return, she'd be permitted this one small corner of the outside castle wall to bury her secrets.

Suddenly, gravel and rock shifted.

Heart hammering, she plucked the dagger free from her leg and stormed to her feet.

Stealing a frantic gaze about, she pointed her blade at the air in front of her.

"Who is there?" she demanded, her breath stirring a little cloud of white.

Her question echoed around the empty grounds.

Then, from the tunnel, a tall figure emerged in the distance.

Terror gripped her, and she took a reflexive step back. As for the first time, she acknowledged the folly in having set out by herself, without the protection of a servant or *anyone*. Her previous promise to the ghosts here forgotten, Beatrice turned on her heels and bolted toward the castle door.

"Halt," that booming voice filled the air, briefly staying her.

A *familiar* booming voice.

And for a long moment, she considered pretending she'd not heard him, disappearing inside the castle walls, and staying there until he left. Even as she knew he wouldn't leave.

Alas, she was many things. A coward, however, was not one of them.

Tamping down a sound of frustration, Beatrice plastered a smile on, turned, and faced the worst possible person to find her here. Robert, the Duke of Somerset.

Also, her big, overprotective brother. Her big, overprotective brother who wore a furious scowl and marched purposefully toward her.

Splendid. Just splendid.

The moment he grew nearer, she headed him off. "Robert!" she called gaily. "How lovely to see you."

His expression dark, he ignored that warm welcome, and even as he spoke, he swept his gaze purposefully about. "What are you doing here?"

Beatrice tilted her lips up in a deliberately wry smile. "Why, it is splendid to see you, too."

At last, he turned a look on her. "Beatrice," he said warningly.

She stared at him with wide, innocent, slow-blinking eyes. "Yes?"

Folding his arms at his chest, Robert frowned. "This is where you've been sneaking off to these past weeks."

His wasn't a question, and Beatrice didn't treat it as such.

"*Sneaking* implies I'm a child, Robert," she said with an amazing amount of patience for her brother's insolent statement. "Lest I remind you, I'm a grown woman not much younger than you were when you married."

Color flooded his cheeks, and she relished having knocked him off balance. "It's different," he groused.

"Yes, it is," she calmly explained, "because we live in a patriarchal society, where men decide upon the rules, and what is fit or unfit for a woman."

He grunted—but did not argue. The tension left his shoulders.

"What are you doing here?" he asked, this time his words were framed in the form of a question and not so much a demand.

Of course, the question had been coming.

"Visiting."

When it became apparent she'd no intention of elucidating, his blond brows flew together. "Visiting *whom*?"

She opened her mouth to disabuse him of that assumption he'd reached and then stopped herself. He assumed she'd come here to meet *someone*. Well, *this* could certainly prove useful.

"*Beatrice*," he prodded, stretching her name a whole extra syllable.

"The…castle, of course."

The suspicion in his eyes deepened.

"It is magnificent here, is it not?" she said. It was the first truth she'd uttered to her overbearing if well-meaning brother.

Robert cast a dubious glance at the place around them. "I'd have opted for cold and dark and lonely."

"Yes, well, you would. I quite adore the untamed feel of it." Nor was her defense of this old castle feigned. She had come to love this land and would miss it when they left, and she'd continue longing for it until they returned.

"Bea…"

Here came the lecture.

"It is not safe for you to come here alone. In the future, I want you escorted by your maid and a groom."

"A groom?" she drawled, knowing precisely what he alluded to.

"One of the men from the Hell and Sin."

The club owned by his wife and her family only employed some of the most ruthless, but also loyal, lot of men.

"A guard, Robert," she said dryly. "Call it what it is. You want me with a guard."

"A guard," he said, blunt and unapologetic in that clarification.

Beatrice lifted her jewel-studded dagger. "I am properly armed."

"And could be properly disarmed were you to run across the wrong sort," he said, and even as he spoke, he again skimmed his gaze over their surroundings.

She opened her mouth to protest.

"It is done, Beatrice." He spoke with a finality only a duke could manage. His words a warning that hinted at the fact he'd already decided the matter was settled in his mind.

Because to him and to most, she was still nothing more than a younger sister, in need of the same looking after that she had as a girl. She'd never be seen as anything more, and that reality sent a familiar frustration roiling through her.

"Bea?" he urged. "If you cannot promise you'll—"

"What? Behave?" she snapped, cutting him off. "We're leaving at the end of the week. I hardly think you need to assign a team of guards to look after me."

Muttering to herself, Beatrice sheathed her dagger, then yanked her skirts back into place. When she straightened, Robert caught her lightly by the shoulder. She glared up at him.

"I didn't say it would be a team. Just...one will do," he said.

Beatrice narrowed her eyes. "Is that an attempt at a jest?"

"No good?"

"Not even close," she said under her breath.

"Bea," he said quietly, in softer tones. "I merely wish to see you safe and happy."

"I am perfectly safe."

He was suffocating her. All of them. Her brother. *Society*. Each day she found herself amongst members of the peerage, a pressure threatened to swallow her whole, and there were more times she wished it would so that she didn't have to contend with the empty, repetitive lot of a lady to be courted. Over and over and over and—

"Happy," Robert said quietly.

Beatrice looked quizzically at him.

"I said I want you to be safe *and* happy."

"I am," she said belatedly. And she was.

Somber eyes met hers. "Are you?"

"How can I not be? I have everything I want or need," she continued, finding her voice enough to cut off any further probing from her well-meaning brother.

In the end, she was saved, by the sudden ping of errant raindrops.

"Come," her brother urged, gesturing her ahead. "I wager a storm is coming."

Grateful he'd let both matters rest, she didn't fight him. Beatrice joined her brother, beginning the march toward the tunnel.

She'd not lied to her brother. Beatrice had *everything* she needed. And that now included a devoted sweetheart—one to keep all other potential suitors at bay. Another slow smile formed on her lips.

It wasn't until after they'd gone, that a figure emerged from the castle, headed to that loose stone, and extracted the notes from their previous hiding space.

CHAPTER 1

Dearest Hamish,

I have waited my entire life for you. I long for the day you declare yourself and make me your bride, so that we can live side by side, together, forever, without ever being parted.

With Love and Longing,
Beatrice

Fall, 1830
Scottish Highlands, Near Dunnottar Castle
Aberdeenshire coastline

SEATED ASTRIDE HIS ENORMOUS BLACK mount, and with Broden Burgess, his only friend in the world at his side, Hamish Brewster, the 12th Great Marischal of Scotland, surveyed the land holdings.

Nothing had changed. And yet, at the same time, everything had. The now empty keep still stood, as it had for centuries prior, with the same vast and turbulent waters of the North Sea battering against the jagged cliffs below.

His late da had oft spoken to Hamish of the significance of the name he'd been given—supplanter. As Scots, their people knew too much about brutal English kings who'd come, pillaged, and laid claim to these very lands he now surveyed.

The 11th Great Marischal had instilled in each of his sons that they'd a responsibility to care for and never take from those who dwelled on their lands. The irony of this moment was not lost on Hamish. This once great land of the noble Campbell family whose hereditary hold of that distinguished title extended all the way back to Malcom IV and William I, with King Robert the Bruce himself cementing that ancestral office, had now been taken from him.

Through Hamish's long evaluation, Burgess remained silent. They both did. Years of hard labor, and beatings bestowed for even the slightest infraction like talking made a man quiet quick and kept him that way.

Hamish swung a leg over the side of his midnight horse and dismounted. Burgess followed in rapid succession.

Absently petting the horse who'd ridden hard to get here, Hamish continued his study, more than half-expecting Ma, Da and his brother, Finlay, to come racing out, arms outstretched, welcoming Hamish back from his long stay away. Even as he knew the impossibility of those imaginings. His mother had died many years earlier, back when Hamish had been but a boy. And his da and brother…

While in prison, Hamish hadn't allowed himself to think about that day of the Radical Rebellion and the ones that followed. To do so would have left Hamish weak, and certain to succumb to the miserable conditions and hardships thrust upon him, and he'd been hell-bent on returning to the beloved lands of his ancestors. Nay, he'd shut out every last thought, keeping the memories buried in the name of survival.

Until now.

Now, with solid, Scottish land under his feet, and his oppressors an ocean away, Hamish squeezed his eyes shut. For the first time since he'd been imprisoned and forced aboard a penal ship to that always-hot colony of Australia, he allowed the memories in.

The well opened, and each agonizing thought swelled to the surface and exploded forth…along with the crushing weight of grief…and loss. Hamish let it all in, the terror as armed soldiers stormed their family's household, thundering his da's and Finlay's names in those crisp, cool tones every true Scott hated by birthright. His father's fury and shock and then panic as they'd carted him and Finlay off, to be tried with false charges of high treason. The hasty trial which had been decided from the start.

Then, the hanging…and…

Hamish's breath grew shallower, and this memory he fought back. This one, that he avoided in daylight, but when sleep had claimed him, always slipped in—haunting him.

He wrenched his eyes open. The resolute castle stared back. The angry wail of the wind, however, proved a welcome companion. Rage had sustained him. It had kept him from crumbling.

"They've all gone," Burgess remarked.

"Not all of them," Hamish said, his voice rough, low, and ragged from years of ill-use. "There are ghosts here." Ones of old…and now the more recent Campbells had since joined them.

To Burgess's credit, he displayed no outward reaction to Hamish's visible suffering. His heavily bearded face and his hooded eyes concealed any emotion he might be feeling. Even so, he paid Hamish the same respect Hamish gave when Burgess looked down at the crooked headstone of his late sweetheart's grave.

"Come," Hamish urged.

Clicking his tongue, he collected the reins of his horse, and he and Burgess fell into step, leading their mounts onward to the stables, ones which were no doubt in as equal disrepair as the rest of this abandoned land.

They reached the courtyard, and Hamish's steps slowed to a stop. Burgess came to rest his mount beside him.

For all the disrepair of his family's estate, the solidly brick-built stables gleamed as red as the day they'd been put into place by their mason and brother to Hamish's father, Angus. Unlike the overgrown grounds leading into the castle, the ones here appeared a still image from Hamish's childhood. But then, this had been his father's great joy…the construction of new stables by his loyal mason, Angus Galbraith…and through his noble construction, Ole Angus had displayed the same pride of the castle owner himself.

Wordlessly, he and Burgess, side by side, made their way through the passage that provided access to the keep and stables. The space, only slightly dimmer than the grey of the late autumn day, had once bustled with grooms and stableboys and holsters and a farrier. Now, but for the occasional whinny of his and Burgess's mounts, a like silence filled this space, too.

A loud, nervous neigh went up from the back of the stables.

Hamish stiffened, his shoulders tensing, as he and Burgess looked toward that stall. Hitching their mounts to a nearby post, they made their way slowly and soundlessly to the back of the stables… and stopped.

A gleaming chestnut mare stamped her foot nervously. Burgess stretched out a hand and stroked her withers until she'd quieted. Both men exchanged a like-look.

Someone was here.

Hamish did a swift sweep of the room. The fodder was stored in the haylofts above the stalls and living quarters. Sliding the knife he'd secured on his escape from Australia free of its place in his boot, with Burgess following suit, they made their way stealthily to the living quarters once inhabited by a good many men and boys.

Now empty, the space, however, proved cozy and clean.

Hamish entered the room, looking quickly behind the door for the potential threat lurking there.

Empty.

All the beds were neatly made, with warm-looking wool blankets pulled tightly upon them. Plain white porcelain wash basins and chamber pots rested in their respective places. But for the errant cracks and chips within some of the pieces, they may as well have been as they were all those years ago. Hooks hung upon the walls where caps had once rested.

Only one tam o'shanter remained.

His gaze locked on that small, plaid article, its bright indigo and blue hues long since faded. Hamish drifted over to the familiar flat bonnet. His knife still in one hand, with his other, Hamish touched the felted piece, and the small woolen ball at the center.

His hat.

Perhaps, he'd died after all, and his soul had been set free. Perhaps, his ghost had hung its hat upon this very hook to claim a place with his family, once more.

Footfalls echoed from the passage leading into the stables. Instantly, Hamish dropped the hand touching that beloved hat.

As one, he and Burgess tensed. In one fluid motion, turned, and pointed their daggers at the giant, orange-haired figure filling the doorway. The old man's cheeks were sunken. His eyes slightly rheumy. But even age could not erase the familiarity of that craggy face. He stood there, his arms filled with an enormous sack.

Fear filled the old man's eyes. "Yer a ghost," he whispered.

Ole Angus—his da's younger and only brother and best friend. Also, Hamish's godfather, the big man had been like a second father to Hamish and Finlay. Another powerful swell of emotion crested within him, and had he been a man capable of tears or feeling anything really, in this moment, he would have been moved to them.

"Do ghosts talk?" Hamish asked, and that emotion pulled out more of the brogue which had become buried in his years away amidst foreign people in a foreign land.

The item slid from those always capable, strong, and now heavily wrinkled hands, hitting the floor with a big thump. The wild-eyed, wild-haired old man closed his eyes. "Jaysus, ye've returned."

Hamish managed a nod. "Aye, Angus. Ah'm home." Only, a home is what he'd left when his kin still dwelled within the keep.

"It canna be. It canna," the mason whispered that litany over and over. As he spoke, Angus's eyes filled with a fear belonging to a man who'd seen a ghost.

And in this, his da's brother was not wrong. Hamish was a ghost of who he'd once been.

"Aye, it is, Angus. Ah am here." Back for revenge on those who'd betrayed him and his family.

Angus sobbed and caught that sound with a wrinkled fist. "Ah never thought to see you again," he said through that emotion.

Through the exchange, Burgess remained silent.

Hamish had sustained himself these years with the thoughts of returning to his family and his homeland. And yet, in this moment, with Angus freely crying, Hamish silently acknowledged the truth—he'd not truly believed he'd make it back from the world away he'd been shipped to.

As if only just noting Hamish's silent companion, Angus looked over at Burgess. A wary expression settled over Angus's heavily wrinkled face.

"Who is this?" he asked with the same bluntness he always had, and for a moment, it felt so very normal…things being the way they'd once been.

"I'm a friend," Burgess said quietly.

At hearing those crisp English tones, Angus's thick, bushy brows snapped together. A frown formed on his mouth.

"He *is* a friend." Hamish spoke quietly, assuring his godfather.

That did little to ease the suspicion in the old man's eyes. An ancestral hatred for a people would have that effect upon a man.

"Where is my mother?" Hamish asked.

Angus's gaze grew stricken.

All the muscles in Hamish's body seized…as his uncle's look confirmed what words didn't even need to.

"Dinna survive, she did." Pain and regret leant an added layer to Angus's already thick brogue. "Died of a broken heart shortly after you…left."

Hamish looked away, composing himself. Even as he'd known as much in his heart and anticipated that obvious fate to befall his mother when he'd been gone, hearing Angus speak it aloud, leant a finality and realness to his ma's passing that hadn't been there until this very moment.

For, if he were finally being honest with himself, this moment, he'd secretly imagined his ma would still be here, and when Hamish had found the castle had gone dark and the grounds still, he'd carried a hope, and thought that the anguish of being with the memories here had driven his mother away to someplace else where the pain was less.

"When?" he asked, his voice thick to his own ears.

"Died just six months after you left, she did."

Left. Funny how his uncle continued to use that choice of phrase. It suggested that Hamish's leaving had been a decision.

"After ah was wrongly imprisoned and carted off, in chains for crimes ah dinnea commit," Hamish said coolly.

Angus blanched and then gave a shaky nod. "Aye. Aye. After… that."

Hamish forced himself to release the rage in him that now came so easily. His godfather didn't deserve that anger directed his way.

Wind knocked against the stable walls, battering at the roof.

"Ah'd see my family's home," Hamish said.

Angus grunted. "Ain't nothing to see in there. Come, have a seat here, and ah'll prepare a meal for you."

Hamish flexed his jaw. "Ah'd take my first meal back on Scottish soil in the keep."

He turned, and headed for the keep, with Burgess falling easily into step at his side, and Angus shuffling along at a slower pace behind them.

A short while later, they reached the inside foyer and made their way in silence through the barren stone halls. Much the way he'd done when first thrown into the hull of a prison boat, Hamish's eyes struggled to adjust to the darkened space.

As he walked, Hamish took it all in. At some point, the family tartans and embroideries that had once adorned the stone walls had been stripped away. Likewise, the parlors and drawing rooms had been emptied of their furnishings. All the crystal and porcelain were gone.

Someone had looted the place. His ancestral home, it'd belonged to the Campbell family since the 15th century, when the first Great Marischals had fortified the castle, turning it into an impenetrable keep. In 1652, this household had been the only place in Scotland to still fly the royal flag, and yet, given that magnificent, proud history, this is what it'd become.

At last, they reached the kitchens.

Hamish did a slow turn about the room. He absently touched the bowls and pans and forks that rested upon the long wood table. It was as if the last people to dine here had dropped it in haste.

"What happened?" he quietly asked.

Old Angus paused and looked to Burgess—his meaning clear. That suspicion for an Englishmen was as part of a Scot's body as the blood pumping in his veins.

"You can speak freely with him," Hamish assured his godfather.

Angus hesitated a moment more. "Not soon after you'd gone, the British, they…came…"

An ominous darkness descended over the room.

Hamish narrowed his eyes. "What did they do?"

The knob in his godfather's throat jumped several times. "British troops, they took it over. Invaded it and set up a garrison."

Hatred, shock, and fury converged, as all that emotion coursed through.

"Tossed your ma out. She didn't have the will to fight." A sheen of tears glossed the older man's eyes. "A broken heart is what everyone said," he said, thickly. "Losing you and your brother and father was too much. And then her home…"

Aye, it would have been. Maeve Campbell's boys had been her world. She'd have grieved terribly at losing not just one, but all? His jaw tensed reflexively, sending a welcome pain shooting along the bone. It hadn't been enough that they'd killed the laird, heir, and imprisoned his youngest son, they'd taken his family's holding, too?

The thought of revenge had sustained Hamish. The idea of finding out exactly who it had been that betrayed Hamish and his brother gave him renewed life, and purpose, and he feasted upon just the promise of it.

His stomach rumbled.

"Come," Angus said gruffly. "Ah've got some food for ye and the other lad. Let us sit 'n' we can talk more."

Reluctantly, he took a place at the long oak table, with Burgess sliding onto the opposite bench.

His uncle Angus proceeded to fetch a pair of plates and set them down before Hamish and Burgess. Then, dipping into his big sack, his godfather withdrew two loaves of bread, and gave one to each man, along with an apple and pear. Hamish and Burgess hesitated a moment, and then without ceremony, they devoured the modest feast Angus had supplied.

How long it had been since they'd been able to eat freely without fear of having to fight another prisoner for rations? At that, meals which had consisted of a crusty slice of weevil-filled bread and porridge.

Now, Hamish bit into the crimson apple and at last understood why Adam had sinned in the name of a mere piece of fruit. When his initial hunger pains had been sated, Hamish ate more leisurely of his loaf.

"You remained," Hamish remarked after he'd swallowed another bite. "You always were loyal to this family. On behalf of my father, brother, and ah… thank you."

Color splotched the gruffy Scot's cheeks and he waved a hand the way a bashful lad might. "Go on with ye now. Dinnae need any gratitude. Certainly not from ye, lad."

How bold and proud all Scots were. But then, that part of the Scottish spirit had also been that which sustained Hamish these years.

Still, as discomfited as the old man may be, Hamish and his family owed him a debt of gratitude.

"It doesn't escape me that this place isn't in disrepair, Angus," he said solemnly. "And that it's been well-tended is a testament of you."

Unnerved by that praise, Hamish's godfather glanced down at his big feet. "Don't deserve that," he whispered, tears thick in his voice. "If ah'd truly been great, this place would not have been run over."

Hamish scoffed. "Do you believe you, one man alone, could fend off the advances of an entire British army?"

Angus grunted. "Ah couldn've done more than ah did." The old man's brogue had grown so thick anyone else would have struggled to make sense of those syllables.

As he and Burgess continued eating in the familiar and comfortable between them silence they'd grown accustomed to over the years, Angus reached inside his sack. He withdrew a thick stack of notes and then set it down beside Hamish's plate.

Swiping a hand across the back of his mouth, Hamish reached for the pile, tied in a pretty pink bow. An ever-so-faint hint of lavender clung to the notes.

"What are these?"

"Not long ago, a bonnie blonde lass would pay daily visits." Angus nodded at the envelopes. "She'd leave those and cover them with a loose brick."

Frowning, Hamish loosened the ribbon and tossed it aside. He proceeded to sift through the pile; each envelope bore a matching elegant scrawl.

Setting aside the stack, he unfolded one of the notes, and read.

> *Dearest Hamish,*
>
> *I wander these beautiful, untamed lands of the Highlands. In my head, I will forever see you here. I will forever see us, here. Laughing at sunrise. Sprinting in summer through the craggly hills, frolicking like dolphins—*

Frolicking like dolphins?

Hamish looked up at Angus. "What the hell are these?"

Angus shrugged. "The bonnie lass left them. At first, ah thought she was cracked in the head, talking to herself she did as if someone lived here."

With Burgess looking on, Hamish proceeded to sift through the notes once more.

"Never took anything, she did."

"Because there's nothing left to take," Hamish muttered, opening another note, and skimming his gaze over the page. This one, even more theatric, and over the top than the one before it.

Angus shifted on the bench. "Here's the interesting thing,"

"And here I thought a pretty blonde woman hiding notes in the keep would have been the interesting thing," Burgess drawled.

"The last time she came," Angus said, ignoring the other man completely, "another fellow arrived, he did. They were trussed up all fancy, they were."

"The dear heart, Hamish," Hamish surmised.

Angus shook his head, his overgrown orange-red hair fell over his face, giving him the look of a big lion. "This is where it gets more curious..." he murmured, leaning in the way all old Scots did to shore up the most interest in whatever tale they spun. "He wasn't. He was curious about her being here, too. Told her he didn't want her riding out anymore without an escort."

"There's nothing curious about that." Clever was what it was. Every man, lass, and bairn born to the Highlands knew in these untamed lands, one should never set out alone—unless they were prepared to meet the danger that dwelled in these ancient lands.

"The man was likely a brother," Burgess ventured.

"Or, *more* likely a husband who went spying on his unfaithful wife," Hamish muttered.

Burgess pointed at Hamish. "My purse would be on that one."

"The pair of them are new neighbors—Sassenachs ones. But the gadgie, well, he wasn't the lass's husband." Angus sat up a little straighter, smug as only a Scot could be at being the first to spawn a never before heard yarn. "Did a wee bit of research, ah did."

Burgess trained his attention on the old man.

Hamish, however, grunted. "Ah'd not fought my way from a life sentence, on the other side of the globe, to come back and care about any bluidy gossip about a pair of Sassenachs who laid claim to land that isna theirs." Such was a tale as old as Scottish time.

"The gadgie is an English duke, and the lass, in fact, his sister. And from what ah gathered in speaking to the villagers who spoke to the Sassenach's servants, there's been no sweetheart."

"So she's an eejit." All the English were. This one was just more so.

"Ach, but there's a history that follows the lass," Angus went on, undeterred by Hamish's disinterest in his telling. "She's cursed, she is. They refer to her as the one who'll never wed."

"Why?" Burgess asked and continuing to put in enough interest for both he and Hamish to keep the old Scot's yarn going, his Sassenach friend helped himself to the forgotten notes and began to read.

Old Angus shrugged his enormous shoulders; his already heavily-wrinkled brow, furrowed further. "Ah…dinna ken."

"It doesna matter," Hamish said, rubbing at the back of his sore neck muscles. "Ah've na interest or use in another man's gossip."

"Actually, this one you might…" Burgess said, studying the page in his hand.

Hamish sharpened his gaze on his friend.

Wordlessly, the other man turned it over.

Dearest Hamish,

This will be the last letter I write. As much as I feel utterly silly having invented you and writing daily letters, to a man who doesn't exist, I'm grateful for your invention…

Hamish swiftly read the remainder of the letter. So, the lass had invented an imaginary beau. That wasn't information that benefitted him in any—

He stilled. Only, the woman wasn't just any lass—she was the sister of a powerful English duke, and a powerful duke would be in possession of connections and information that ordinary sorts couldn't otherwise come across—ordinary sorts like a convicted Scot's whose family had been declared traitors, and then he, shipped overseas to a penal colony.

Burgess slowly grinned and nodded his head.

With a big frown, Angus looked back and forth between the two men, before settling his stare on Hamish. "Ah dinna like the look in yer eyes. Recognize it from yer youth. Whit scheme are ye cookin?"

An eagerness and the same sense of purpose that had allowed him to survive and escape, lent Hamish's lips a rusty smile. "Ah think, ah'm long overdue for a visit to London to visit my chridhe."

Angus's eyes narrowed, and then understanding flashed within their rheumy depths. "Ye canna be thinking to—"

"To what?" Hamish impatiently interrupted. "Discover the ones who wrought shame to our clan and have my vengeance upon them?"

His godfather's cheeks grew florid. "Ye should be grateful to be alive and back in Scotland," Angus snapped. "Find yerself a good Scottish lass to wed and move on with your life."

A mirthless laugh spilled from his lips. "Grateful," he spat, and he closed his eyes as the memory of that distant day came flooding back to the surface, as it so often did.

Fully cloaked and hooded, Hamish had stood on the fringe of the solemn gathering that wintry day, forced to hide in the shadows to pay witness to his brother and father's hanging. Hamish had stayed through it all: from the moment his da and Finlay made a slow, dignified march up the dais to meet their executioners, to the last words they'd been allowed to utter to the crowd, and then the instant they'd slid that noose about his big neck, and then kicked the block out from under him so that his form writhed and twisted from that rope.

As if the agony of watching his brother strain for his last breath hadn't been suffering enough, Hamish had felt hands clasp him at the shoulders, where he'd then been carted off to meet his fate.

Hamish's eyes snapped open, and the somber, silent countenances of the two men before him stared back.

"Do you truly believe ah should let this go, Angus?" Hamish quietly asked, not allowing him a chance to answer. "That isn't our way."

The old Scot tugged free his cap and twisted it in his hands. "Nay, but mayhap…mayhap it should be. Mayhap you should just be grateful at having what most men do not have—a second chance."

"Aye, ah've a second chance, all right," Hamish said in low, steely tones. "A second chance to avenge the wrongs done to his family that day.

"What do you want to do?" Burgess asked gravelly, speaking with the same knowing only one bent on the same revenge as Hamish himself could.

"Why, ah ken a trip to London is in order. Aye, the visit to my bonnie Bea is long overdue." Hamish curled his lips in a mirth-free grin that, if seen, would have chilled the lass who'd no idea what was coming for her.

CHAPTER 2

My Dearest Hamish,

I yearn for the days we can be together. I would wait forever for you, though I wish I did not have to. My heart is only complete when you are near.

With Love and Longing,
Beatrice

GENERALLY, THE TON WAS ALL abuzz with talk about the gentleman who'd passed Lady Beatrice Dennington over for another lady who'd landed his heart. This time, Polite Society continued their whispers—but whispers of a different nature—fascinated interest.

And sometimes, with the bolder ones, it wasn't even whispers.

When she'd created a pretend sweetheart, and almost betrothed, she'd intended to reveal his existence in a more measured way; dropping mention to some carefully selected someones, so that information could then slowly trickle throughout London.

Alas, that had been before the latest determined prospective bridegroom seated at her shoulder, suffocating her. And then, here, in the midst of her family's dinner party, the words had just slipped out…

"You must tell us more about the man who's stolen your heart, Lady Beatrice," Lady Jersey called from down the middle of the dining table where she'd been seated. "How did you meet?"

In an instant, two dozen sets of stares from the invited guests swung Beatrice's way. Of course, there'd been questions about the news that had been printed earlier that afternoon about Lady B, sister to the Duke of S, and the gentleman whom Lady B was purportedly betrothed to. A man whom no member of society—polite or otherwise—had met. It's all anyone wished to speak of since someone had shared that information with the London Times.

Not even a glare from Beatrice's brother, the fear-inducing-when-he-wished-it duke, and his equally terrifying wife Helena could manage to quell those questions. Fortunately, Beatrice had grown well-accustomed to stares being trained upon her. This time, she welcomed them.

Beatrice made her features grow soft and her gaze distant as she breathed the made-up connection into existence.

"I was off sketching as I often do. There is no more magnificent subject to capture than the wilds of the Scottish islands." Her quiet murmuring contained the only real truth to any of this—that wild, untamed land had stolen every corner of her heart and soul. "And then…it happened," she said.

All the guests strained forward, leaning in.

Even the ever-composed Lady Jersey clutched at her heart. "What did, my dear?"

Beatrice stretched the silence a moment more, adding to the gathering's anticipation. "The skies opened up in a deluge, and I found myself caught in a violent storm."

"Did he carry you home?" one of the younger ladies down at the opposite end of the table called over, her voice imbued with a soft wonderment.

Beatrice shook her head. "Oh, no. I raced home. In my haste, I abandoned my things. Only the next morning, when I returned with my maid to reclaim my belongings, I discovered him there."

She caught her sister-in-law's gaze—sharp, astute, one that missed nothing, and Beatrice briefly faltered.

"Him?" another young lady amidst the crowd of assembled guests pressed.

"*Him*," Beatrice repeated.

Every pair of eyes grew more riveted. That was, all except for her brother whose narrow-eyed stare radiated a healthy suspicion.

Resisting the urge to squirm, she made her features go softer. "Lord Hamish. He poured through my pages and was so absorbed in my work he failed to hear my approach, and when he did… when he looked up…it was…"

The guests leaned in, and once more Beatrice stretched the moment, holding onto their interest and wonderment.

"Magic," she whispered, and the lie came so very easy as it was borne of the dreams she'd allowed herself through the years.

Sighs circulated around the table, with even the cynical, always-skeptical Lady Jersey joining in. A fork scraped noisily upon a porcelain plate, and she slid her gaze over. His eyes thin, his attention trained on her, Beatrice's brother popped a bite of meat into his mouth and chewed angrily.

There'd be even more questions following the guest's departure. The timing when the gossip had dropped hadn't been a coincidence. There'd been no time for questions from either her brother or Helena.

Beatrice took great pains to avoid her brother's razor-sharp focus.

"How is it no one has ever met him or seen him?" Lady Jersey put forward that question.

Beatrice had been prepared for that exact and obvious query. "Lord Hamish is very much a Scottish Highlander and takes care to avoid Polite Society affairs."

"As all Scots do," Lord Trowbridge drawled, earning a bevy of laughter from the other guests.

That was, all except Robert and Helena, whose expressions remained unnervingly set and serious.

Lady Jersey spoke, granting Beatrice a reprieve from her brother and Helena's probing looks. "Doesn't take part in *ton* events?" Lady Jersey bristled. "What does he *do* with his days, then?"

Of course. Because to lords and ladies, the only life with any real meaning was one where one partook in High Society events.

Beatrice kept her features even. "He is attempting to restore his ancestral state to its former glory for the day we call it home."

The Marquess of Townsend lifted his nose. "Gentlemen charge others with that task," the old marquess, a pompous, though generous beneficiary of Helena's brother's school for children, said.

"Yes," Beatrice conceded. "That is generally the way."

Lord Townsend lifted his glass and tapped the bottom of it to the tabletop. "That is *always* the way.

"It is also something that set him apart from all other gentlemen I've ever known," she murmured softly. She eased her lips up in a soft, wistful smile, and allowed her eyes to go soft. "He is not like all men. He doesn't turn his nose up at hard work." In short, her imaginary beau possessed the exact qualities she'd longed for in a real sweetheart.

Sighs from the less cynical guests went up around the table.

Lady Jersey added her voice to the group. "I'd expect a sweetheart so ardently in love would face anything…including joining *ton* events for the pleasure of your company."

When she'd been a lady of eighteen, just out for her first Season, such a blunt judgment would have cowed her. She was not, however, a young girl nor afraid of the leading peeresses.

"My love for him is so great, Lady Jersey, that I'd not ask him to abandon his important work improving his family's estates and come to a place he'd rather not be, for my own selfish wish of seeing him."

The older woman opened her mouth to direct another question her way. Fortunately, Beatrice was spared from answering; her rescue came in the form of her sister-in-law.

"May I suggest we adjourn to the parlor? Lady Beatrice has agreed to grace us with a song upon the pianoforte." It was a lie her sister-in-law spoke, and also a declaration, more than a request from the duchess. "Isn't that right, Lady Beatrice?" Helena directed that her way.

"Nothing would bring me greater pleasure," Beatrice demurred, with a fib of her own.

She and Helena shared a slight, sardonic smile; one that came from two friends who knew one another so well as to be able to pick up on the unspoken thoughts between them.

With an obvious reluctance, the guests came slowly to their feet, and, taking painstaking care to avoid Robert's intent stare and Lady Jersey's attempt at cornering her, Beatrice hastened over to Helena.

"My apologies," Helena murmured as they fell into step beside one another, leading the ladies onward to the parlor, while the men adjourned for drinks. "I considered the current circumstances and made a decision that your performing might be preferable." A twinkle lit Helena's pretty brown eyes. "At least, *this* night."

"Indeed," Beatrice muttered, which was saying a good deal.

During her first Season, the papers had declared her a diamond who sang like a songbird, heaping praise upon praise on Beatrice for not only her proficiency but mastery of all ladylike skills. From that moment on, at every affair she attended, Beatrice's respective host and hostesses had requested she perform.

It was also the moment her joy in singing had died.

"Your brother will have questions." Helena spoke in low tones that even Beatrice strained to hear.

"You can tell him," she said from the corner of her mouth, "I've settled on 'As I Walked Forth'."

Helena's lips twitched. "I wasn't referring to your song selection."

"I know."

They shared another grin.

Undoubtedly, there'd been ten thousand questions in his eyes. Her brother's questions had been the one thing she'd known she'd had to face, and absolutely dreaded. Not because she feared her big brother. Anything but. Robert had always been a kind, loving, protector and friend. It was the protective aspect of her only sibling's personality, however, that proved a bother.

Helena gave Beatrice's arm a light squeeze, drawing Beatrice's gaze up to the taller woman.

"You may rest assured," her sister-in-law said quietly, "I shall remind your brother you are a woman, and therefore he is only entitled to information you wish to impart."

So much love for the woman who'd been like the sister she'd always wished for filled her breast. "Thank—"

Helena gave her arm a slight squeeze. "Oh, hush. I may be in love with your brother, but in this man's world, women must look after one another."

They arrived at the parlor; and as all the ladies went about claiming seats in the parlor, and her sister-in-law joined them, Lady Jersey, with a singular intentness in her gaze headed Beatrice's way.

Quickening her steps, Beatrice hastened over to the pianoforte. She stopped at the instrument. God, how she hated playing publicly. She almost preferred being peppered with questions by the gossip.

Almost.

Alas, Beatrice's hesitation proved a dangerous misstep. Lady Jersey joined her at the instrument.

"Lady Beatrice," she greeted as if this was their first time meeting for the night, and not as though they'd been seated opposite one another at the dining table for the entirety of the evening.

"Lady Jersey." She cut the tenacious woman off before she could launch into further questions Beatrice wasn't wholly prepared to answer at this moment. "Have you come to join me in a duet at the pianoforte?"

Nonplussed, the silver-haired matron blinked several times. Alas, one who'd been around Polite Society as long as Lady Jersey would collect herself in an instant.

"My days of public performance are at an end," the countess declared. "No, I wanted to speak with you away from the prying eyes,"

Beatrice peaked over the woman's graceful shoulder to where nearly every guest present stared baldly at them. "Too late."

"I cannot even begin to tell you," Lady Jersey went on over Beatrice's droll pronouncement, "just how very happy I am that you've *finally* found love."

With the passage of time, Beatrice had become a self-confident woman, undaunted by most. She'd come to accept what society had not, that there simply wasn't a suitor for her, and had even found peace in that realization. Even so, Lady Jersey's slight and very deliberate emphasis sent more heat climbing from Beatrice's neck to her cheeks, and all the way up to her hairline.

Like a predator who'd sensed weakness in its opponent, Lady

Jersey's expression grew sly, and she angled herself closer. "Why, after Lord Sinclair's defection of affections, I and the rest of the world dismissed that rejection as extraordinary, a product of the fact he was a scandalous rogue who would, of course, do something so outrageous as fall in love with his sister's governess. But then time after time, after *time*," she went on, spiraling her gloved index finger, with an enormous diamond upon it, exaggerating that subtly spiteful phrase, "you were passed over, so that with Lord Exmoor's latest rejection, well, I and the rest of the world came to believe it just would not happen for you, my dear."

And the older woman and the rest of the world had been correct on that score. Hence the reason for Beatrice's fictitious beau.

"Ah," she said softly, "but as Keats said, 'no love worth having was had without waiting'."

The older woman blinked slowly. "How very lovely and accurate considering your changed circumstances. I…I fear I do not recall those lines of his."

No, she wouldn't. Considering, Beatrice just created that quote and attributed it to the late, great poet, no one would.

"Surely your Lord Hamish will join us for some of the Season?" the relentless matron pressed. "How could he not, when so many gentlemen wish to court you?"

Court, but never marry. The truth of her circumstances had once been a physical pain. One that had faded to only annoyance at all those wondering and talking about her wedded—or as the case may be, *un*wedded—state.

"My betrothed is confident in my love and has no reason to doubt my faithfulness." Beatrice infused a frost meant to deter further questions, and mayhap in any other lady she would have been successful.

"Yes, but that is neither here nor—"

There came a commotion in the hall. The frantic rise and fall of footsteps, and all eyes went to the front of the room, just as Jax, the unconventional butler who'd previously been employed at Helena's family's gaming hell, exploded through the entryway.

Gasps went up. Relatively new in his role, the former gaming hell guard still struggled to navigate the formal customs that existed in this new-to-him world.

"Visitor's arrived," he said, slightly out of breath, his exertions having leant an even thicker quality to his cockney.

All eyes flew from Jax to Helena. "And?" she asked gently of the unconventional servant.

He dropped his voice slightly. "Asked that he be allowed the honor of surprising his…betrothed."

The gathered women collectively looked around at one another.

Helena puzzled her brow.

The big, burly servant grinned and stepped aside.

There came a long, stretch of…nothing, as the women stared expectantly at the empty doorway. Even Jax's brow dipped, along with his smile, and he glanced over his shoulder. A moment later, a tall, midnight-haired figure clad in dark from his head to his toes, entered, and Beatrice found herself silent and gawking like every other lady present.

In the years since her brother had married into the Blacks, Helena's notorious gaming hell family, Beatrice had become accustomed to all manner of unconventional servants and people. Usually big, often scarred, and rough spoken, Beatrice had ceased to be surprised by people.

That was…until now.

The man soared over Jax—a tall man by any and every standard—towering at some four or five inches past six feet. His shoulders were broad. His chest, too. But for the fine cut of his evening clothes, he may as well have been a warrior of old brought to the present. His biceps strained the immaculate fabric of his wool jacket, and his thighs were the size of trunks she'd scaled as a child.

The stranger's blue eyes leant a shade so very dark as to be black, moved slowly but methodically as he took in every occupant the way a gentleman might seek a person in a crowded room.

Only, this room was not crowded.

And then, his gaze landed and locked on Beatrice. He assessed her, taking her in, and for an instant, it was as though she was the only woman in the room…which was a foreign place to find herself. All the men who'd ever courted her did so not because of any passionate desire for her, but rather, for the benefits that came from such a match.

Despite herself, a hand came up reflexively and fluttered at her breast. She pressed it there briefly in a bid to still her pounding heart.

The ghost of a hard grin played at his lips, and a flicker of *something* glinted in his eyes, a flash of recognition, and for a wild instant, she could almost believe he'd come…for her.

"May I help you?" Helena said, finding her voice first, as she invariably did.

"Ah've come to claim my betrothed," he spoke in a thick brogue, his, a lyrical Scottish lilt that captivated.

Even as Jax behind him smiled and clasped his hands like one bearing witness to the world's grandest romantic gesture, Helena narrowed her eyes. "Claim?

The gentleman briefly looked in Helena's direction. "Aye."

Beatrice should pity the woman who found herself betrothed to a man so primitive as to speak about laying claim to her. Strangely, that primality stirred a dangerous, forbidden thrill, and she proved so very pathetic responding so to a man betrothed to her family's guest.

"I could no longer bear to be parted," he said, and then his gaze landed on Beatrice. "Mo chridhe, Beatrice." His brogue thickened, obscuring those two syllables, and it took a moment for the name of the recipient of his Gaelic endearment to register.

And then…

"*Beatrice*?" Helena asked incredulously, her voice crept up an octave and she squeezed an extra syllable into Beatrice's name.

Beatrice's gasp was swallowed by the collective ones that filled the parlor.

Then, with slow but confident steps, the gentleman strode forward, only stopping when he reached Beatrice. Her ears buzzed and her mind whirred, and in a reflexive move, so she didn't have to crane her head, she came to her feet. Only, he still soared over her by a good half foot.

Helena jumped up beside her.

He reached inside the front of his jacket and withdrew a stack of notes—a stack of very, very, *very* familiar notes. Ones that were written in an even more familiar hand.

Mine. Beatrice's heart knocked sickening against her rib cage. *They are my notes.*

She whipped her neck back so quickly her muscles screamed in protest, as she sought to make out from his eyes what game he played…

Nay, it was obvious. He'd come to humiliate her. But why? She was a stranger to him, and he was a stranger to—

"Beatrice," he murmured. "I have missed ye, lass."

Every pair of eyes were upon them. She felt them searing into her back, burning a hole into her.

With his spare hand, he cupped her cheek; his gloveless, big, callused palm cradled her in a surprisingly tender touch that muddled her senses and replaced her earlier panic with the sort of dazedness to befall the heroines in the romantic tales she'd read through the years.

The gentleman wasn't done.

"*Like ye, Ah've yearned for the days we can be together. Ah would wait forever for ye, though Ah wish Ah did not have to. My heart is only complete when ye are near.*"

As their audience collectively sighed, Beatrice's mind scrambled.

Her words. Those were the ones she'd written upon those pages in Scotland and hidden behind a crumbling stone in that falling-down keep.

"It is, I, mo chridhe, your Hamish, returned."

Beatrice's tongue felt heavy, and her mouth went dry, as dread took solid root within every part of her. *Her* Hamish? As in, Hamish Hamish…her fake sweetheart. What game had this menacing stranger come here to play? Only one certainty existed: the only way it ended was with her being an absolute laughingstock of society.

Here, you believed there could be no greater humiliation than being constantly thrown over by suitor after suitor for other women.

A noiseless giggle gurgled in her throat and remained trapped there, threatening to choke her, which, in this instance, a quick death seemed vastly preferable to a death by slow shaming.

"Beatrice?" Helena's pointed questioning slashed through

Beatrice's rapidly spiraling panic.

And in a bid to escape the room of guests, and to find herself more time, Beatrice did whatever any English lady would have done long before now—fluttering her lashes, she made her entire body go limp and forced herself into a swoon.

CHAPTER 3

My dearest Hamish,

There is no one like you. As you know, I have never been the manner of lady given to fainting. But I must confess, the moment I first laid eyes upon you, I nearly succumbed to a swoon.

With Love and Longing,
Beatrice

SILENTLY CURSING, HAMISH CAUGHT THE well-formed lass before she hit the floor.

Only, because he'd been anticipating such an expected response from an English lass who'd had a stranger—and a Scottish one at that—join her and her fancy guests, under the pretense of being whichever fictional lad she'd penned her letters to.

To a bevy of more of those ridiculously romantic sighs, Hamish caught the lass up and cradled her in his arms.

The tall, interestingly scarred hostess of this group eyed Hamish with all the suspicion he'd been deserving of since he'd set foot inside her room, before turning her focus to the noisy gaggle around them.

With the dark-haired lass distracted, Hamish gave the woman

in his arms his full attention. Given Angus's description, it'd been easy to identify the golden-haired woman he'd sought within the crowd. *Find the most bonny one*, his godfather had advised and Hamish had done just that.

Only, 'the most bonny one' had been an understatement of the century. The lass possessed an otherworldly beauty: creamy white, satiny-soft-looking skin. She'd a slim face, arched golden eyebrows, and sensuous red lips that formed a perfect bow.

He narrowed his eyes on her tensed features. Just now, her impossibly long, flaxen lashes twitched slightly. Flaxen lashes that were not at all relaxed as they would be in a woman who'd had herself a full dwalm. She'd feigned a swoon, the lass had.

The duchess spoke loudly to the room at large, pulling Hamish's attention from the comely beauty in his arms. "Given Lady Beatrice's shock at seeing…at seeing…" The woman paused and looked hopelessly at Hamish.

"Lord Hamish Campbell," he supplied. "The lady's betrothed," he added for good measure.

His latest declaration was met with another swirl of frantic, noisy whispers.

The lass in his arms tensed. Aye, as he'd expected she'd merely pretended to faint. Hamish drew her closer, holding her curved-in-all-the-right-places form snug to him.

The duchess lingered a distrustful look on Hamish.

Canny lass.

The duchess snapped her attention back to their audience. "Given the shock of Lord *Hamish's arrival* might I direct you to another parlor?" Sweeping an arm out, she gestured to the door.

With obvious reluctance, the dozen assembled ladies rose in a flurry of ridiculously garish skirts and headed for the door. But for one, an older, grey-eyed woman with a shrewd gaze, and a clear appetite for gossip.

"Given the years I've been out in society, and witness to young ladies in a full swoon, perhaps I may stay and help the gel."

"That will not be necessary, Lady Jersey," the duchess said, gently but firmly taking the lady by the arm, she steered her to the entrance.

"But..." As the woman was ushered from the room, her protestations faded.

The moment the pair stepped outside, Lady Beatrice opened her eyes, and they were the prettiest eyes he'd ever seen—the prettiest eyes, he'd wager, *anyone* had ever seen. Hers were every shade of the purest blue sky that had ever smiled down at the Highlands.

Shock, suspicion, and anger all roiled around those revealing irises. Ach, she'd more emotion there than he'd ever thought a Sassenach woman might possess.

"Surprised to see me, lass?" he asked in a husky voice.

The bonny lass's eyes flared wide; fire flashed in their depths.

Her perfectly formed eyebrows climbed to her hairline. "Put me down this instant," she hissed.

"Och, and here I would have expected the woman who would happily sail to the ends of the world forever, as long as I was at your—"

Her gasp swallowed the remainder of those words he'd memorized from her notes.

She pushed against his chest. "I said, put me down, you lying, deceitful fustilarian with—"

Alas, he was denied the rest of that fiery insult by the return of the duchess. Lady Beatrice instantly went soft and pliant in his arms.

"Lord Hamish," the woman said stiffly, and with a suspicion he certainly deserved.

From the corner of his eye, Hamish caught the butler's mood shift from jubilant to rightfully—though, belatedly—leery.

Digging deep for the long-dead charm from his more innocent, affable days, Hamish bowed his head deferentially. "It is an honor to meet a dear friend and sister of Beatrice's, Your Grace," he murmured. "I've heard countless stories about you."

The lass in his arms twitched.

Some of the other woman's wariness, however, faded—just, slightly. "Indeed?"

"Aye." Countless stories—useful ones—he'd managed to gather from Scottish servants in the lady's employ. "Beatrice has regaled me with so many happy stories of ye and she's friendship, and the tale of your own romance with His Grace."

As the duchess's suspicion continued to recede, Hamish gave thanks for those useful pieces of personal information Lady Beatrice had inadvertently shared.

"I am honored to meet the woman who has been like a sister to her."

If the lass he held grew any more rigid, she was going to find herself stretched out like a taut plank. As it was, if any guests remained, they'd have spotted the lass's ruse in an instant.

"And much the way His Grace believed *ye* saved *him*," Hamish glanced down at the woman in his arms, "the same can be said for me and my Honey Bea."

Those words were the truest he could speak, for the lass who'd left those letters was his greatest hope for retribution and justice.

Lady Beatrice fluttered her lashes, and their gazes clashed once more.

She glared, and hers was an impressively black scowl any other man would shrink from, and under ordinary circumstances—under any circumstances, he would have felt an appreciation for such a lass. But it was her eyes: sparkling blue irises with mesmerizing green inner rings. All at once, her eyes managed to conjure thoughts of celestial skies and lush Highland glens.

Those eyes, which in this moment radiated both fury and fear. Fear that he'd come here with harmful intentions.

In this instant, he braced for her screams and charges calling Hamish out as the charlatan he was. That fear of discovery hadn't been one he'd dwelled overly on. A Sassenach cared more about pretense than anything else, and before coming here, he'd bet his entire plan on her not fingering him as a stranger.

His muscles coiled tightly, and he braced for impending disaster—an end to his plan before it had even begun, and the return of that big butler and other big servants to cart Hamish off.

Suddenly, unexpectedly, the lass's lustrous eyes grew soft.

"H-Hamish," she whispered, in some of the falsest, over-the-top reverence, it was a wonder the duchess didn't summon that butler who even now stood in wait, prepared to toss Hamish out if his mistress so ordered. "Is it really *you*?"

Ach, it was a good thing the lass had been born to the lap of luxury and hadn't been forced to rely on her acting skills for either the stage or survival.

"Aye," he murmured, "tis I, mo ghràdh."

All the while, the woman beside them took in their entire exchange. Her gaze, a good deal less suspicious than it had been, passed back and forth between Hamish and Lady Beatrice.

He placed his lips close to Lady Beatrice's ear, but paused, momentarily distracted. She'd the scent of heather, a magical scent that harkened back to Celtic times. The wariness in her gaze redoubled. Her big, berry-red lips quivered, and even bigger tears filled her eyes.

All his muscles went taut, and he felt the duchess's keen gaze boring into him and Lady Beatrice. This was it. This was the moment the lass in his arm screamed the household down. He'd give her credit for keeping it together longer than any other wilting English lady, or for that matter, Scottish lass, would.

"Helena," Lady Beatrice said in a surprisingly calm voice, "may I have several moments alone with… mo grad."

And despite the fact Hamish found himself one wrong word from swinging from a rope this time, his lips twitched at her awkward attempt at Gaelic.

The door shut with a firm, but quiet click, leaving him and his betrothed alone. Lady Beatrice remained silent and still and for an instant, he thought this time she may have truly fainted.

Glaring at him, she pushed at his chest. "Set me down now," she whispered furiously.

He clucked his tongue. "And here I'd thought you wished to spend forever in my ah—"

The lass slapped a palm over his mouth and scowled that black scowl of hers. "I said put me—"

"Och, I'd nah have you faint again on me."

"I didn't faint *on* you," she muttered, stealing a glance at the doorway.

Nay, she'd collapsed *into* his embrace, and she'd felt surprisingly good pressed against him. But then, it'd been years since he'd had a woman in his arms or in his bed.

"Though, I'm nah surprised. I expected an English lass would faint," he drawled.

Her eyes flashed fire, and with a grin, he, at last, set her down. This time, she remained impressively steady for one who'd been dealt the shock he'd handed her this evening.

Lady Beatrice pursed those big lips that put him in mind of thoughts he'd no place having. Not when he'd matters to see to.

She jabbed a finger at his chest. "Give me that, this instant."

Hamish touched a hand to the space where his heartbeat. "This, mo chridhe? Don't you know you already hold my heart?"

"Not…that," she whispered. "My stack of notes."

Hamish withdrew them from his jacket. "These?"

Lady Beatrice gave a curt, angry nod. "I just said so."

"You wrote them to me," he said, returning them to the place where he'd kept the letters since Ole Angus had laid them before him.

She sputtered.

Hamish cast a pointed glance at the door, and the lass instantly stopped.

She dropped her voice to a furious whisper. "I most certainly did *not* write them to you."

"You placed them in my keep."

That managed to silence her—for a moment. "*Your* keep?"

"Well, it isn't yers," he said. "At least, not until we wed."

"We most certainly are not marrying," she said, her voice creeping up.

As one, they looked to the door.

"—Until your family has arrived," Lady Beatrice called more loudly for the benefit of whichever kin had no doubt stationed them outside. "We *must* wait until your family and for you to properly meet mine."

The moment the lass returned her attention to him, she caught him by the hand and tugged him forward. Instead of marching him right to the exit as he expected she would, she maneuvered to the furthest corner.

She drew her hand back and folded her arms at her chest, bringing his gaze to the lush, plump mounds of creamy white flesh straining against the neckline of her gown.

A wave of lust bolted through him.

"That castle is abandoned," she said flatly.

He narrowed his eyes, and he lowered his voice. "That castle along with the *verdant virgin land*," her cheeks went red at the latest quote he'd borrowed from her notes, "belongs to the Campbell clan whose hereditary hold of that distinguished title extended all the way back to Malcom IV and William I, with King Robert the Bruce himself cementing that ancestral office."

She eyed him warily. "You speak those words like they were memorized from a script."

"I speak them like they were words passed down to all the lads and lairds of the Campbell clan," he corrected.

"And is that what you are?"

He'd hand it to the lass. With the fearless, no-nonsense questions she'd level his way, she proved to be a brave thing.

"Aye, that is what I am," he said, in a low voice.

Lady Beatrice ran her long, clear-eyed gaze over his face; she lingered briefly on the scar at the left corner of his mouth, that livid white mark a gift of the Sassenach who'd put Hamish in chains. The men he'd been imprisoned with had borne scars of their own. The men and women whom he'd crossed paths with, however, had gone out of their way to avoid looking at his face altogether.

This woman, however, did not. She stared at him as if he were no different from the once unblemished lad he'd been.

The lass returned her gaze to his. "Who are you?" she asked quietly.

Her fearlessness, coupled with her ability to look at him and speak to him, as if he were a man and not a monster, unnerved the hell out of him.

Tauntingly, Hamish pressed a hand to his chest. "Never tell me ye've forgotten me. It is I, Lord Hamish Campbell."

"*Stop*!" A bright crimson blush flooded her sharp cheekbones. "What *game* are you playing?" she demanded, no-nonsense and very much the duke's sister she, in fact, was.

"Isnae game," he said.

He had been baiting her, which given the gravity of what brought him here and the dark memories that lingered in his mind, had been an…unexpected pleasure.

Before she had him tossed out once and for all, he got to the reason for his seeking her out and continued. "My name is Hamish Ian Campbell, the Earl of Brewster, and, as ah said, the rightful owner of the keep you trespassed upon…the keep and all its belongings, including those missives ye penned to me."

"I did not pen them to *you*," she said between gritted teeth.

"My name is Hamish."

"I did not know that." She flared her delicate nostrils. "Nor, for that matter, do I believe that."

She'd question his honor? Rage briefly darkened his vision, and a growl worked its way up his chest. His honor, which had been ripped to shreds by the Sassenachs, and which he desperately sought to restitch in the name of his father and brother.

"Ah've no reason to lie to ye, lass," he said on a steely whisper. "As ah said, that keep is the Campbell's, given to my ancestor, the First Laird of Brewster, by Robert the Bruce himself."

A long overdue fear lit her eyes. "You are mad," she whispered.

Aye, he was mad, in every way a man could be: enraged over the betrayal that had taken his family from him and mad from the effects of what he'd seen and done.

Lady Beatrice took a step around him.

Hamish caught her gently but firmly at her wrist.

Worry flashed in her big blue eyes. It was replaced in an instant by a glitter of defiant fury. "Release me this—"

"You think I'm doolally why? Because ye find it so hard to ken that my family's holdings were taken from me? That it's unfathomable for the Sassenachs who've, since the beginning of time, pillaged and stole everything from the Scottish people, to have done so?"

Lady Beatrice tugged her hand, and at that show of resistance, he let her free. She drew that slightly quaking palm protectively close as if she sought to keep him from snatching her wrist once more. But she did not flee.

Fighting with the lass would get him nowhere. Whether he liked it or not, he needed the lass's cooperation.

BEATRICE SHOULD SCREAM THE HOUSEHOLD down. She should have done so the minute the big, burly Scot had sauntered into the parlor, centered his gaze on her, and laid claim to her name and story like he was pillaging people he now spoke of.

Something held her back—a glint in his eyes. Those cobalt blue irises that leaned closer to onyx radiated with an emotion different than the previously teasing glimmer that had been there the dozen or so times he'd managed to needle her since he'd stepped foot inside this parlor.

He spoke of injustice and wrongs done to him and his family.

And no, despite his clear disdain for her and all things English, she was not so naïve as to believe her people were morally just and only good. Since her brother's marriage to Helena, Beatrice had her eyes opened to the wrongs around her. While the *ton* lived lives of lavishness, the majority toiled and struggled for the smallest scraps on which to survive.

Perhaps that was why she didn't call for Helena who undoubtedly stood just outside. Mayhap that was why she wished to hear this angry Scottish stranger out, anyway.

"Were you spying on me?" Beatrice asked, quietly, somehow her voice emerged even.

"When?"

"All the times I visited the keep."

"*My* keep," he clipped out.

"You let me believe I was alone."

"Ye were alone. I'd not yet returned."

Why was she still talking to this man? She should summon Helena and Jax. She should run. So why then did she find herself standing here, continuing to ask him questions? "Returned from where?"

"Prison."

She recoiled and then found her footing. "You're trying to scare me."

"Why would ah want to scare ye, when ah've a need of ye?" he asked flatly.

Well, *that* was certainly honest. "You have a need of me?" she repeated.

He nodded.

Beatrice eyed him closely. Something had brought him here. Initially, the only thing that made sense was he intended to extort her or humiliate her or both. Her intrigue redoubled. Silently she cursed that part of her which had always longed to know some manner of mystery, wished to know…more about what he'd shared regarding his imprisonment.

"Don't ye want to at least know what need ah have?" he asked, unnervingly accurate in his read of her unspoken musings.

"I do not," she said in hushed tones, layering the cool indifference an earlier governess had taught Beatrice, which she'd vowed to never use with anybody.

This man and this situation, however, certainly called for an exception.

What had she been thinking engaging him as long as she had?

Mad, you are utterly mad.

Giving her head a clearing shake, Beatrice lifted her chin to meet his gaze—a near impossible feat, even for one as tall as herself.

"Your business is your business, sir, and it does not involve me."

"Aye, but that is where yer wrong, lass." When annoyed, his brogue thickened. It was an intimate detail to note of a man who was a stranger. "Ah'll have yer help."

"Or what?" she shot back on a furious whisper. "You will now use my own words against me?"

"I'll use your words for me," he said without missing a beat.

She spoke through clenched teeth. "That's the same thing."

"Not to me, it isn't."

No, it wouldn't be because he'd be saved and spared from the shame staring down at her. Whereas Beatrice? She would once more be made the fool, all over again, but for different reasons *this* time. When it was said and done, she'd be the one made a fool, not him. Nay, men were always spared the humiliations and injustices leveled on women.

Despair, fury, and frustration roiled inside. Her legs twitched with the need to move…flee. This time, as Beatrice moved out from around him, he made no move to stop her.

His shrewd gaze, as powerful as a physical touch, however, followed her restless journey over to the windows that overlooked the London streets below. With fingers that shook, she grabbed the filmy white curtain and yanked the material back and stared sightlessly out at the brightly lit townhouses across the way.

Sorrow threatened to choke her. As a duke's daughter, she'd been expected to behave a certain way. She'd known early on that any connection people wished to have with her stemmed from her birthright. As such, she'd never had real friends, and she'd never shared her hopes, her dreams, and secrets with anyone. Instead, she'd put them down onto pages and pages of paper, and—

Those most intimate, personal letters…which if—when?—revealed by him, would be the final coup de grace—her latest but ultimate humiliation before Polite Society.

It was one thing being thrown over. Those rejections had come about through no fault of her own. Rather, those gentlemen had simply fallen for grander, greater women. As a romantic, Beatrice had well understood the heart wanted what—and who—the heart wanted.

But this? This would be a disgrace of a different sort. This would be Beatrice, pathetic, and pitiable, making up a suitor.

Desolate, she closed her eyes and pressed her fingertips sharply into her temple and rubbed. Damn him. And more, damn herself for having ever written those notes and daring to think they'd not eventually be found by someone, if not now, then some other day. She'd been careless and imprudent, but she was no coward.

Beatrice let her arms fall to her side. "Are you here to bribe me?" she asked icily, imbuing as much frost as she could, even as she shook inside.

"I dinna need to bribe ye."

That blunt reply came so close, she gasped, and spun about.

At some point the dangerous, black-eyed stranger had moved to a point just beyond her shoulder, but out of reach of where she'd have seen his figure reflected back in the glass.

"Ah'll have yer cooperation."

"My cooperation?" she spat.

"Aye." He spoke with both a confidence and automaticity that only a man could manage. "Ah'm needing yer help…and ah will have it."

And here she'd always thought the brogue musical and captivating. That had been before one of those gentlemen had wielded it with dire threats.

She gritted her teeth. He was a beast of a man, and yet, in this instant, she didn't care. "And that's all that matters, isn't it?" she spat. "What *you* want and what you intend to have."

That was all men had ever cared about where Beatrice was concerned—how they stood to benefit through their connection to her.

"As ah see it, lass, ah'm not the only one who stands to benefit by our betrothal."

She eyed him warily. "We are not betrothed," she said for good measure.

"Nay, but we can be, and ye can have what ye wish for, and ah can have what ah want."

Even closer than they'd been before, she noted the sharp glint in his nearly jade-black eyes that sent a shiver through her.

She dampened her lips. "You, a stranger whom I've known but a handful of minutes who, by your own admission is a criminal, only just returned from prison, presume to know what I want?"

He nodded. "Aye, lass. Ye've covered the whole of it."

"The Scots are as arrogant as the world says, then," she said under her breath.

"Dinna forget stubborn, too, lass." A muscle rippled along his jawline. "Ah'll not be deterred."

The steely resolve in his deep brogue should have her shouting down the rafters for the servants.

So why didn't she? Why did she remain less than a pace away, locked in a debate and discussion with the man in possession of the most personal words she'd ever written, who now sought to use them as leverage over her?

"What do you want?" she asked bluntly.

"Ah've already told ye—"

"No," she cut him off. "Actually, you haven't. You've told me you'll use my words to benefit you, but for what purpose? Money?" she supplied, not allowing him a chance to answer.

He scoffed. "Only a Sassenach worries about money and power."

"Men of all backgrounds and origins do," she said. This man was no different. When he made no attempt to defend himself or his people, she quirked an eyebrow. "You'll not deny it."

The dark-haired stranger lowered his sooty black lashes. "Why should ah, lass? Ye've already formed yer opinion and it disna matter to me? What matters is having your cooperation." He steeled his jaw. "Ye can open doors for me no one else can."

And there it was. As she'd said, they were all the same. A sound of disgust escaped her.

"You believe I'll wed you to keep my words secret? That I'd tie myself to a coldhearted stranger out of sake of my own vanity?" Beatrice shook her head. "We're done here." She took a step.

The big Scot—Hamish, if that was even his name—latched long, strong fingers about her upper arm, again staying her, preventing her from leaving. Once more, there was a surprising *tenderness* to his touch and an unexpected warmth in hands that were so scarred and heavily callused.

Her belly fluttered and her senses grew muddled all over again, but this time, for different, confusing reasons. He, however, on the other hand, seemingly remained wholly oblivious to her body's response to him.

"You've been courted nearly a dozen times, and yet, you've never been betrothed."

Beatrice found her voice. "And you think I would want to be betrothed to you, a man I've never met, an absolute stranger who invaded my family's home and presented yourself with a false name and identity."

"It's nah false name or identity. My name *is* Hamish Campbell, and Ah'm the Earl of Brewster."

Her jaw slackened. There was no way in God's green earth he possessed the same name as her make-believe suitor. "*Impossible.*"

"Aye," he said, once more, unsettling her with how closely he read her thoughts. "Ah assure ye, it's not only possible, it's verra much true." The dark stranger lifted his lips in a cool smile that sent a chill up her spine. "My kin, my clan, were wronged, and ah seek justice in their name. Ye will help me achieve that."

Beatrice eyed him incredulously. "You speak like you're some kind of warrior of old, set to battle neighboring foes." Beatrice shook her head. "Such wars, they don't still exist."

A muscle at the corner of his eye twitched. "Not everyone enjoys the benefits ye know as an English lass. Ye come from a powerful family and can't fathom there are people still fighting those same battles ye talk about as if they're dead and over." Contempt dripped from every terse syllable he spoke. "Ye have luxuries ye dinnae even realize ye have."

Beatrice's face went warm. "I assure you, I'm not blind to the advantages enjoyed by me and mine, while others know different struggles."

He scoffed. "Because yer sister-in-law belonged to a gang and happened to grow up on the streets, ye think yer afforded some greater understanding of the way the world really is?"

Her face went warm at that not erroneous accusation he'd leveled her way.

Hamish, *supposed* Laird of the Campbells wasn't done. "The duchess's experiences aren't yers. Ye may ken someone whose suffered the harsh reality of life, but that isn't yer truth. 'Tis theirs."

Had his tone been snarling and mocking it would have been easier to take than that matter-of-fact deliverance; one in which he aptly, and accurately called Beatrice out for her privileged lifestyle. At every turn, he was smug, arrogant, and condescending. Why then did she wish to know…more about him and what role he possibly believed she could play in his scheme?

"For a man seeking my help in your madcap plan, I'd expect you to be a good deal less insulting."

"Do ye not mean a good deal less *truthful*?"

Touché.

"Ah'm not looking to charm ye into helping me. Ah'm trying to reason with ye, and by yer notes," he lifted those letters and she followed their movement with her gaze, "ye are a clever lass capable of reason and logic."

It was all she could do to keep from reaching out and yanking her intimate missives from his fingers. And yet…

That was what his takeaway had been in reading her most intimate thoughts? Not that she'd been a hopeless, pathetic, romantic fool yearning for a grand love, but rather, that she possessed a keen wit?

Beatrice contemplated him a long while and then asked the question which had plagued her since he'd spoken earlier. "Tell me what wrongs were done to you?"

"My kin and ah were accused of crimes we dinnae commit," he said with a black lethality in his words and in his eyes. "A Judas sold us out and ah'd have justice in the names of me, my brother, and Da."

This time, Beatrice couldn't keep herself from rubbing the gooseflesh that dotted her lower arms. Contained within that whisper-soft vow was a promise to those who'd betrayed him…and her mind shied away from thoughts of that inevitable reckoning. No, a man so consumed by revenge was surely a man to be avoided.

Only…a new wave of dread washed over her.

"Your brother and father," she said hollowly. Which meant there wasn't just one who knew of her shame. "They are also aware of my…letters."

"They aren't aware of anything anymore—they're dead." A muscle rippled along his jawline. "Their lives lost for other men's avarice and greed."

This time, however, she didn't imagine that slight but marked chink in his armor.

Anguish so fleeting had she blinked she may have missed it, passed over his blue-black eyes. With Beatrice's mother having died many years ago, and her father more recently, Beatrice knew the sorrow that came in those losses. Despite only having just met, despite the ruthless goal that had brought him here, Beatrice found herself beset by that rush of kindred feeling, forged of loss.

"I'm sorry," she said softly.

"Ye dinnae murder them."

"No, but I am sorry for your losses all the same."

"Because then ye wouldn't have to be tangled up in my plans for revenge?"

"*Because* it is painful to lose those we love." Even though, his had been the logical assumption.

He didn't dispute that point, but neither did he issue an echo of agreement that would have bonded them in that way.

Beatrice dampened her mouth. "And just how do you believe I can help you avenge them?"

"The men who sealed my kin's fate were men with power and influence. They were…*are* Englishmen in Parliament." His eyes grew distant and somehow harder. "Ah'd learn who had the most gain. And who *did* gain by my absence?" His words were a whisper. His breath a steely kiss upon her face that roused a different manner of shiver. One that she couldn't sort whether it was born of fear or…more.

"Ye will open doors for me, lass. Ye will allow me entry into those households, and ah'll have the freedom to search for the information I seek." His brogue had grown thicker, making it harder for her to untangle his explanation.

Entry, then. That was what he sought. It was what all gentlemen who'd ever courted her wished for—the most coveted doors opened. The power and influence that came from one who managed to snare a duke's daughter. Ultimately, this man was no different.

God, how she despised her birthright. Yes, it had afforded her every luxury, but it had also denied her that which all people truly yearned for—a deep, abiding, human connection—love. To be wanted for who she was, and not what she offered.

Hamish broke the silence. He nudged an intractable chin her way. "Well? What say ye, lass?"

What was she doing even still talking to him? He was a stranger in possession of her most humiliating secret, and the idea left her vulnerable, humbled, and cut open. By his own admission, he came from a family who'd been deemed criminals. She'd say she was mad for not having already screamed the household down, and for the next query that came tripping from her tongue before she could apply the reason he'd praised her for, and call it back.

"You have much to gain through this proposed ruse," she said crisply. "What do I stand to gain?"

"Ye'd have a betrothed so ye dinnae have to worry about those Sassenach swains ye detest as much as ah. As soon as ah have justice, ah'll disappear, and ye can mourn as long as ye so wish, the passing of yer beloved."

She considered that.

In the past, suitors had tossed her over. But what Hamish proposed, was far different than a courtship coming to an end. This time—though pretend—it would be Beatrice having fallen in love with a man who loved her in return. They'd be on the cusp of marrying, and then she'd tragically lose him; destined she'd be to never recover.

She could wear black widow's weeds for ton events. No gentleman looking for a wife would be so doltishness as to pay serious suit of a bereaved Beatrice and actually believe she'd marry.

"If I do agree to this…arrangement," she said, "when…and how does it come to an end?" Without her being humiliated by being thrown over once more.

"When I have the information I need. Not a day sooner. When it does, ah will go. Ah'll arrange for a body that the world will take for my own."

She shivered.

He'd thought of everything.

"Whose body will it be?" she asked, her voice emerged as a whisper.

"In other words, will ah kill an innocent man? Nay, ah'm not a savage, lass."

No, but he was a stranger, a man she didn't know at all.

Beatrice's thoughts clashed in her head. The logical side of her said the man was mad, and she should have him thrown out this instant. The *other* part of Beatrice, however, stood by silently contemplating everything he'd shared—and sought.

If he were truly a criminal, would he go to such efforts to avenge his family's name? And what was more, if he'd been betrayed as he claimed, then by partnering with him, she'd be doing something meaningful. Something valuable. In short, something she'd never truly done in her nearly thirty years on this earth.

Beatrice worried her lower lip between her teeth. From the

moment he'd stormed her family's property, proclaiming to be her love, and armed with the letters she'd written, she'd been filled with a franticness and panic. What if, however, this man's arrival as he said, could be used to her advantage?

For, there'd be no pretenses with this man's courtship. There'd be no expectation of a relationship that progressed to the cusp of a betrothal…for this stranger, unlike the other men who'd come before, had no interest in that. With him, she knew exactly what he wanted…and there was something…empowering in that.

As she contemplated his proposition, she felt his keen, clever stare, assessing her.

"And if I say no?" she asked cautiously. "What then?"

"Do ye mean will ah expose ye?"

The moisture leeched from her mouth, and unable to get a word out, she managed a tight nod.

He reached inside his jacket, and she stiffened. But he only pulled out a small circular scrap of silver, tarnished with age and lack of care. "Ye know of the thistle and how this prickly flower became the symbol of Scotland?"

Beatrice stared at the ancient-looking brooch, hesitated, and then shook her head.

"Long, long ago, the Vikings sought to conquer the Scottish clans. They landed on the Coast of Largs and chose the dead of night to launch their attack."

She should be focused on his underhanded reasons for being here. Instead, she listened on, riveted by the story.

"At the start of their invasion, the Norsemen took off their footwear to make their approach in silence but were thwarted when they stepped in a patch of thistle and cried out. That flower, it came to represent devotion, bravery, determination, and strength."

The big Scot paused in his telling, and before she knew what he intended, he was affixing the old brooch to her dress. The brush of his fingers, both intimate and purposeful sent her heart into a quick double-time rhythm.

When he'd finished, Beatrice touched her fingers reflexively to a metal now warm from this man's touch.

"The Scots?" he murmured. "We aren't underhanded, lass. We're people of our word. Ah'll only have yer help if ye'll freely give it."

Beatrice glanced down at the silver piece upon her dress, both a brand and a promise.

She must be mad. Or desperate. Or mayhap both. After all, desperation made people do crazy things. And there could be no doubting, this was the most outrageous thing she'd ever done in all her years.

In fairness, she'd never done anything wicked or scandalous or remotely improper. Which was, also, mayhap why she entertained the idea put to her by this man who was a stranger. A stranger who intended to one day disappear, but not before he procured a dead body and feigned his own death.

"Very well," she said before logic reigned her in. "I'll assist you." And in so doing, she'd secure *his* help.

He gave no outward reaction, not a hint of relief, joy, not even smugness. Hamish's powerful scarred square face remained impassive; his hard, sharp jawline may as well have been chiseled from granite.

"But I shall set the terms," she said, in a bid to elicit some response—any response—from him.

Hamish grunted. "Out with it, lass."

"I'll not have you take," she searched her mind for the politest, prettiest way to say it, "*liberties*."

The ghost of a smile curled his hard lips. "Liberties?" he drawled. His brogue managed to add layers within that word.

Heat exploded on her cheeks, and she cursed her fair skin. "When we are together, you'll not touch me or…embrace me."

"Fine." That assurance came so swift, so absolute and definitive, the blush spread across her entire body.

She should be relieved at the resoluteness of that pledge. So why then did she feel the oddest…regret?

Because it's just one more reminder that you've never been the manner of woman to inspire desire or passion in a man. It was why they'd invariably all chosen other ladies.

"What else?" he asked, prodding her back from her own pitiable musings.

Beatrice gave her head a slight, clearing shake. "The arrangement ends when I—"

"Ah say when it's over," he interrupted, in that low, Scottish rumble. "When ah have what ah need, ah'll disappear."

She eyed him with renewed suspicion. "If you find what you seek quickly, then the ton will not have the opportunity to see you and I, madly in love, together. It is only believable if they see enough of our courtship play out. Otherwise, I'll be—"

Humiliated, once more. Beatrice instantly clamped her mouth shut.

"Aye?"

She shook her head.

He slid closer; surprisingly stealthy and sleek of steps for one so broadly muscled. "Verra well. Ah'll promise to stay for a minimum of a fortnight. Ye have my word, and as ah told ye, we Scots are men of our word."

"Men are men," she muttered.

Another one of those grins teased at his lips; those muscles twitching as if it'd been so long since he'd formed a full smile, they'd long since forgotten the movement.

"Ye've never known a Scot, have ye, lass?"

"I've met—"

"*Known* one," he corrected. "Because if ye did, ye'd know, we are honest, reliable, but compassionate—something the Sassenach aren't. Unlike a Sassenach, when a Scot makes a vow, he honors it until he draws his last breath, and then holds onto it long after in the grave." Hamish pointed to the brooch he'd affixed to her breast.

Beatrice touched it once more and then gave another little nod. "I'll have you know something else."

His thick lashes swept down, once more. "Aye?"

"I'm not given to fainting. I did not swoon earlier." Suddenly, it seemed important he know that. "I did that intentionally before."

Only silence met that admission.

"Is that all?" he finally said.

"Yes." She wrinkled her nose. "No."

"Which is it?"

Did she imagine the faint twinge of amusement in his tone? Surely, she did. "My letters…"

"Aye?"

"You may have read them,"

"Ah *did* read them."

"Yes," she gritted out. "I'm aware. As I was saying…you read my letters, but you don't know anything about me. Not really." Suddenly it seemed very important that he know that.

"Is that all?" he asked, with his usual impassivity.

Another blush warmed Beatrice's cheeks. "That is all," she said, with as much dignity as she could muster.

He bowed his head. "'Tis done."

At that icy declaration, Beatrice shivered, now understanding all too well what those desperate souls who'd made a deal with the devil felt after inking his pages.

It was done.

CHAPTER 4

How is it I do not know if you paint or sketch? For everything I do know about you, there are a thousandfold more I wish to.

With Love and Longing,
Beatrice

THE NIGHT HAD BEEN A success.

Sprawled on his back in the middle of the floor, with his hands folded behind his head as a makeshift puzzle, Hamish smiled and stared at the pretty pastel mural overhead; just as he'd been staring at it since he'd laid down in his chambers at Burgess's fine, fancy townhouse to sleep some eight hours earlier.

From the moment they'd met, Burgess had proven a solid, loyal friend, and that held true since they'd arrived in London. In addition to helping Hamish with his plan, the other man had also offered Hamish a permanent place to stay in his household. The Mayfair residence, grander and more gilded than any home he'd ever set foot in, afforded greater warmth, security, and comforts than the hell they'd endured during their time in prison.

The considerable changes in Hamish's circumstances, however, weren't what accounted for his smile.

Bonny Beatrice.

Before he'd first met her, Hamish had done his research on

the lass. He'd scoured papers new and old about the Duke of Somerset's sister. The gossip pages had printed about her beauty, her status as the Rare Diamond who'd yet to wed. The gentlemen who'd courted her and then went on to wed others. But not a word on those scandal sheets had contained a hint about the lady's character.

Och. Only a Sassenach could commit such an oversight.

He'd been braced for her tears and horror, but he'd never expected her to be so feisty or spirited. Anyone else would have had a full, true drawm. She'd been almost more affronted at his having dared thought her weak than the outrageous proposition he'd put to her. She'd been tenacious and bold and hadn't been afraid to go toe-to-toe with him. In short, she'd been everything he'd expected an English lady wouldn't.

I'll have you know something else…I'm not given to fainting. I did not swoon earlier…I did that intentionally before…

Aye, the lass had proven to be an unexpectedly, fitting partner.

His gaze settled absently on two cherubs twined in a celestial dance overhead; the pair of them twisted and tangled not unlike Hamish now found himself joined with a Sassenach.

A lifetime ago, even English born, she'd have been the manner of lass he would have thought of making his. He narrowed his eyes on the patch of grey painted upon the cloud those cherubs danced.

But that had been before.

Back when he'd been a young man, without the responsibilities of future laird awaiting him. He'd envisioned a modest lifestyle, serving his clan. There'd never been a thought in Hamish's head that he'd one day inherit any of it. And in the end, even with his brother's passing, he hadn't. Everything had been ripped from him.

Today marked the path forward—a new beginning, one that would be born of revenge and right. With that sobering reminder fresh in his mind, Hamish straightened. Early on, in the earliest days of his imprisonment, and then sailing across the sea in the tight confines of a ship, every muscle in his body had ached from the unforgiving hard, wooden floor under his back. Now, he welcomed the solidness under him.

Leveraging himself with his palms, Hamish propelled himself upright in one fluid movement and headed for the water that had been left by Burgess's servants.

A short while later, after seeing to his morning ablutions and changing into respectable garments, as fine a quality as the ones he used to don, Hamish made his way through the corridors of his temporary home.

The lavish residence, bequeathed to Burgess by his beloved late aunt, couldn't be more different from the ancient stone keep once owned by Hamish's family than the Scots were from the English.

Ornate, gilded furniture managed to make the wide halls feel narrow, lined corridors done in garish pink wallpaper. The artist had painted each wood panel full to bursting with swans, birds, and beasts in an explosion of nauseatingly bright color.

When Hamish entered the breakfast room, he found Burgess had already seated himself. A plate, filled with a modest fare of bread, cheese, and apple lay untouched before the other man, who stared over folded fingertips at the opposite window. His eyes were blank, dark, and near identical to the empty ones Hamish now saw when he looked in a mirror.

But then, he and Burgess and all the men who'd been shipped off for either imagined crimes, or in most cases, negligible offenses. They'd both lost someone. For Hamish it had been his da, ma, and brother. For Burgess, the woman he'd loved.

They'd both lost everything.

The moment Hamish seated himself near his friend, a servant came forward. With a word of thanks, he accepted a cup of black coffee but waved away the offering of food.

Burgess looked to the young maid. "That'll be all," he said.

The girl dipped a curtsy, hurried from the room, and then closed the door behind her. They waited several moments after she'd gone.

"Well?" Burgess said.

Hamish set his coffee aside, forgotten. "Ah'll speak with the lass this morning and furnish a list of the households ah seek entry to."

Three.

There'd been three men who'd profited from the sale and plunder of Dunnottar. Hamish flexed his jaw. What he'd find out was who'd sold his family out to make that transaction happen.

"I was referring to the lady."

Hamish stared at the other man.

"Is she as lovely as they say?"

Bonnier. They'd not managed to do her beauty justice. He'd wager even a wordsmith couldn't.

He grunted. "It doesna matter what she looks like." Which was true. "It matters what she can," and would, "help me do."

"Yes," Burgess said, picking up his coffee, he cradled it between his hands. "I suspect that is true." He crooked a wry grin. "But it will certainly make your work more enjoyable."

His work. Aye, that was precisely what this was. Hamish had a job to see to, and when it was done, justice would be had.

"Her brother will pose a problem," Burgess was saying.

"Aye."

And the sister-in-law, too. That much had been clear last evening. Not that there'd ever really been a doubt. The English were a supercilious lot, more concerned with their precious bloodlines and even more precious landholdings. As such, the duke would have more than an opinion, he would have a *say* in who his cherished sister wed.

"Not for the reasons you think," Burgess said, accurately following Hamish's train of thought. "The lady hasn't married, but unlike other nobles eager to marry off their sisters and daughters, the current Duke of Somerset, and the duke before him, he is content to let her make a match of her choosing."

Hamish snorted.

"No, it's true," the other man insisted. "The lady is very much the beloved darling of her family."

"Spoiled is what ye mean, isna?"

Burgess chuckled. "It's likely a combination of both. However, might I suggest…if your efforts are to be successful here in London, might I suggest a good deal less antipathy when speaking of the lady?"

Hamish's dislike wasn't necessarily with the lady but with her people, and the power they wielded. But his friend was correct. If this ruse were to work, it required Hamish play a part, and play it fully.

Hamish notched his chin the other man's way. "Ye've my attention."

As the other man continued to reveal details about the Denningtons, Hamish attended to the other man, mentally filing away each detail shared. Having been born the third son of a powerful marquess, Borden Burgess had knowledge Hamish never had and never would of Polite Society. His knowledge, coupled with the property he'd inherited upon his return, would prove essential to Hamish's efforts.

"She's a beloved sister," Burgess concluded. "Which means he'll be watching you closely."

"He can watch all he likes," Hamish said, tightening his jaw. "He won't see anything." That was, he wouldn't see anything Hamish didn't wish to share. As a man who'd become a master of his emotions, he'd honed the art of revealing absolutely nothing.

The door opened, and they looked up. Ole Angus let himself in and limped into the room. "Yer still here," he said, slightly winded and out of breath.

Hamish consulted the pretty porcelain painted clock above the buffet. Not for long. Yanking out the Chippendale chair next to Hamish, his godfather ignored Burgess and seated himself.

"Ah, was hoping ah'd manage to meet ye, and talk ye out of this foolishness," the old Scot groused.

"Ah've already told you, ah'll nah be deterred," Hamish said to his godfather.

For the first time since he'd entered, Angus turned his attention on Burgess. "This is yer fault for nah stopping this."

Despite having vouched for the Englishman's loyalty and friendship, Angus had been suspicious as only an old Scot could be of the Sassenachs.

"You've known Hamish since he was a boy," Burgess said, showing Hamish's godfather a greater magnanimity than most any other man would, particularly one who'd opened his household to. "Does he strike you as one who can be deterred by me or anyone?"

Ole Angus glared through rheumy eyes. "Ye dinna help the

matters, ah wager, encouraging him to find out information he's better not knowing."

"Do ye really ken that?" Hamish asked quietly of his late da's brother, recalling his godfather's attention. "Do ye truly believe we're better off forgetting?"

"Aye," Angus said with a resounding finality that bespoke his conviction. "Ah ken the Sassenachs a good deal better than ye. For every way ye suffered before now, they could make it a thousandfold worse."

"Worse," Hamish murmured. What his uncle did not realize was that they couldn't do more to him than they'd already done. Hamish may have lived, but he'd died in every way that mattered.

Hamish pushed to his feet.

His godfather's ancient features turned pleading. "Please, lad. See reason."

Hamish squared his jaw. "Ah have to do this, Uncle."

Angus briefly closed his eyes, and then his shoulders slumping, he fell tiredly back in his chair. Sitting there, frail and pale and haggard, in this instant, Hamish's godfather looked some three decades older than his sixty-six years. Hamish hadn't been the only one who'd lost all those years ago. His uncle bore the lines of suffering in every harried wrinkle on his face.

Somehow finding a greater resolve, Hamish pushed his chair back and stood.

"Might I give a word of advice before you pay the lady a visit?" Burgess asked.

Hamish looked at him.

"Be charming," the other man said. "Otherwise, no one will believe you really snagged the lady's heart."

Angus scowled. "The lad isna a bluidy Sassenach skilled in the ways of charming. He's always been a crabber, he has."

Sending an apologetic glance Burgess's way, Hamish quit the breakfast room.

A short while later, he found himself returning to the Duke and Duchess of Somerset's palatial townhouse, where he and Lady Beatrice would commence their deception.

CHAPTER 5

My dearest Hamish,

Do you ever wish there weren't so many rules that dictate our every move? I far prefer imagining a world in which we are free to be together, whenever we wish, without worrying about society's recriminations.

With Love and Longing,
Beatrice

IF SHE'D NOT AWAKENED TO gossip page after gossip page detailing the arrival of her beloved betrothed, Beatrice would have believed she'd merely imagined the arrival of the big, burly Scot in possession of her greatest secret.

After a fitful night's sleep, eager to get this charade begun and over with, she'd prepared for the day, impatient to begin. For, at the end of it, she'd at last have what, until last night she'd thought was unattainable—freedom from the steady stream of suitors, and her humiliating fate of being thrown over.

From the corner of her bedchamber window overlooking the Mayfair streets below, Beatrice stole what was surely the hundredth glance at the gilded Louis XVI mantel clock.

Her stomach fluttered with anticipation.

It was entirely too early for his visit. The whole of society knew that first to call were the informal visitors and late to visit, were those whose interest was most serious. It was a lesson Beatrice had learned early on and one that had been solidified time after time by the slew of gentlemen bent on marriage.

No, the thrill of anticipation she felt had absolutely nothing to do with the brooding, surly Scot and everything to do with the freedom from future *beaus* awaiting her.

It was…

She stilled as a rider approached. Tall and broadly powerful, the figure seated upon the enormous black mount, could never be mistaken for any other. Instead of riding up to the front gates, Hamish drew his mount to a halt at the opposite side of the street. As if searching for foes in the shadows, or secrets in the streets, he scanned an intent gaze over the area around him.

Abandoning all attempts at discreetness, Beatrice stepped forward, and studied her accomplice; the term she'd decided to use for their arrangement. For it put them on equal footing.

With his black hair unfashionably long, without the benefit of a queue, and his eyes as hard as the cobbled streets he now stood upon, she'd have been wise to run, but curiosity compelled her, as it had from the moment he'd arrived last evening.

Suddenly, Hamish's stare locked on something, nearby.

She craned closer.

What exactly was he doing?

Puzzling her brow, she peered more closely.

Hamish's lips moved, but the distance between them made it impossible to make out the words he spoke.

A small, waif-thin figure emerged from the shadows. The boy in a tattered cap, and with coal-splotched cheeks approached Hamish. It hadn't been something he searched for, but rather, a someone.

The two exchanged a handful of words. The boy nodded, and then puffing his chest out with pride, he reached for Hamish's reins. He placed several coins in the boy's spare palm, and with a final word, Hamish turned back to Beatrice's residence.

She swiftly dropped the curtain and jumped out of sight. The suddenness of her movements sent the fabric fluttering into place, and she pressed herself against the wall.

The last thing she'd have him do is catch her gawking at him like some lovesick lady. Years ago, she'd vowed that the last thing she'd do was go falling in love with any suitor. Not when they were all certain to choose another. Protecting her heart had been a matter of both self-preservation and also maintaining what pride she could.

No, she'd not have this self-possessed Scot thinking she'd been studying him with fascination—even if she had been…and even if in doing so, it'd go a good deal towards their ruse of captivated couple.

Heart pounding, she peaked down below at the empty stoop.

Gone.

Beatrice craned her neck, searching for a glimpse of him. The boy he'd hired remained holding the reins of Hamish's mount, proving Hamish hadn't left, after all. She should be regretful. She should be desperate to escape this arrangement she found herself locked in.

So why did this thrill of anticipation persist? Why—?

Knock-Knock-Knock

Gasping, Beatrice spun towards that light tapping on the door. A thrill of anticipation? She made a face. Dread was the only sentiment coursing through her. That was it.

Knock-Knock-Knock

Beatrice gave her head a hard shake, and with unsteady palms, smoothed the front of her immaculate silk skirts. "E-Enter."

The door opened, and her bright-eyed maid, Lily, hastened inside. "My lady," she said, slightly out of breath. "Lord Hamish arrived!" she cried, with the same joy a mama would have shown a spinster daughter finally finding love.

So it began.

Or continued.

It was all mixed up.

The girl dropped her voice. "Most handsome he is. *Most* handsome. Dangerous looking like a highwayman," Lily sighed, "but tender on the inside." Her maid's prattling drifted in and out of focus.

Tender? When it came to any form of softness to him, a boulder of granite would be Lord Hamish Campbell's only rival. There was nothing tender, and only everything hard about the man who'd arrived last evening and flipped her world upside down.

But then, people saw what they wished to see. She and Hamish had been counting as much. Why then, was her head all muddled? She was not a young, naïve miss but a grown woman who'd—*Never been kissed or traveled or had a true sweetheart.* Nay, she was a nearly thirty-year-old woman who'd hardly any life experiences. All of which surely accounted for the excitement running through her. Where her brother's life had been filled with adventure and danger and passion, and her cousin Abigail having traveled across the ocean with grand tales of her life in America, Beatrice's own life had only ever been ordinary.

Now, she'd experience something. She, who'd only ever been proper would, like her brother and his wife had done, engage in a ruse. In helping Lord Hamish right past wrongs, she'd take part in something worthy, and possibly dangerous, and she'd do so, with a stranger, no less. Granted, she'd do so with a stranger who by his own admission was a former prisoner, who with one word could expose Beatrice's greatest shame. That in and of itself should have sent her fleeing to the country and away from any and all involvement with the mysterious stranger.

"My lady? *My lady*?"

Beatrice looked confusedly at her maid.

The girl cleared her throat. "Jax has shown Lord Hamish to the drawing room," she said, with hesitancy. One that sensed, she'd at last detected her mistress's unnatural quiet. Which would only rouse questions…and doubts.

"My lady?" Lily ventured.

"I cannot believe he is here, L-Lily," she whispered, adding a deliberate tremble to her maid's name.

Which wasn't *untrue*. Beatrice couldn't believe the situation she found herself in.

Lily's eyes instantly brightened. "I am so happy for you, my lady." She dropped her voice to a whisper. "All the servants are, really. It's all we could talk about for so long. How awful it's been that a woman as kind and gracious and beautiful as you has been forsaken for another, time after time."

Beatrice winced. Even the servants had been talking about her spinster state. Of course, they had. After all, that was all anyone had spoken about. But hearing it confirmed on the lips of her lady's maid leant a realness to it.

Lily blanched. "No disrespect meant, my lady." In her haste to assure Beatrice, the young woman tripped over her quickly spoken words. "It, it is only—"

"It is fine," Beatrice said gently and took one of her maid's hands in hers. She gave it a slight, reassuring squeeze.

Relief seeped from Lily's pale, plump features. "What I'd intended to say," she grimaced, "was that now we understood the reason you never married…because your real love had not come along." Lily brightened. "That is, until now."

"Until now," Beatrice repeated.

More like, *for* now.

And this time when Beatrice's sweetheart perished, the whole world would turn a different type of pity her away. But pity was still pity. The only difference being, when Hamish went, Beatrice would be left broken-hearted, free to mourn, and more importantly, free from the attentions of would-be suitors.

"I'll be along shortly."

Still, Lily remained.

"Is there something else, Lily?" she gently asked.

"It's just…he offered a calling card for you and *not* His Grace." Lily whispered that last part as if the duke were nearby, and they risked his overhearing.

"I see."

Ah, a breach in formality wasn't generally something the Denningtons cared about. However, Beatrice could say with an absolute certainty, that slight from a suitor Robert had never before met until yesterday, would have Beatrice's brother with his guard up.

"Thank you, Lily," Beatrice said.

Her maid dropped another curtsy and then left.

With the young woman gone, Beatrice took a look at her reflection in the vanity mirror. She'd opted for her finest gown, an amethyst satin fabric with a deeper neckline adorned in crystal beading, it favored her figure.

Why had she cared which dress she wore for their meeting?

For the sake of her and Hamish's ruse, it hardly mattered what she donned, and it wasn't as though it mattered either way what he thought of her appearance.

At all. In anyway.

That was what she told herself.

"Why does it feel like you're nothing more than a lying liar?" she said under her breath. Why did it feel like she cared if Lord Hamish found her… appealing?

Perhaps because you're so accustomed to men being wholly indifferent to you, a voice silently taunted.

Her gaze slid to the brooch Hamish had given her. Unbidden, she touched the silver of gilding and glass.

The vow he'd uttered last evening, came whispering forward.

"We aren't underhanded, lass. We're people of our word. Ah'll only have yer help if ye'll freely give it…"

Had Hamish threatened her, had he sought to bend her to his will, it would have been easier to reject the menacing Scot and all thoughts of him. But he hadn't…he'd sought her support and left the decision to Beatrice.

She closed her eyes. "Enough," she muttered.

She *didn't* care one way or another what Hamish Campbell thought of her.

With that, Beatrice made the long, winding walk downstairs to the drawing room.

A short while later, she stopped at the threshold of the door. Staring out the window to the streets below, Hamish stood with his broad back to her, and his hands clasped behind him, and she took the opportunity to further study him.

Attired in a midnight black wool coat, and equally black trousers, and positioned as he was, he'd the look of a fearless pirate at the wheel of his ship, eying the horizon before him. From his woolen trousers to his day jacket, those midnight black garments were perfectly tailored to his big frame. More impressive up close, he exuded power and strength that she'd do well to run from. Such a lethal-looking man wasn't one to tangle with, and yet she'd found herself partnering with him in a game with a definite conclusion, and one that couldn't end well.

His low baritone broke across her thoughts. "Is the view different?"

Beatrice jumped. "L-Lord Hamish?"

He didn't bother to turn. "The view." Just nudged his chin at the window. "Is this one different than the one in yer chambers where ye were watching me?"

Heat blossomed on her cheeks. He'd known she'd been staring at him. Alas, it appeared he'd have her acknowledge it outright.

With all the aplomb she could muster, Beatrice gave a toss of her head, joined him at those windows, and did what any woman would do—she changed the subject.

"Lord Hamish," she greeted. "You've arrived earlier than I anticipated."

Then, he did what no gentleman would do. Slanting a look her way, he dug in on his earlier questioning. "Spying on me, were ye?"

From another man, a less cynical, less life-scarred one, that tone would have been teasing.

"No answer?" he asked, like a dog with a bone.

She'd always prided herself on being truthful. This time, she understood the necessity that drove others to mendacity. "I was not."

He snorted. "Yer a lousy liar."

And apparently, she lied poorly.

"Are all Scots blunt to the point of rudeness?"

"Not all," he said.

"Well, that's affirming for your people," she muttered.

"Some are more direct."

"That I find hard to believe."

He released another one of those snorts. "Then ye arena spending enough time with the Scottish."

Beatrice closed her mouth. She'd not give him the satisfaction of admitting her family, friends, and staff were largely English.

The mocking glint in his eyes, however, indicated he knew as much.

Determined to establish an equal footing with this man so skilled at unsettling her, Beatrice gestured to the parcel-gilt and Egyptian-blue painted banquette.

"If you'd care to sit, Lord Hamish, I'd like to go over several things."

Hamish's jaw tightened, and with the long, impregnable pause, she expected he'd defy her directives. But then, a pugnacious man, he was no doubt unaccustomed to having orders put to him.

"I assure you," she said, teasingly. "I do not bite."

"Ah'm nah afraid of ye, lass."

"No, I expect one such as you is afraid of little, as such, I'll again ask you to take a seat."

They remained at an impasse. Beatrice, however, had no intention of backing down from Hamish Campbell. She'd have herself on equal footing with him. If she didn't establish that now, she'd never attain it.

With a sound somewhere between a grunt and growl, Hamish crossed over and sat—on the matching blue, sofa bench. As she availed herself to the banquette he'd declined, her lips twitched. Let him have his small protest.

Beatrice's maid appeared in the doorway with her embroidering.

"Lily," Beatrice said. "Would you arrange for refreshments for Lord Hamish and myself?"

The girl dropped another curtsy, and hastened off, leaving Beatrice and Hamish alone once more.

"Now, we do not have much time before she returns," she said, the moment Lily had gone. "I'd have us—"

"Go over several things. Aye, ye said as much." He gave an impatient wave of his hand. "Get on with it."

"There are certain rules of etiquette," she began.

He chuckled. "Yer givin' me etiquette lessons?"

"It may seem like a waste of time to you,"

"It is."

Any other time she'd agree with him on that. "Given the nature of our arrangement," she continued over his interruption, "we must follow certain strictures."

"*Strictures*?"

And if he were a man capable of humor, she'd have sworn there was a wealth of mirth contained within those two syllables.

"Yes, *strictures*," she said impatiently. "If we are to," she stole a glance at the front of the room, and dropped her voice to a hushed whisper, "dupe the *ton*, then we'd best adhere to societal rules of what constitutes a courtship."

He grunted. "Well, out with it, lass."

Beatrice proceeded to tick off a list. "Exchanging letters by post is an indication of a serious stage in our courtship. As such, we should begin…or given the fact society believes we exchanged letters before, we should *resume* doing so."

"And what do ah say in these letters?"

"I…"

She'd not a deuced clue. She'd been courted what *felt* like a hundred thousand million times before, and of all the men who'd sought to marry her, not a one of them had put a pen to paper.

"Lass?" he asked, with his usual impatience.

"I don't know…*romantic* things."

"*Romantic things*?" he repeated.

Again, she felt her face go warm. Here she'd believed having no true suitor would be the pinnacle of humiliation, only to have been tasked with giving a step-by-step lesson to a make-believe beau on how to court her.

"Or, that is what is usually in them." She suspected. "Sonnets. Poems. Odes." That was, anyway, what she'd gathered from other women and books she'd read.

" 'Ah'm nae romantic."

"That I believe," she said under her breath.

He cupped a hand around his ear. "Whit wis that?"

"The letters should include details about ourselves and our dreams of the future and the time we've shared."

"We havena shared any time, and that isna what ye said."

"If you knew that," she said in exasperation, resisting the urge to stamp her feet, "then why—"

The faintest silver flecks within his blue-black irises glimmered, stealing the rest of her retort, and thoroughly befuddling her. No man had a right to eyes that magnetic.

She sought to steady her heart, sought to regain her footing. "Where was I?"

"Ye were giving me course work."

She puzzled her brow.

"Telling me wit to write," he clarified.

"You strike me as a clever man," she gritted out between her teeth. "I'm sure you can figure it out, Hamish."

At her use of his Christian name, his dark brows flared slightly. Good, let him have a taste of being unnerved. Even as the case would have it, only for an instant.

"Why thank ye for that compliment, lass."

She opened her mouth to tell him the last thing she'd intended was to flatter him when that same distracting glimmer in his eyes stopped her.

"Why…why…You're *teasing* me," she blurted.

"Aye, 'n' haein a deuced guid time o' it, tae."

Would wonders never cease?

Then, he winked. It was a slight, up and down sweep of impossibly long, ink-black lashes, and it was a simple gesture and yet, she'd never before properly appreciated how very sensuous that movement was…before now.

She'd expected he'd be incapable of levity. And yet…he'd proven himself one capable of humor, and it put him in a new light. It made him more real and sent her senses topsy-turvy.

He tipped his chin Beatrice's way. "What else?" he urged.

What else, indeed?

Reigning in her thoughts, she brought her focus back to the lecture she'd prepared. "There is the matter of your visits."

"What about them?"

"They are generally no more than thirty minutes in length."

"Hmph."

"Hmph 'what', Hamish?"

"Tis just, given that silly rule, Ah'd think ye'd make more haste after spying on me at the window."

"I wasn't…" Refusing to let him get another rise out of her, Beatrice continued. "I'd be remiss if I didn't inform you that serious suitors intent on marriage, do not arrive in the morning."

He looked at her as if she were sporting two heads. "Now, ye'r joking me."

"I'm not." She explained, "Etiquette dictates you arrive later in the afternoon."

"Only a Sassenach would come up with rules so stupid," he said under his breath.

"If we intend for this arrangement to be believable, then you'd do well to neither be so apparent in your disdain of all things English,"

"That's a difficult feat, lassie."

"*Or* question the rules of society, no matter how stupid they may be."

"So ye agree they're stupid?" he drawled.

"Yes. No." Actually, she did agree that the rules of the *ton* were archaic and ridiculous. But in the scheme of their ruse, that was neither here nor there. She spoke through clenched teeth. "My opinion has no bearing on the matter."

He shot her a smug, all-knowing look.

Her patience snapped. Beatrice stormed to her feet so she had the height advantage over him. "Need I remind you that you sought *me* out, Lord Hamish? You were the one who pilfered my letters."

"Pilfered implies ah stole them. Ye left them for me."

God, he was as infuriating as the English day was rainy. "For a man who has such stakes in this arrangement, I'd expect you wouldn't act as if all of this is a game,—*Hamish*."

The height advantage she'd snagged over him proved short-lived, as he slowly stood, unfurling each inch of his six-foot, four-inch frame. His dark eyes clouded.

"Ah dinna take any of this for a game, Beatrice, and ah do ken the rules of yer *ton*," he said quietly. "Ah'd a mother, and then tutors who advised me on all of them. And before my family was betrayed, and my world turned upside down, ah verra much lived like any fine English gentleman."

She started. She'd not known that. Of course, she hadn't. Until just recently, Hamish Campbell had been a stranger to her.

He shifted closer, and the hint of tobacco, that masculine scent, clung to him and filled the air and her senses.

"Ye ken ah arrived here without a thought of what ah was doing?" he asked, bluntly, his harsh tone at odds with the strange things his surprisingly intoxicating scent did to her.

"No," she said, weakly.

Only, she had.

"The rules *are* stupid. A man who hasn't seen his true love for months, and is suddenly reunited, wouldn't wait to be with ye. He'd be here the minute he knew ye were awake, and soak in every single second of ye, lass."

Her lips slipped apart. "Oh," she whispered, her voice as weak as her knees.

Only, he wasn't done with her.

Hamish continued in that low, sonorous, entrancing way. "He'd nah wait for some respectable hour when all the other suitors converged upon ye," he said, his voice a sough upon her flushed face, "and he'd certainly never relinquish that time to them, because the thought of ye with another would be too great to bear. He'd sooner fight them than allow them the chance to woo ye, Beatrice Diana."

In her mind, she knew Hamish's words were an explanation and nothing more. But her heart didn't care anything about that. That wildly beating organ fluttered under his hypnotic telling.

Hamish slowly glided his knuckles along her cheek, further confounding her senses.

Her gaze locked with his, and the world stood still. The earth forgot its job was to spin, and time meant to march onward.

" 'N' he certainly wouldn't stay for just twenty or thirty minutes. He'd stay longer because the idea of being apart from ye for a moment more was a fate he couldn't bear."

Beatrice's breath caught.

His distracted caress came to a slow stop, and he lingered his fingers there upon her cheek. His sapphire blue eyes darkened, and his ink-black lashes swept down, obscuring whatever emotion existed in those depths.

Nay, she recognized that emotion, with Eve's intuition.

Desire.

But this was not a hunger for her rank or station or even this ruse she'd become a partner in, but rather for Beatrice, herself. And for a woman who'd never truly been sought for anything more than her birthright, the evidence of his passion for her had a dizzying effect.

Beatrice lifted her head slowly, and Hamish dipped his lower.

They hovered that way, their breaths mingling, their chests nearly touching.

A flurry of footfalls sounded from the hall.

Still, they both remained locked in a like trance; two people who defied time to cease existing, once more.

They managed to find their way back to the moment and took their seats just as Lily came rushing back to the drawing room.

Beatrice's maid curtsied, then continued over to an armchair in the far corner of the room. All the while, Beatrice struggled to put her mind to rights. Her efforts were in vain, and she was grateful when a moment later, another maid entered, bearing refreshments.

Beatrice used the opportunity to compose herself. Or, attempted to. Her hands would not cease their trembling. He'd almost kissed her. Not because doing so helped further advance his plans of revenge. There'd been no reason other than, at least, in that moment, he'd longed to. And she'd longed for it, more.

"Thank ye," Hamish said as the maid set down the silver tray.

"Yes, Mary," Beatrice managed to say. "Thank you." Had she known a single British lord who'd ever thanked a servant? Her beloved brother, included among those ranks?

After the girl had taken her leave, Beatrice cast a discreet look in Lily's direction. The woman's focus remained fixed on her embroidery frame. With her hands now steady, Beatrice reached for the teapot, and knowing it was a detail the world would expect she'd already possess about her betrothed, she spoke quietly; "How do you take your tea, Hamish?"

He stole a glance at their chaperone. "As all good Scots do, with plenty of sugar, and then milk added last," he said, in equally hushed tones.

For an English lady, pouring tea was as common as rain. As such, she'd never before considered just how intimate an act it was…

until now. As she made Hamish's tea—Hamish who preferred his tea with plenty of sugar and milk and added in just that order—she discovered the act provided a revealing glimpse into his likes and preferences.

Beatrice offered him the teacup and as he accepted it, their fingers brushed. Riveted, Beatrice stared at their hands. Hers unblemished and smooth, his bigger, more powerful, and scarred, stood in stark juxtaposition. His long fingers, that dwarfed the delicate porcelain cup, bespoke a life of struggle and strife. Those blemished palms contained stories of the man before her, and dangerously, Beatrice found herself yearning to know each of them.

While Beatrice made herself a cup of tea, Hamish's piercing gaze remained upon her.

They took a sip at the same time.

Hamish's eyes widened.

"It isn't good?" she said quickly. "I can make you another."

" 'Tisn't good."

Beatrice tensed.

"Tis perfect," he spoke with an almost boy-like wonder that left her all warm inside.

"Ah haven't had a dram of tea like this in years," he said in hushed tones, his low voice, faraway and distant.

His lips curved up at the corners, in the first relaxed, uncomplicated smile she'd seen from him, and the sight of it wrought further havoc on her heart's rhythm.

Hamish glanced down into the contents of his cup. "My mum would insist all her lads join her for tea. My brother and da despised tea, but we were want to deny her anything."

As he reminisced, his brogue grew so thick, Beatrice had to concentrate to make out each word.

"Ah on th' other hand enjoyed it. Bit, ah think, whit ah enjoyed most wis th' time we spent together doin' something so simple, something ah didnae properly appreciate. 'til 'twas gone..."

Beatrice's smile faded, and without thinking, she reached out and covered one of his hands with her own. "I am sorry," she said softly.

His answer came as fast as a reflex. "Tis braw." He grimaced. "It is fine," he clarified.

Beatrice shifted closer so that their knees touched. "It's not," she said in hushed tones. "And it is all right to admit that it's not."

His jaw flexed. "What does that change?"

"Not the past." She paused. "But acknowledging your feelings on the past, it speaks to who you are and who you've become… and what you have done in your life, Hamish."

"What ah've done," he spat. "For almost ten years, my life hasn't been my own because of the wrongs done my family. There's no good in any of that."

Hamish tried to pull his hand away, but she kept it covered and brought her other palm under his to hold him in place.

"We look before and after,
And pine for what is not;
Our sincerest laughter
With some pain is fraught;
Our sweetest songs are those
that tell of saddest thought."

He peered at her. "What's that?"

"Shelley. I don't believe I ever understood that stanza, until this moment," she murmured. "Sadness and beauty…we cannot separate them. For good or bad, they are part of the human experience, and denying either does not erase those emotions inside you."

Hamish glanced down at their still-joined hands. The heat of his touch warmed her in ways she'd only read of in the romantic tales she'd read, and then in stories she'd secretly penned and subsequently burned because surely no touch could elicit such a feeling.

"Ah've something for you," he murmured.

Her heart galloped. "Y-you do?"

Reaching inside his jacket, Hamish withdrew a small, folded sheet of parchment. Beatrice set her teacup down and accepted the proffered page. With her hands unsteady once more, she opened the note, and read.

"Names," she blurted and then promptly looked across the room at where her maid sat.

Lily remained with her head down, and all her focus on her embroidery frame.

Beatrice returned her focus back to Hamish. "These are names," she repeated, this time, her lips barely moved when she spoke.

"Aye," he said, hushed. "Those are the men whose homes ah'd have ye gain me entry to."

What did you think he was giving you? A page of romantic sonnets he'd penned himself?

Beatrice looked down again at the list written in Hamish's hand; those bold, confident slashes of ink were as powerful as the man himself.

The Earl of Shaftesbury
Viscount Scarborough
Baron Roxburghe

"There are only three," Beatrice said.

She should have been relieved. More names would have meant more time spent with the enigmatic Scot, which she certainly did not want. Did she?

He nodded. "It willna be long. Ah'll have answers and then justice, and then, ah'll be gone."

She should be relieved. So…why, wasn't she?

"But…how can you know these are the suspects?" she asked, earnestly. "Mayhap there are others?"

He banished that thought. "These are the ones. Shaftesbury wasn't an earl at the time. He took part in the arrests of my family. He was and is a second-born son, without a title, *until* he served in the," Hamish's lips pulled in a sneer, "*King's* army. "For his efforts in service to His Majesty, Shaftesbury found himself with the title he now carries."

Hamish continued. "Scarborough," he pointed at the page, "Is a collector of Scottish artifacts. He's in possession of the widest accumulation in England. After my family was—" A muscle rippled along his jaw, and pain flashed in his eyes.

Instinctively, she touched a hand to the top of Hamish's, even as her mind hurriedly pointed out, he'd mistake her compassion for pity, and a man so proud would reject that showing—and any offering, for that matter.

Only, he didn't pull away or lash out. Instead, he continued speaking in that near-soundless murmur. "After we were removed from our home, the Campbell's belongings were partitioned off."—His hand tensed under hers.—"Most of them went to Scarborough's vast collection of Scottish relics."

"And Baron Roxburghe?"

"With the exception of the Campbell Keep which served as a British military post for a number of years, Roxburghe found himself the proud new owner of the remainder of the Campbell's holdings."

Beatrice processed all that information he'd imparted. After Robert's marriage to Helena, who'd previously lived on the streets, Beatrice had prided herself on seeing more clearly the world and all the injustices done so many. But this? What Hamish had revealed here proved how very little she still saw. How little she knew. And her heart hurt for the wrongs which had been committed against Hamish's family.

"How do you know all this?" she asked quietly. When, by his admission, he'd only recently returned.

"Ah know a man, who'd also been wronged. His late aunt was an English lady, with a fondness for her nephew, and a firm belief in his innocence. Her rank also afforded her the ability to send and receive letters while we were in Australia. She provided those details about the men who'd gained from my family's misfortune. Had she lived, she would be the ones to open those doors for us."

The ones he now needed Beatrice to open.

And she and Hamish would have never crossed paths. Why should that thought leave her oddly bereft?

Beatrice folded the paper and tucked it inside the pocket sewn along the front of her gown.

As if they'd shared a chat about the weather, and not talk of treachery and evil, they returned to their refreshments. And as she and her imagined betrothed, who'd turned suddenly real, sat with a comfortable silence, sipping their tea, Beatrice discovered there was a far greater danger than being exposed as a fraud who'd made up a suitor—it was falling for a rugged, proud Scot bent on revenge against those who'd wronged him.

CHAPTER 6

I long for us to run wild in the midst of a rainstorm and take shelter and find warmth within one another's arms. As long as I have your embrace, I will always know home.

With Love and Longing,
Beatrice

HIS FIRST VISIT WITH THE lass done, Hamish walked at a brisk clip through the Duke of Somerset's home. All the while, his exchange with Beatrice played over and over in his mind.

When he'd set out this morning, he'd thought only of executing his plans for justice. He'd been solely focused on providing her with the names of the lords whose households he sought entry into and securing an entry with her assistance.

Instead, there'd been talks of how he'd taken his tea and owning one's emotions, and her recitation and their discussion of Shelley, all details which collectively made Lady Beatrice, Hamish's means to an end…more. Their morning visit had revealed her to be a woman of intellect, who read the romantic poets, and who though fully aware of societal dictates, chafed at the rules of decorum.

In short, she was a real woman…not that that had ever been in question from the moment they'd come face to face just last evening. But, where before there'd been a wave of desire for the voluptuous Athena, today, there'd been that primal hunger, and…

more. There'd been an emotional connection, which he'd not anticipated and one Hamish neither wanted, nor for that matter, needed. He needed to be focused. He needed all his energies and attention on—

Hamish sensed a presence behind him—too late.

"Lord Hamish,"

Even as that voice called out, staying him in his tracks, Hamish silently cursed his uncharacteristic distractedness. Hell's bells, the lady was already wreaking havoc on his focus.

Schooling his features, Hamish turned and faced Beatrice's brother who stood a short distance away. A smile wreathed the duke's face. That smile, however, failed to reach the other man's eyes.

Hooding his lashes, Hamish remained silent and waited as the other man approached.

The duke stopped a pace away.

Both men sized one another up.

Near in height, Hamish still had a two-inch advantage over him, and though Hamish was a stone or two bigger, the Duke of Somerset's build better suited a working man and not a lord just a step beneath royalty.

Beatrice's brother spoke first. "Might I say I'm disappointed that you'd taken your leave before we'd a chance to speak, Lord Hamish."

Another man may have taken that casual drawl as a friendly tone. Hamish wasn't most men. Furthermore, he'd experienced enough with the English to ken their favorite pastime was playing with Scots like they were prey. Add a cherished sister into the proverbial mix, and they toyed with one like a cat with a canary.

The duke arched an arrogant eyebrow. "What? The feelings are not mutual? I'd expect the gentleman so ardently in love with my sister would care to meet her family."

It wouldn't do to bait the man, who, with his influence and power, could put a quick end to any arrangement Hamish and Beatrice had come to. And yet…

"Ah came to see whom ah wished to see, Duke."

Beatrice's brother narrowed his eyes into dangerous slits any other man would have feared. "May I speak plainly, Lord Hamish?"

Hamish inclined his head. "Here, ah thought the Sassenachs weren't capable of such a feat."

That taunt didn't get the rise Hamish expected it would from an English duke. Instead, the other man eyed him closely. "One would expect with your apparent disdain for all things English, the last person you would have fallen in love with would be an English woman, Lord Hamish."

"Beatrice isn't most women," Hamish said solemnly in that deliverance. "And ah'm not referring to the lass's beauty—though she could put a selkie to shame," he murmured that last part more to himself. "She's clever, quick-witted, spirited, and resourceful; a veritable Medb Queen of Connacht."

Nor did those words he had for Beatrice's brother come from a place of pretense. From the start, she'd proven herself intrepid and forthright he'd never known any woman to be.

The duke contemplated Hamish with a penetrating stare that would have unnerved any other man. But just as Beatrice was no ordinary lass, neither was Hamish a man like any other. Nay, he'd been shaped by betrayal and bore witness to the death of his own brother and father. A duke's glower couldn't induce a single dash of terror within him.

Beatrice's brother broke the seemingly impregnable silence. "You are saying the correct words, Lord Hamish, and yet, you, by your and my sister's own admission, have conducted yourself in a way that was anything but aboveboard." The duke lowered his voice so that his not incorrect charges were barely audible. "Never once did you pay her an open visit nor seek my approval."

"Mm, of course. How could ah forget in all Beatrice shared, that your first order of business when courting the current duchess was to seek your sister's approval."

"It's not at all the same," the Duke of Somerset said, between clenched teeth.

Hamish winged a brow up. "Why, because yer a man and Beatrice is…what? A child who requires her brother to make decisions for her?"

"It wasn't *just* a secret courtship—though that would be bad enough. You *became* betrothed."

Hamish couldn't resist. "Without yer permission."

The duke's impressive stretch of patience snapped. He took a step closer to Hamish and stuck his face in his. "Because it is *my* responsibility," Beatrice's brother jammed a finger against his own chest, "to see she is cared for and safe, and that you don't gather that *simple* fact suggests you are a man who'd not put her well-being first."

"Expecting the lass should be free to make her own decisions doesna mean ah dinna care about her well-being. It means, ah respect her, and see her as an equal. As for, yer approval? It didn't matter then, and it matters even less now. All that matters is that which Beatrice wants." Hamish sneered at the arrogant English lord opposite him. "Ah'd also remind ye. Yer sister? She is a grown lass capable o' making her own decisions and doing so without her brother's *approval*.

That managed to silence the seething Englishman, for a moment. But only a moment.

"As honorable and liberal as that opinion may be, Lord Hamish, women *are* held to different standards. Loving my wife, sister, and daughters, as I do, I *wish* the world was both fairer and different. However, that isn't the case."

Hamish had spent such a large part of his life seeing the English as less than human, and as such, he found himself jarred by how freely and sincerely Beatrice's brother spoke about the love he had for his family.

"The fact remains, my sister *isn't* allowed the freedom to carry on as she pleases without consequence. To do so risks her reputation and her very future." He stuck his face in Hamish's again and spoke in lethal tones only a big brother could perfect. "Based on your clandestine meetings, I can only speculate that they occurred without the benefit of a companion or maid for accompaniment, all of which are grounds for me to call you out and kill you at dawn."

Hamish opened his mouth to point out he'd be part of the lady's future, and therefore the threats this man feared were not ones that would ever be realized. The taunting words died on Hamish's tongue before he could utter them into existence. For the lass's brother may be an overbearing, bumptious fellow, but, in this? In the accusations he'd leveled and the concern he had for Beatrice, the man wasn't wrong.

Hamish had become so caught up that reality had gotten all mixed with fiction. For the first time, he found himself confronted with a thought of Beatrice…navigating Polite Society after he was gone. She'd become prey to those English gents she'd written about in her letters.

A scorching rage slithered around like a serpent in his mind.

"Nothing to say, Lord Hamish?" the duke jeered.

A flush heated Hamish's neck. *God, what the hell is wrong with me, woolgathering about the lass?*

He reigned in his emotions…emotions which only posed a dangerous distraction. "Ah ken the reason for your worrying," Hamish allowed.

At that concession, disbelief flashed in the other man's eyes.

"If ah had a sister," Hamish went on, "well, ah'd respond the same." If not worse. "But if ye think to deter me from marrying yer sister, then ye'r bound to be disappointed."

The duke flattened his mouth into a frustrated line. "I want your word she won't be hurt."

Hamish started to offer that vow but stopped.

Can you really promise that? a niggling voice silently derided. Ultimately, the very nature of Hamish's plans for revenge made the lady a target.

Beatrice's brother thinned his eyes another fraction.

Hamish was saved from answering.

"Papa!"

Both men looked to the owner of that exuberant little cry. A child, a little girl, no more than six or seven came hurtling over. Behind her, a taller little boy walked at a more sedate pace, with a swagger that marked him as a future duke.

The girl launched herself at the duke, just as the man opened his arms to catch her up. "Aila," the duke greeted with a boisterous welcome, in a display that could only be genuine affection and love for his daughter.

Hefting her high, Beatrice's brother protectively angled the dark-haired child away from Hamish's view. The little girl, however, was having none of it. She arched around the duke and peered baldly at Hamish.

Hamish inclined his head in a silent greeting.

Catching that unspoken exchange, the duke frowned. "Why aren't you in your lessons?" he asked, directing that question to the blond-headed heir apparent.

"Aila insisted on being present, and I followed to ensure she didn't get herself in trouble."

Beatrice's niece gasped. "How dare you?" Squiggling out of the duke's arms, she shimmied to the floor. "Darragh is *lying*, Papa."

"Takes a liar to know a liar!"

She stuck her tongue out at the older boy.

The boy responded in kind.

As brother and sister launched into a noisy argument, Hamish felt himself knocked off-balance. Had he ever been so innocent? It'd been a lifetime and the memories were so distant—distant, buried, and replaced by reminiscences of death and betrayal.

Hamish stared wistfully at the bairns before him. Watching the duke's son and daughter spar, forced to the front, recollections of another time—quarrels between he and Finlay. How many spats they'd had over who received the last of the cranachan. And chases and full-out brawls, which had ensued when a quicker, fleeter of hand and foot Hamish managed to snag the prize.

Hamish tensed. They'd company. He felt her presence even though he didn't need to see it. Even though the lass's own kin dinna sense her standing there.

"Children," the duke raised his voice to make himself heard over the argument in progress. "*Children*."

When his address had no impact, Beatrice's brother pressed his thumb and index finger together and put them in his mouth, until the digits formed a ring shape, and then he blew. That piercing whistle shattered the argument and effectively silenced the pair. Brother and sister instantly fell into a line of two; all the while, they shot sideways glares at one another.

"Now," the duke said. "May I advise that you return to the

nursery?"

"No," Aila responded.

She immediately caught an elbow in the side from her brother. "It wasn't really a question Aila," he spoke from the corner of his mouth.

"Well, it went up at the end as questions do, *Darragh*."

Another lord would have chafed at being challenged by a child, in front of a foe. The duke, however, only gave his head a wry shake.

"Either way," the little girl carried on, "*this* seemed far more important." She waved a small hand Hamish's way. "Are you he?" she asked with all the unrestrained curiosity, only an innocent child could muster.

The duke stepped between them, but Hamish and Aila took a step around him.

"It depends," Hamish said, sinking to a knee before the girl. "Which *he* dae ye think ah be?"

"Aunt Beatrice's sweetheart?"

He bowed his head. "One 'n' th' same."

"My father doesn't trust you," she confided in a noisy whisper.

"Aila," the duke chided.

Hamish and Aila continued to ignore him. " 'N' whit do ye think?"

The girl angled her head the opposite direction Hamish had cocked his. That small movement brought the brown ringlets bouncing at her shoulder. "I believe if my Aunt Beatrice trusts you, then he should, too."

Hamish smiled. "Clever lass."

Aila cast a glance over at her father. "I know you said you don't like him or trust him, but mmmffffmff."

The remainder of Aila's words were lost to the hand Darragh placed over his sister's mouth.

Like a naughty child caught with a hand in the cookie jar, the Duke of Somerset, with flushed cheeks, looked up at the ceiling.

Another grin tugged at Hamish's lips.

Slamming a foot hard against her brother's shin, Aila followed that blow with an elbow to the lad's side.

Beatrice's young nephew gasped and lost his grip enough upon Aila that she wrestled his hand back to his side…but not before she pinched his forearm hard enough to ring another exhalation of pain from the lad.

"Impressive wirk, lass," Hamish said when she'd properly dispelled of her brother and father's interference.

With a toss of her dark brown curls, Aila sank into a perfect curtsy. "Thank you."

"Ye were saying before, lass?"

Aila cleared her throat. "What I was saying before I was so *rudely* interrupted," she directed that last charge to her brother, "is that my father may not like you, but I approve of you just fine."

Hamish bowed his head and touched a hand to his chest. "Aside from Lady Beatrice's, yours is the only approval that matters," he said with a deserved solemnity to his statement.

Instead of being further enamored, the lass thinned her eyes and looked out at Hamish from under the slits those lashes formed. "Are you attempting to charm me, Lord Hamish? If so, you're bound to be disappointed as I'm not a lady who can be charmed."

He touched a hand to his chest. "Though bonny ye may be, A'm a loyal lad, and my affections are reserved fur just one—yer aunt Beatrice."

"Yes," Darragh shot back. "Well, I do not trust you, either."

As one, Hamish and Aila looked to the ruddy-cheeked lad.

Aila cupped a hand around her mouth and spoke in a brazen whisper. "Don't mind him. He's just angry you praised me for besting him."

"You didn't best me!" Darragh snapped.

"Did, too."

"Did not!" the lad shouted.

"Did—"

"That will be enough, children."

Hamish glanced to the owner of that command, which unlike the lady's husband who'd relied on a shrill whistle to gain his children's notice—and then, only with mild success—was quietly delivered but stern enough to penetrate the latest row between brother and sister.

The duchess.

The lady moved with a stealth befitting the time she'd spent surviving on the merciless streets of London. She briefly touched her eyes on every member of the party present. Her children had the good sense and grace to drop contrite gazes to the pale blue carpet under their feet.

The Duchess of Somerset then moved her attention to her equally sheepish-looking husband. She quirked an eyebrow, and that slight upward arc sent deeper color rushing into her husband's cheeks. A silent look passed between the couple, whose thoughts appeared so in harmony they neither relied on nor needed words.

It'd been that way with Hamish's mother and father. They'd shared a closeness and a love that ran deeper than Loch Lomond. A bond that as a lad, made Hamish cringe. In time, however, when he'd been coming to manhood, he'd imagined finding and knowing that same affection with a good wife. That'd been one more unrealized dream taken from him that day.

"Lord Hamish?"

Having been caught up in memories of old, Hamish started and swiftly switched his gaze from the floor to the duchess patiently staring back. There was an intelligent glint in the woman's eyes. That, coupled with the sizeable scar on her cheek, bespoke a person whose own life experience had left her able to discern the men and women around her with tragedies…and secrets of their own.

A slight tug on his sleeve brought Hamish's focus away from the duchess's unnerving stare.

"Did my Papa and Darragh upset you?"

Hamish sank to a knee so he could look the lass in the eye. "They dinna upset me…" His words trailed off.

The wee lass had Lady Beatrice's eyes—irises flecked with hints of greens and golds, and for an instant, they offered Hamish a glimpse of a *different* wee lass; a daughter with Beatrice's golden curls and brilliant blue eyes.

Aila cocked her head. "Are you sure they didn't upset you because you seem upset? You've gone all quiet and look funny."

"They didn't upset me. They love yer aunt and are worried about her. Ah'd never find fault with them for that."

And that much was true. As it was, the duke and duchess were right to their suspicions. Hamish's intentions were not the honorable ones he said they were. "It was seeing ye and yer ma and dad had me thinking o' my own parents."

"They are in love, too?" Aila said with a child's intuition.

"Aye. Very much so." He paused. "Or, they were."

"They died?"

"Aila," the duke and duchess said sharply, at the same time.

He glanced over the lass's shoulder to her red-faced parents. "'Tis fine," he said and returned his attention to Aila. "Aye, they died," he murmured.

Beatrice's niece rested a tiny hand on his shoulder. "I am sorry you're sad."

He shrugged. "Twas a long time ago."

"Yes, but no matter how old one is, I don't believe one ever gets over losing their mama or papa."

A pang struck. No, the pain of losing his da, his ma, and his brother would be with Hamish always. "Yer correct on yet another score, lassie."

Aila beamed. "Well, I for one am *very* happy you'll be marrying my Aunt Bea. All the gentlemen who've come before you *never* talk to me or my brothers. And they *always* act like silly boys afraid to look at my mama and papa." She leaned in and whispered. "I like that you're not afraid of them."

He matched her whisper with one of his own. "*Should* ah be?"

"Yes!" Darragh called over.

The duke rested a hand on his son's shoulder and gave it a light squeeze.

The lass considered him a moment. "You don't strike me as a man who is afraid of anything…even if there are times you should be."

Hamish gave Aila a small wink.

Aye, she was right on that score. There wasn't any greater misery or struggle life could heap on his shoulders than had already been done. He'd lost everything. He'd lost everyone. And when a man lost it all, well, there wasn't much to fear after all that.

"Yes, well, I know who he should be afraid of," the duke's distrustful lad interjected. Staring straight at Hamish, Darragh made a fist and sent it sailing slowly into his other palm with a noticeable *thwack. Thwack. Thwack.* "And you have my vow, if you hurt my Aunt Beatrice, you'll be answering to him."

"Don't you mean *'her'*, Darragh?" Aila drawled. "Because the Good Lord knows I've thumped you more times than the cock crows, and I'll be the one to do Lord Hamish in if he hurts her.

"You have not trounced me *once*," Darragh gritted out.

"No," Aila allowed. "I've trounced you six times," she clarified, holding up that respective number in fingers.

Bright crimson circles exploded on the lad's cheeks. "Have, not."

"Have, too."

Just as brawl seven was set to erupt, the duchess collected each child by an arm. "If you'll excuse us, Lord Hamish. We look forward to seeing you soon, but we must be getting these ones back to the nursery. Isn't that right, my dear?" She gave her husband a pointed look.

"Lord Hamish." Reluctantly, the duke dropped a curt bow, and, making equally brusque goodbyes, he followed after his wife.

Bemused, Hamish stared after the noisy family as they took their leave—and waited for Beatrice to show herself.

BEATRICE HAD FOLLOWED HAMISH ON his way out.

She'd *only* done so to ensure her family had not waylaid him—which she'd expected they would do—and which they *had.*

The moment she'd come upon her brother haranguing Hamish, she'd intended to step forward and intervene, but then Hamish had begun speaking about Beatrice, and then her niece and nephew had appeared…

Everyone knew eavesdropping was a sin to be avoided…that was unless one was prepared to see or hear things they'd rather not see or hear. Governesses and mothers and people everywhere swore nothing good could ever come from spying on others.

Only to learn, those trusted ones had been right.

After Helena dragged Robert along, and the two ushered their precious but precocious children off, Beatrice came to an eye-opening discovery—the world had proven right about listening in on other people's exchanges.

For watching Hamish with her niece and nephew, Beatrice had seen a new glimpse at Hamish Campbell, and there could be no unseeing or forgetting the endearing tenderness he'd shown Aila and even the defiant Darragh.

With her back pressed against the corridor wall, Beatrice borrowed support from the painted panel and attempted to get her racing heart back into a semblance of a normal beat.

She tried…and failed.

Closing her eyes, she rested a hand against her chest.

First, there'd been her overhearing his defense of her character to Robert. As though, that beautiful enumeration of her traits hadn't been enough, he'd gone and charmed her niece—even as he'd claimed to not have thought of doing so, there could be no disputing he'd done just that. Talking with her niece and nephew, and showing them kindness, served no purpose in Hamish's crusade for revenge against those who'd wronged him and his family.

Were he a ruthless bastard, driven only by his own quest, he'd never have spared a thought for Darragh and Aila. He'd have come and gone, just as all the many other suitors who'd come before, courting her, but not ever really caring about her or those in her life.

Unlike the previous gentlemen, Hamish hadn't been so single-minded in his goals as to fail and see those little children as people who mattered so very much to her. He'd dropped to a knee so he could meet their gazes and…Her chest hitched. God save her, she'd lost a part of her heart to him in an irrevocable loss there could be no recovering. She—

"Leavin' me to my own devices, were ye, lassie?" That deep Scottish brogue rolled around the corner and slashed clear through her romantic musings.

Gasping, Beatrice's eyes flew open.

Hamish ducked his head around the corner and flashed a teasing half-grin that sent her heart galloping all the faster.

"It appeared you had the situation well under control, Lord

Hamish," she said, with all the grace and aplomb she could muster after being caught skulking in the shadows.

He smirked. "So ye don't deny spying on me for a *second* time now?"

Beatrice was going to die, here in her family's hallways. Cause of death: fire from a blush that would not quit. If she'd learned nothing else, however, from years of rejection and societal embarrassment, it'd been to confront people head-on.

"I was spying on you, yes."

"Afraid ah'd get into a rammy with yer folks?"

"I'm not entirely certain what a *rammy* may be, but I did wish to make sure you were able to escape without being cornered by my brother."

Surprise stamped his features. "Ye thought to protect me from yer brother?"

He'd obviously expected Beatrice's concern would have been reserved for Robert, like logic said it should be. After all, Robert was family, and this big Scot had entered her life in possession of her most shameful secret and solicited her help in ferreting out those who, by only his admission, had wronged him.

She may not know Hamish well or long, but she did, however, know her brother.

"I love my brother," she said. "But having been born to be a future duke and now serving in that role, he's long been three things: overconfident, overbearing, and overprotective."

"While ah agree with ye on the first two, ah'd say yer brother is maybe not protective enough. Were our roles reversed, a'hd not let me near ye."

Hamish's admission gave her pause. Beatrice touched her gaze upon his harshly rugged features that were tanned by the sun, and scarred by stories she didn't know, but wished to.

"Should I fear you?" she asked quietly.

His expression grew shuttered. "What do ye think?"

What she thought was that for some reason, her answer seemed to matter to him. "You wouldn't hurt me," she finally said, that admission coming from a place deep inside. "For some reason…I trust you."

Instead of being pleased, his eyes darkened. "Ye are too free with yer faith, lass."

"Shh," Beatrice whispered, and then catching him by the hand, she proceeded to show him how little she feared him, by tugging him into a nearby parlor. After she closed the door behind them, she inclined her head.

He gawked at her. "Whit do ye ken yer doing?"

"Securing us some privacy with which to speak." She gave him a pointed look. "Unless you'd rather we return to the corridor and invite my family and passing servants to listen in on all that?"

"Ye wanted to speak with me?"

She nodded. "My cousin Abigail is hosting a music recital tomorrow evening, and I thought it would be a good event to mark our entry into society as a couple."

"A music recital," he repeated as if he'd never before heard the phrase.

"Yes, I share your feelings on that score," she muttered.

Did she imagine the ghost of a smile upon his lips?

She cleared her throat. "But, I thought, given Abigail is one of my relatives, that you being in attendance—"

"At a recital."

"—At a recital, would lend further credibility to the serious nature of our courtship."

Hamish said nothing. And then…

"Is that all?"

It was on the tip of her tongue to ask whether he'd be there, and yet, she swallowed that question to keep her pride. "That is all," she said.

Then, without so much as a goodbye, the mystifying Scot took his leave.

And after he did, Beatrice remained there, with the echo of his earlier warning replaying in her mind.

CHAPTER 7

My dearest Hamish,

Envy is a terrible sin, and yet to you, I can confess, for so long I was besieged by that sentiment. I longed to know a loving relationship like the one shared by my brother Robert, and his wife, Helena. And my cousin Abigail and her husband, Lord Redbrooke. I could not understand why I was destined to be passed over time and time again…until I realized, it was because of you.

With Love and Longing,
Beatrice

THE FOLLOWING EVENING, WITH GUESTS of the Viscount and Viscountess of Redbrooke's milling about the candlelit music parlor, Beatrice stood beside her chair and discreetly stole glances at the front of the room.

Knowing her sister-in-law and brother despised social events and only did so with the frequency they did because of Beatrice, she'd excused them from accompanying her and welcomed the companionship from her cousin and dearest friend, Abigail.

Beatrice forced her gaze away from the entrance and glanced over to where Abigail and Lord Redbrooke now conversed with several guests. The viscount and viscountess proved as in love—

mayhap even more so—than they had years ago when they'd first met…back when Lord Redbrooke had been just another gentleman who'd originally set his sights on Abigail; a fate which would have perhaps stung had she ever fancied or favored the fellow.

Now, Beatrice took a moment to observe the viscount: the way his gaze remained locked on his wife as she gesticulated wildly. Still as reserved as he'd been when Beatrice had first met him, the gentleman hung upon the viscountess's every word like she spun a poem to rival the Great Bard, and Beatrice would wager her very soul that to the gentleman, Abigail did.

Nay, perfectly proper and respectable for her cousin, he was decidedly not the man she looked for this evening.

Restless, she scanned the entry of the room once more.

Another guest appeared, and Beatrice arched on her tiptoes at the arrival of the tardy gentleman. Tall and muscular, wearing a rogue's grin, and decidedly not the one she sought. Except, why *would* he be here? A silent voice both needled and reminded. Nothing could come from Hamish attending her cousin's intimate event.

That was, *he* stood to gain nothing by being there. Hamish had provided Beatrice with a list of the contacts he sought to make; various men who were connected to his suffering, in some way that merited his suspicion. Neither Abigail nor her husband had wronged Hamish's family. Nor did the men or women on their guest list include anyone linked to Lords Shaftesbury, Scarborough, or Roxburghe. Even knowing that didn't diminish the pathetic hope in her breast.

A shadow fell over her shoulder, and she spun quickly. Disappointment immediately replaced an all-too-brief, but very much real, anticipation.

"Lord Landon," she murmured.

Slapping a hand to his chest, the gentleman staggered back a step. "Egad, disappointment like that is sure to kill a man's self-esteem."

"Don't you mean, a man's 'ego'," she drawled.

"Ah, but I'm not like other chaps." He waggled his blond eyebrows. "I'm a modest fellow."

"One might argue a man who claims to set himself apart from all other men is anything but." Her lips twitched. He was charming. There was no disputing that fact. She'd always *wanted* an amiable, dashing rogue ready with a clever quip and able to pull a laugh from her. So why all of a sudden should it be…different?

Nay, she knew why.

Despite herself, her focus crept back to the still-empty doorway. Lord Landon followed her stare.

"You know, my lady," he murmured, leaning close enough that she caught the citrusy hint of bergamot on him. Why could that scent not stir her the way Hamish's more primal tobacco and leather did? "It is a certainty that if you were my sweetheart," Lord Landon went on in that familiar way, "I'd never leave ye alone for any rake or rogue to prey on.

Her shoulders came up, and she met his gaze squarely. "And is that what you are doing, Lord Landon? *Preying* on me?"

He flared his golden brows and slammed another hand against his chest. "La, you wound me a second time this night, thinking I'm nothing but a rake or rogue."

She gave him an incredulous look. He was rumored to be in outrageous debt—a hefty debt helped along by the many mistresses he kept, the scandalous parties he hosted, and the wagers he loved to place at his *many* clubs.

Lord Landon flashed an endearingly boyish, albeit false, sheepish look. "All rogues eventually reform."

And there'd come a time when she'd longed to be the one who so moved a gentleman. Alas… Something shifted over the room; a palpable energy that exploded to life and commanded the whole world's focus.

And she knew. Even as the marquess picked up from his brief pause and continued with his diatribe of charming words…because *somehow* she'd come to sense his presence before she even saw him. A glorious warmth radiated through her being. And it was only because he'd come, and the looks people had been stealing at her would now take on a less pitying quality.

Liar. She was nothing but a big, lying liar.

He stood at the front of the room. Attired in his customary black from his unfashionably long hair down to his boots and his scarred visage carved of stone, he put Beatrice in mind of an ancient medieval warrior who'd returned to face his foes—and in a way, he was.

"Hamish," she mouthed.

His harsh, direct stare skipped over the rest of the guests, and locked and lingered on…Beatrice. It was her cousin who broke the impasse. With the viscount following close, an always smiling Abigail rushed across the room to greet Hamish.

Just like that, Beatrice came whirring back from the dazed place his presence had left her, and while her cousin went out of her way to make Hamish feel welcome, Beatrice was beset by a wave of shame. How hard it must be for him to join not only this event, but all the ones to follow.

And then there was she, Beatrice, who lamented the discomfort that followed her, as a woman on the shelf year after year. But what it must be for Hamish, a stranger to these people who looked upon him like an oddity.

Lord Landon spoke, drawing her back from her ponderings. "He seems like a rather severe fellow," he murmured as if they shared some intimate secret—about Hamish.

Fury snapped through her.

Beatrice shifted her gaze away from where Hamish stood speaking with Lord and Lady Redbrooke and turned a withering glance on the marquess. "There is something to be said for solemn gentleman, Lord Landon."

Color splotched the marquess's cheeks. "I'd not intentionally offend the gentleman."

"Good. I'd suggest you don't."

Instead of being further chastened by her frosty response, Lord Landon looked upon her with a renewed…and different interest than that which had brought him her way this night. Of course. Leave it to a gentleman to only be *truly* interested in a lady when she was offending him.

He flashed an urbane smile. "There's a good deal more to be said for an affable fellow, too."

She'd have once been of that same opinion. That was before—
Unbidden, her attention slid across the room to where Hamish

stood conversing with her Abigail and Lord Redbrooke—Before she'd met Hamish and discovered one who'd been shaped by hardship and life's cruelties, a man who'd emerged stronger, more resilient for that pain. When presented with an agreeable lord who'd only enjoyed the comforts afforded him by his birthright, she'd far rather have a man so real and raw than a rogue whose words were as empty as his nearly empty pockets.

As he spoke with her cousin and Lord Redrooke, some of the tension left Hamish's face. Abigail, with her warmth, always had a way of setting people at ease and Hamish was no exception. At that moment, whatever Abigail said elicited a laugh, not one that resonated about the room, but rather, a chuckle that slightly shook his broad shoulders. And even as the sight of him so transformed wrought mayhem upon her heart, Beatrice proved to be a small, petty person for the red-hot jealousy that slipped through her.

After an almost farcical number of suitors' defections, she'd believed herself accustomed to the feeling of being thrown over for another.

She'd been wrong.

She now knew she'd never given a jot about the Earl of Sinclair, Viscount Redbrooke, the Marquess of Exmoor, or anyone else for that matter, falling for another, because her heart hadn't been engaged—that was, engaged in anything other than a dream of being loved.

With Lord Landon droning on at her side, and Hamish still engrossed in conversation with her cousin, Beatrice discovered this was different. Her fingers curled into small fists at her side. Had Hamish ever been so relaxed in her company? Had he smiled so or—

As if he felt her eyes upon him, Hamish glanced over.

Beatrice's heart quickened.

She dimly registered Lord Landon still speaking, but she couldn't make sense of a single word he uttered. It was as if she and Hamish were the only two in the room, and she wished it were so. For in this instant, she could be true with herself—she enjoyed being with him. She longed for his company, for reasons that had nothing to do with their arrangement and everything to do with how wonderful it was being with him. For when they were together, he didn't treat her as Beatrice the Diamond to be claimed, but as an equal to talk with and spar with, and she wanted that.

She wanted...*him*.

Beatrice reeled.

Oh, God.

"My lady?" Lord Landon asked concernedly, with more seriousness than she'd ever believed him capable of.

He cupped her elbow in his palm, steadying her. "Are you all right?"

No. Her heart knocked around for altogether different reasons—terror. She'd never be all right, again.

"Fine," she said, her voice thin, and high, and reedy to her own ears. And like any proper English gentleman, Lord Landon knew better than to question a lady on matters of her appearance.

From across the room, Hamish narrowed his eyes into thin, dangerous slits upon the place where Lord Landon still cradled Beatrice's arm. Abigail said something that recalled Hamish's attention. And for an instant, she thought she recognized that glint as jealousy. Only, that couldn't be. She was nothing to him. That was, aside from a means to an end. Wasn't she?

Then, the pair started across the music room.

As they walked, Abigail spoke. Hamish's lips, however, remained in their usual severe way; only moving ever so slightly when he did respond. Of course, he'd not been so solemn when it had been just him and Abigail. It appeared Beatrice was the only woman who elicited that grimness from him. Her and all the English, that was.

Perhaps that was what accounted for the difference in his attitude with Abigail. Mayhap the fact that Abigail was American by birthright made it so that he didn't hold her in the same contempt he did everyone else.

And then he was there.

They were—Hamish and Abigail.

She'd eyes, however, for only Hamish. Her heart beat wildly and excitedly for him.

He, *on the other hand*, stared back with his usual scowl, and not a hint of the same warmth whipping through her.

Tension sizzled among them. Not a single word was spoken.

Abigail glanced between the two gentlemen and Beatrice, then returned her focus to the pair.

"Allow me to perform introductions," Abigail said in her flat, slightly nasally American tones that had forever been more interesting to Beatrice than the clipped ones of the English.

All the while her cousin saw to the formalities, both men sized one another up; one only slightly shorter, wiry, and blonder, the other tall, dark, and heavily-muscled—muscles he'd acquired from the time he'd spent in that penal colony he'd only occasionally spoken of.

Lord Landon held out a hand to Hamish. "A pleasure," he said, with his usual urbane charm.

Hamish stared at the gloved fingers a moment, and for a longer moment Beatrice thought he'd ignore that offering, but then, he placed his palm in the marquess's and shook. It did not escape her, however, he didn't return Lord Landon's words.

Abigail cleared her throat. "Lord Hamish has been incredibly patient with me as I prattled, however, I trust he was far more eager to see his betrothed," she said, subtly declaring her allegiance. "Lord Landon, if you would care to join me, I'd like to introduce you to my sister and brother who are newly visiting from America."

Lord Landon hesitated a moment, and then, with a courteous bow for Beatrice, he accepted Abigail's elbow and allowed her to escort him to the opposite end of the room where Beatrice's cousins appeared to be plotting an escape.

And then she and Hamish were…alone. Or, as alone as one could be during an intimate gathering. Why did she suddenly find herself tongue-tied around him?

Because you now realize he means more to you. Certainly, far more than she would ever mean to him.

"I…see you met my cousin, Abigail," she said lamely after it became apparent Hamish wouldn't speak first.

Hamish grunted. "Aye."

That was it—*Aye.*

She tried to make out more, to make out *anything* from that single syllable response rolled in his husky brogue but came up empty. Rocking on her heels, she glanced in her cousin's direction. She was in the middle of ushering her siblings and Lord Landon to the chairs arranged in neat rows.

Hamish followed her stare.

"My cousin Abigail is lovely, and charming," Beatrice murmured.

"Aye."

His was yet another curt reply, only…the meaning behind it was far more than just a casual confirmation. It implied Beatrice had spoken with certainty, and he'd emphasized his agreement.

"We should take our—"

Hamish was already extending his elbow to escort her.

"Must give everyone the show they expect," she muttered under her breath and wholly unable to keep that bitter disappointment from seeping into her voice.

Hamish dipped his lips close to her ear, and his mint-scented breath tickled that overly sensitive skin of her nape, bringing her lashes fluttering and her heart—

"It'd be helpful for the both of us if ye dinna refer to our courtship as a show, in the middle of an event."

He may as well have plunged her into the frigid waters of Durness Beach where she'd once swam on a dare from her brother.

"And it would be equally helpful if you referred to our arrangement as a betrothal and not a courtship," she said archly.

Without another word exchanged, Hamish escorted her to their seats at the front of the room. And as Hamish joined her, she felt a silly, and overwhelming urge to cry. Pitiably, she had been pining for his presence, and he should arrive, not indifferent as he so often was, but coldly distant.

Her cousin took to the front of the room, welcoming the first performer of the evening. As Lady Nora took up her place at the pianoforte, Beatrice kept her gaze unswervingly straight on; her stare directed just above the young woman's head.

Then Lady Nora raised her fingers and launched into a haunting rendition of 'Sumer is icumen'.

"Summer has arrived,
Loudly sing, cuckoo!

The seed is growing…"

Lady Nora possessed a husky contralto, a rich, warm, open singing voice that under any other circumstances would have enthralled Beatrice as much as every other guest absorbed in her performance.

Hamish shifted, that slight movement brought his enormous thigh flush against Beatrice's. The black hue of his wool trousers may as well have been night to day of Beatrice's pale yellow satin skirts. How could the mere press of his leg send this sea of butterflies fluttering and dancing in her belly?

"Yer cross with me." His was an observation delivered in tones so hushed she could easily pretend she'd not heard them.

"The ewe is bleating after her lamb,
The cow is lowing after her calf;
The bullock is prancing,"

"Well?"

And for a moment she considered ignoring his prodding altogether.

He nudged her.

Beatrice kept her eyes on the front where Lady Nora performed.

"Oh, I'm sorry," she whispered from the corner of her mouth. "Yours didn't strike me as a question."

From the corner of her eye, she saw his lips twitch. Her contrariness was what should elicit a smile? What a peculiar humor the Scots had.

"It wasn't. Yer angry," he repeated, in a different way.

This time, she shifted her gaze from the first performance of the evening. "*This* from the man who glowered at me from the moment you entered the room. I'd advise, Lord Hamish, if you're concerned with the world believing our ruse, then you'd do well to put a good deal more effort into being remotely charming."

THE LASS WAS CARNAPTIOUS THIS night. In fairness, Hamish

himself was in a fine temper, too. He didn't know why he'd come. There'd been nothing for him to gain by accepting the invitation from Beatrice's cousin. None of the gentlemen whom he sought information from would be in attendance. And yet…he'd come, anyway, *and* standing at the entrance of the room and watching her while that bluidy Sassenach with his scoundrel's grin charmed her, he was glad he had.

He seethed. Why did he seethe?

Nay, he knew. Just as he knew why he'd been deuced awful since he'd walked into Lord and Lady Redbrooke's music room.

And nay, it had nothing to do with having to suffer through the misery of an inane Polite Society affair and had absolutely everything to do with the fact Beatrice had been smiling and smitten as she'd conversed with Lord Charming-Trousers Landon and then frowning and scowling across the room at Hamish. The moment he'd spied that blighter's fingers upon Beatrice's sleeve, he'd wanted to detach the Sassenach's limb from his person.

He slid a cold look across the aisle to where the Marquess of Landon with his loose golden curls, and unscarred features sat, looking impossibly bored with the performance but also looking… perfectly unblemished and unscarred and able to charm a lass—a lass like Beatrice who was so very deserving of *being* charmed.

Whereas Hamish? Hamish bore the stain of sins—many false that had been painted upon his name, and then others real, deeds committed in his hands in the name of survival. And in the end, he'd survived… Nay, he'd no claim to Beatrice Dennington. Not really. Not based on anything more than the mutually agreeable arrangement they'd come to.

"If you were going to scowl the whole while, why did you come?"

He stiffened and glanced down at the lass who'd been occupying his thoughts.

A ruddy flush heated his cheeks. "Because I wanted to," he muttered, giving her the truth.

She released a nearly imperceptible and unladylike, but endearing for it, snort, earning a look from an older lady in the opposite row. After the guest's attention turned face-forward once more,

Beatrice continued in a soft whisper. "No one wants to attend music recitals."

It was another revealing piece she'd let slip about herself. One of those slight but important details that made this woman who she was, and for some reason, like all the other many interesting bits she'd revealed, he stored this one away for later.

The lady performing at the front of the room raised her voice, as she reached the crescendo of the song.

"Cuckoo, cuckoo,
You sing well, cuckoo,
Never stop now."

Reaching up, he gave that lone curl draped artfully over Beatrice's shoulder a gentle tug, bringing her focus back his way. She glanced up at him; annoyance and confusion creased her high, noble brow.

"Never tell me ye dinna enjoy singing a good song, lass?"

"Music only serves one purpose."

A grin pulled his lips up. By her arch tones, the lass was still cross with him.

When it became apparent she didn't intend to add anything else, and that she went out of her way to avoid looking at him, he drew her gloved hand into his. Slowly, carefully, and discreetly, he peeled the satin article free.

"What are you d-doing?" Her whispery soft voice trembled faintly.

Ach, the lass may pretend to be indifferent, but she was aware of him.

"Getting yer attention," he murmured, caressing his fingertips in a smooth, slow circle over the satiny softness of her inner palm.

"You h-have it."

"What's the purpose?" he asked, reversing course and trailing a backwards circle upon her hand.

She quivered. "I d-don't know, Hamish. You tell me. You were the one who wants my attention."

"I referred to your earlier statement, your claim that music only serves one purpose."

A pretty blush spread over her high cheekbones. "Oh."

Another smile formed on Hamish's mouth. Funny, how with every quirk of his lips, the motion and muscles grew less rusty, more natural, and…more the way it had before his life and family had fallen apart.

Memories that were never far crept in. The sounds of that dark day amplified in his mind: the groan of the wood parapet as Finlay took his last steps. The whistle of the noose being tightened around his brother's neck, before—

"Hamish?"

The cheerful lyrics sung by the performer at the pianoforte filled the air around them, in an ironic contradiction to the thoughts that would forever haunt him.

"The stag cavorting
Sing merrily, cuckoo!

"Hamish," Beatrice repeated, and it was the sound of *her* voice—soft and musical and filled with concern that yanked him away from the precipice of misery.

"What's the purpose of song, then if not to sing?" he asked, desperate for this inane dialogue to continue with her, because somehow, for some reason, this woman was the only one who managed to chase the demons away.

"Cuckoo, cuckoo,
You sing well, cuckoo,
Never stop now."

"It *should* be. One would think." And then her whispered words came frantically and furiously. "But all pleasures are taken by English society and warped and twisted so that they are no longer pleasures that exist for the sole purpose of being pleasures, but rather become devices, used as tools to secure matches."

As she spoke, and her whispered words grew more impassioned, her chest rose and fell with the force of her emotion. "To you, and other men, the purpose of song may exist for only the pleasure to be had in it. To women, it is nothing more than a means of putting us on display, so that we might sell ourselves like pretty songbirds to interested parties, destined for their gilded cages."

"Sing, cuckoo, now; sing, cuckoo;
Sing, cuckoo; sing, cuckoo, now!"

As if abashed by all she'd revealed, Beatrice's enormous blue eyes grew all the wider, and a blush stained her high, proud cheeks.

Hamish slid his gaze along the graceful planes of her face.

"I said more than I should have," she whispered.

"Ye dinna," he murmured, sliding his fingertips along the seam where her wrist met her palm. In fact, she'd not said enough. "Ye spoke yer truth, and there is a good deal to be said about a person who does."

Their gazes locked on one another, and the room melted away so that it was just he and she in it, and he found he preferred such a world. Whatever else she intended to say, was cut off and drowned out by the swell of applause that went up around the room. They both whipped their gazes forward and belatedly Hamish and Beatrice leant their clapping.

The lady who'd just concluded her performance gently pushed the bench back, took to her feet, and sank into a graceful curtsy. Then, gracefully, she quit her place and returned to the vacant chair alongside an older woman who appeared only an aged version of the lass.

Their hostess, Lady Redbrooke traded places with the young woman, and after speaking several words of praise for the earlier performer, looked to Beatrice.

Beatrice's entire body tensed, and, having come to know her body's nuances so well in such a short time, he felt the frustration and panic building in her before her cousin even spoke.

"I know I'm not partial when I say one of my favorite voices to regale music rooms all over London belongs to that of my cousin." The viscountess's declaration came with the same pride a mother or older sister might show a beloved child or favored sibling.

All eyes swung to Beatrice. Her perfectly even, porcelain white smile dazzled as the lady herself did. Only, seated at her side as

Hamish was, he caught the stiffness at the corners and a dread which glimmered in her eyes.

Even with the handful of paces between them, Lady Redbrooke too must have sensed something. The viscountess wavered.

A murmur rolled over the crowd as the guests glanced about, before ultimately all settling on Beatrice.

Cornered. Trapped.

It was a feeling Hamish knew all too well, and how he could recognize when another being found oneself surrounded and robbed of options.

Beatrice made to stand.

Hamish surged to his feet; the suddenness of his movement sent the legs of his chair screeching along the hardwood floor, and as he stood, every gaze in the room swung his way.

"If ah can lend my voice in song?" Hamish directed that question not at their hostess, but at the woman beside them.

Shock and relief all rolled together to replace the anxiety that had existed the moment Lady Redbrooke's focus had honed on her. Only, she wasn't so selfish as to throw him to the London lions.

"You do not have to do this, Hamish," she said in hushed tones, her lips barely moving.

"Ach, but ah want to."

"*No one* wants to be on display, and I'll not have you put yourself up there for me."

"Hush now, lass or ah'll be thinking ye dinna want to hear me sing."

"Never that," Beatrice said on a rush. "I—"

Hamish winked.

"You're teasing me."

"Ah'm teasing ye."

Something softened in her face. In her eyes. Something he could not quite name, or mayhap that he didn't wish to because of dread with what that look meant.

Hamish forced his gaze from Beatrice's and headed to the pianoforte.

CHAPTER 8

My dearest Hamish,

I love to sign and play pianoforte but despise performing before an audience. The only audience I would ever find joy in playing for would be an audience of just you.

With Love and Longing,
Beatrice

AS HAMISH SETTLED HIMSELF ONTO the bench of the boxwood and cyprus Cristofori instrument Lord Redbrooke had gifted Abigail some years earlier, Beatrice sat motionless, her gaze forward.

Her heart beat erratically within her chest.

Hamish, the big, burly, brooding Scot had taken to the front of her cousin's music parlor to perform a song, in front of a large gathering of Polite Society. And more…he'd done it for her. Was there any man who'd have ever made that sacrifice? Certainly, there'd never been one who'd do it for Beatrice—until Hamish.

She kept her eyes on him as he examined the keys. Had he ever played before? He must if he'd taken up a seat on the bench. What if he hadn't? Panic settled in her gut. This time, far worse, and all because the thought of him being an object of disdain and amusement.

Or…what if he did play and this was just another detail she'd uncovered about Hamish Campbell, the Scot who'd stolen her heart?

Hamish raised his hands, his fingers poised over the keyboard when another slight din descended. She dimly registered someone claiming the spot beside her, and she glanced up.

Helena and Robert. At some point, the couple had entered the room and had discreetly sought to claim their seats—that was, as discreetly as a duke and duchess were able.

"What…?"

Helena interrupted Beatrice. "It occurred to me you despise music recitals, and your brother and I thought to come to your rescue."

"Little did we know, there'd be someone else rescuing you this night," Robert drawled.

Unbidden, her gaze flew to Hamish, who remained on display. For her. Because of her. His gaze on her, patiently waiting for her, as if the song he was about to perform was for her, and in every way, it was.

Her sister-in-law and brother forgotten, Beatrice smiled softly. "I'm sorry," she carefully mouthed.

Hamish gave a little wink; one that indicated he'd read her lips perfectly and found her apology unnecessary. That second flutter of his lashes, both playful and seductive, softened him in ways she'd been so very certain he could never be softened.

Hamish began to play, and Beatrice's breath caught and held, and remained suspended, and she'd wager her very soul on Sunday, her heart would never return to a normal cadence.

She'd wondered at his playing skills—worried, even.

Beatrice, however, had worried for naught.

His fingers glided over the keys of that instrument with familiarity and grace and ease, and sitting there breathless while he played, she marveled that it was possible to be envious of an inanimate pianoforte.

Then, he began to sing. His husky baritone a shade away from a bass swelled around the room. Euphonic and deep, Hamish's voice possessed a sonorous quality that entranced.

"O, my luve is like a red, red rose,
That's newly sprung in June;

Oh, heavens. Not only did he sing and play, but he sang *romantic* ballads.

"O, my luve is like a melodie
That's sweetly played in tune."

The whole while he did, Hamish's gaze never left Beatrice.

"As fair art thou, my bonnie lass,
So deep in luve am I;"

Every single gaze of every single guest present moved between Hamish and then Beatrice, and Beatrice couldn't care.

She couldn't care if there were a thousand stares upon them or none.

She didn't care how or if Hamish's serenade played perfectly into the arrangement they'd come to.

She didn't care what had brought her and Hamish to this moment, only that she was in it with him now.

"And I will luve thee still, my dear,
Till a' the seas gang dry.

Breathless, Beatrice moved to the edge of her chair and hung upon every enchanting lyric sung so beautifully from his lips.

And I will luve thee still, my dear,
Till a' the seas gang dry."

That she could remember, her brother had never sang a song. Nor had her father. Nor, for that matter, had any of the gentlemen who'd courted her.

"Till a' the seas gang dry, my dear,
And the rocks melt wi' the sun;"

All of those lords had devoted themselves to their clubs and brandies and horseflesh and hunting and sparring—those masculine pursuits where they each vied as master of their male-centered universe.

And I will luve thee still, my dear,

While the sands of life shall run.

The ones who'd read poems had halfheartedly recited the words of other men.

And…

But fare thee weel, my only luve!
O, fare thee weel awhile!

And Beatrice stilled. In this instant, it was all too easy to imagine that he *could* be what none of her previous suitors had been, which was preposterous. Ultimately, he didn't sing as a suitor so desperately in love with Beatrice. She knew his only reason for being here in London. Just as she knew better than to allow herself to daydream.

And I will come again, my luve,
Tho' 'twere ten thousand miles.

Her chest hitched painfully, and she held herself absolutely motionless where she sat on the edge of her chair, afraid, if she moved wrong, she'd fall to the floor, and keep on falling. And for the first time, she found herself acknowledging that mayhap the walls she'd erected to keep her heart safe weren't so very sound, after all.

Tho' 'twere ten thousand mile,
And I will come again, my luve,
Tho 'twere ten thousand mile.

Hamish stilled his fingers on the key, and his song came to a close.

Silence filled the hall, as each guest alongside Beatrice, held their collective breath: they in wonderment, and she with a host of swirling emotions. Then, explosive applause broke out among her cousin's guests.

With a slight bow of his head, Hamish headed back to join Beatrice.

HE'D LOST THE LASS AMONGST the crush of guests who'd swarmed them.

Hamish was surrounded by no fewer than a dozen gray-haired societal matrons falling all over themselves in praise of his performance. And Beatrice, by a like number…but as her case would have it, gentlemen who took advantage of Hamish being waylaid, to press their suit.

Ignoring one of the English women going on about her daughter's musical accomplishments, Hamish craned his head, and then he found her…still at the center of men who circled her the way he'd observed sharks swarming unsuspecting prey on his return journey from Australia.

He scowled. The lass was a leery-loonie if she believed Hamish's eventual death would be met with anything but relief from the lords of London and their renewed attempts to woo her.

At last, the lass managed to disentangle herself from her bevy of would-be suitors.

Making his excuses, Hamish stepped around some Lady Battersby or Battleby or another and made a hasty retreat.

Keeping both a careful eye on Beatrice, along with a measured distance, Hamish set out in pursuit. He turned a corner of the palatial townhouse, just as Beatrice's seafoam green skirts disappeared within a room. She shut the door quickly but quietly behind her.

Hastening his steps, Hamish headed for the room, and let himself in. He did a sweep of the dimly lit library; a handful of bronze sconces remained lit upon the walls, while the remnants of a fast-fading fire danced in the hearth, bathing the room in flickering shadows.

Hamish closed the door soundlessly behind him.

Beatrice called out. "Spying on me, are ye?" she called in a lilting, near-flawless, brogue.

His lips twitched, and he found the lass perusing one of the floor-to-ceiling shelving units containing hundreds of leather tomes. She plucked a book from the shelf, skimmed the front page, and then returned it to its place.

"No answer?" she asked, turning those familiar words back on him, once more.

"Aye."

Beatrice paused. "Aye?" she repeated.

"Aye, ah was spying on ye, lassie."

That brought her around to face him, at last.

"Did ye ken ah would or should deny it?"

"Another man would have certainly done so to save face."

"A *Scottish* man doesn't worry about how the world sees him. And as ah told ye afore, lass, we dinnae lie."

She cocked her head. "That isn't quite true."

He frowned.

"Isn't the very nature of our relationship predicated on a lie?"

His frown deepened. "Tis different."

"Is it?"

It wasn't. "Matters of justice trump all else."

Beatrice showed no reaction to that statement. Instead, she turned and resumed her study of Lord and Lady Redbrooke's collection.

"I wanted to thank you," she said softly.

"For what?"

"For singing so I didn't have to."

He made a dismissive sound. "Twas but a wee thing to do."

Beatrice turned her focus back on Hamish. "Not to me," she said softly. "Gentlemen? They don't sing. Not usually and not often, and certainly not out of any enjoyment."

"More of the silly Sassenach ways. We Scots, however, on the other hand, enjoy a good song."

Something akin to disappointment flickered in her eyes. She tugged another book free. "Did you…wish to speak with me?"

His mind went momentarily blank. When he'd given chase, he'd not been motivated by a need to speak about their ruse. He'd… wanted to see her.

Balking at that realization, he drew back.

"Having second thoughts?" she asked curiously.

First, second, third, and then some.

"Ah should be the one asking that question, Beatrice."

"Mm, but you didn't…" Pausing in her search of whatever book she now held, Beatrice cast another glance his way. "*I* did."

Saucy lass.

Hamish reached her, stopping a pace away. "Ye were wrong, lass."

She tensed. "*That* is why you sought me out?"

"Aye." Nay. But he'd sooner voluntarily climb aboard a prison vessel bound for Australia than admit a genuine desire to see her is what accounted for his presence.

Fire flared in her eyes. "Oh, and exactly what have I been incorrect about, Lord Hamish?"

She Lord Hamish'd him when she was cross. It was an intensely intimate habitude, that left him with a queer warmth in his usually cold chest.

"Ye ken when ah'm gone that ye'll be protected by yer grief over my loss. And yet that isn't the case."

Black, unreasoning jealousy rooted around inside and Hamish brought a hand up, possessively cupping her nape.

"Those men before may have been fools, but the ones who'll come after me, willna desist until one of them wins yer heart."

"My heart can't be won," she said, her voice slightly tremulous.

It could and one day it would. An overwhelming hungering to tear out the limbs of that nameless, faceless bastard consumed him, and Hamish's hand curled reflexively, tightening his hold upon her. He forced himself to lighten his touch.

"I'm never going to fall in love," she said.

"Aye?"

"I'm not." The lady bristled. "I've resolved not to."

"Ah'm not sure ah ken that is how love works exactly," he said drolly.

"Oh, it does. If I never let a gentleman too close, then I cannot be hurt."

She sounded so very pleased with herself; Hamish felt another smile building.

Then the latter part of what she'd revealed inadvertently, registered. "Ye've been hurt before then." By one of those many suitors she'd mentioned. More of that slow, and deathless fury filled him.

"Oh, no."

Juxtaposed against the volatile emotion raging inside, Beatrice's casual declination proved disarming. "Nay?"

She shook her head.

What accounted for this rush of…relief? With his thoughts in tumult, Beatrice wandered away, and resumed scanning the pages of her book. Snapping it closed, she placed it back on the shelf and exchanged it for another heavy-looking volume.

His intrigue won out. "What are ye looking for, lass?"

"My cousin, Abigail," she explained, "has always had a fascination with Greek mythology, with any mythology, really," she mused aloud. "Prior to marrying Lord Redbrooke, she lived in America and came with tales of Native American myths. Now, she has shelves filled with those stories and legends."

Hamish attempted to follow Beatrice's seemingly disconnected response to his question.

" 'N' ye have a similar appreciation."

"I have a curiosity."

"About?"

"I overheard you speaking with my brother—"

"When ye were spying on me."

"Yes, when I was spying on *both* of you," she clarified.

Hamish dropped a hip along the curved and gilded beechwood back of Lady Redbrooke's silk damask sofa. "Well?"

"You said a number of…things about me." A rose-pink blush splashed her cheeks. "You mentioned, Mebd, the Queen of Connact."

"Connacht," he murmured.

"Yes, Connacht," she corrected, and was this time perfect in her delivery of the Celtic goddess's name. "I'd not ever heard of her and searched my family's library but could not find anything about her. I know if anyone had any books about her, it would be Abigail."

"That is what yer wondering about?"

She nodded.

"Ye could have just asked me."

"Yes, well, I *thought* about that but then I would have had to admit I'd been spying—"

"Which ye just did, anyway."

"And that I was curious about what you'd said…about me, which I, of course, know was only for my brother's benefit."

She really believed that?

Running a distracted finger over the gilded lettering upon the title, Beatrice looked with a renewed, intense, and unflagging interest at that book she held protectively close.

He searched his gaze over the top of Beatrice's bent head: her hair, the color of spun gold and sunshine had been woven into a coronet, giving her the look of one of those mythical queens she spoke of. The lass didn't ken how extraordinary she was in both beauty and courage and wit? Any other woman in possession of Beatrice's vast loveliness alone would've left her gallus.

"Medb was a fair-haired wolf queen," he began softly, and Beatrice brought her head slowly up. "Legend has it, her form was so beautiful that it robbed men of two-thirds of their valor upon seeing her. She possessed a beauty so great *men* would battle one another for her favor, and the right to possess her."

Beatrice remained motionless, as if she was as riveted by Hamish's telling as he was by the lass's rapt expression.

"Only, no mere man could." Drawn like all those hapless men who'd fallen for the Celtic queen, Hamish palmed Beatrice's cheek, her skin soft as satin. "For beauty wasnae, all she was." Hamish rubbed the pad of his thumb over the place in her neck where her pulse throbbed.

"N-No?" she whispered.

"Nay. Medb demanded to be equal in power and in wealth to

any man, and when her husband proved richer by a bull, she waged war in the name of parity."

The air pulsed with a charged energy, like the still and silence before a lightning strike. Captivated, he and Beatrice, studied one another. Time stood still as they continued that same back and forth, silent search.

Laird help him, he wanted her.

He is going to kiss me.

She'd never kissed a suitor, and she'd never been kissed by them. At first, she'd been eager, yearning to know her first kiss. With time, as each suitor had come and invariably gone and along with them, the hopes of her first embrace, she'd come to the realization it was best she to not know the kiss of a suitor. There was an intimacy to that meeting of the mouths, one that deepened connections, and she couldn't afford the inevitable hurt that would come.

Those other men, however, Beatrice hadn't possessed a hunger to know as she did this man.

His lips, straight and incisive, and more beautiful than she knew a man's mouth could be, the lower angle of his lip perfectly aligned with his bold, angular chin. The slight cleft at the center there leant the only hint of softness to an otherwise rugged face.

Hamish...Hamish was different. Which was mayhap why she moved nearer him.

And as his broad palm cupped her cheek, bringing her eyes again closed, she leaned into a touch so phantasmal, it silenced even nature's sounds to a distant hum.

She and Hamish met at the same time, in a hungry kiss.

His arms were around her, folding her in a powerful embrace and she clung to him.

There'd be time enough after to panic at all the rules she'd put in place to protect herself, that she'd gone and broken this day. In this moment, in this *instant*, there was only she and Hamish, and his kiss. *Their* kiss. And this was the one she'd dreamed of and imagined but had ceased to believe she'd ever truly know. Only it was more. It was fire and fire and passion, and fears be damned, she wanted it all.

With a primal touch that enflamed her, Hamish gripped her at her nape, angled her head, and deepened the kiss.

"A'm waantin' to taste ye, lassie." Desire deepened his brogue, and drove her mad with a deeper hunger for this raw, virile Scot. "Let me in."

She couldn't have denied him anything in that moment.

Moaning, she parted her lips, and he swept inside, devouring her, branding her, marking her his. Their tongues danced in a primitive battle in which no party lost, and where both she and Hamish emerged triumphant victors.

Beatrice twined her arms about his neck, and the book she'd been holding tumbled with a muffled thwack to the floor, where it lay forgotten. She pressed herself against his powerful, contoured frame; from the sculpted plains of his flat stomach to each clearly defined muscle of his chest, he oozed masculine perfection.

"Yer so bonny," he whispered against her mouth.

Many men had uttered similar words, but none of them had rung with the sincerity of this man's passion. He wanted Beatrice. And that realization enflamed her, emboldened her.

Hamish lightly sucked at the tip of her tongue. She moaned and moved her hips, rhythmically against him. Other men stank of brandy and cheroots. Hamish tasted of oak and spice and vanilla. She loved the taste of him. She loved the feel of him. She loved being in his arms. And she wanted this moment to last forever.

Hamish filled his hands with her buttocks and the muslin fabric of her day dress gave a hedonistic rustle as he crushed that material. Of its own volition, Beatrice's head fell back, as with a long, desperate mewling she further opened herself to his exploration.

Hamish sank his fingertips hard into her hips and pressed her against the long ridge of his manhood. The evidence of his desire for her unleashed an even wilder fervor inside. That sharp ache, both exquisite and excruciating, grew between her legs, and in a bid to find some relief, Beatrice moved against him.

A guttural groan shook his chest, and that slight rumble thrummed within her.

She wanted more. She wanted so much more.

Her legs went limp, and Hamish was there to catch her. He brought her back flush against the bookshelf, and she sagged against it.

"We should stop, lassie," he said in between kisses.

Beatrice panted. "Should we?"

"Aye."

"Why?" she asked in between each possessive slant of his lips over hers.

"Don't ye fear letting yerself too close to a man?" he murmured against the side of her mouth.

Had she said that? She didn't recall much of anything at this moment. In fact, she'd be hard-pressed to dredge up her complete name.

"Sweet Bea." Hamish brought the kiss to a stop.

"I'll make an exception in this instance."

"By yer orders, ah'm not to take liberties."

"Fair, but I'm freely giving them."

"Ah'd nae hurt ye by letting ye fall for me, lassie."

"Scots are bold, stubborn, and a-arrogant," she teased. "I cannot be made to fall. It has never happened, and it never will." Beatrice turned her mouth up to his.

He evaded her efforts, proving his obstinance had no limits.

Then, she froze; horror rolled together with humiliation. He, not unlike all her other suitors, found himself unmoved by her.

She let her arms fall to her side. What a fool she was. No man had ever been consumed by any real passion for her. What had made her believe Hamish would be any different?

"Oh, dear," she said, her voice threadbare. She made to step out of his arms.

Frowning, Hamish shifted and blocked her attempt at escape. "What is it?"

He'd force her to say it. Beatrice directed her gaze up at the crystal chandelier overhead, and its dozens of unlit wax tapers.

"You do not enjoy kissing me." Was it possible to die of shame? If so, it wasn't a quick demise, but rather an agonizingly slow, miserable one.

"*That* is the conclusion ye came to, lassie?" He tweaked her nose.

"Ah might have to reassess my earlier opinion on yer wit."

Beatrice swatted at his hand. "What other conclusion *should* I draw?" she asked between gritted teeth.

"That ahm enjoying it a tad too much."

"So, kissing should only be enjoyed *a little*?"

"Nay."

"I was teasing, Hamish."

"If yer capable of making jokes," he whispered against her lips, "then ah'm clearly not doing a good enough job of it." Hamish returned his attention back to the long, graceful line of her neck.

She closed her eyes and angled her head to allow him better access to that skin he now worshipped. He certainly didn't kiss like one who didn't like kissing her.

Her reservations melted away and she sighed under his ministrations. "You are doing a very nice job."

Hamish touched a finger to the corner of his brow. "Ah'm glad ye find my work adequate, lass."

He lightly suckled her skin, biting and licking that spot, driving her mad with wanting.

"Oh, f-far more than adequate."

"Aye?"

"O-Oh, yes. In fact, I'd say it'd be a shame and we'd be remiss if we stopped in the midst of doing something we're both doing exceptionally w-well." Her words dissolved into a mewling little whimper as he cupped her breasts in his palms.

"Och, who ah'm ah to argue with that logic?"

"You can't."

With that, Hamish took her lips again, this time, a gentler kiss; one that was still seeking, and yet, he did so with the tenderness of one who sought to take his time learning the taste and feel of her.

And as she kissed him in return, she silently admitted the truth to herself. She'd lied to him. If she weren't careful, Beatrice rather feared she might be capable of falling for him.

CHAPTER 9

My dearest Hamish,

I used to think it silly the way my brother would walk around with his head in the clouds, because of that emotion called love. Now, I understand it.

With Love and Longing,
Beatrice

FOR THE NEXT WEEK, SLEEP eluded Hamish.

Nor was that insomnolence a new state he found himself in. A man didn't witness what Hamish had and ever again know a restful day *or* night. This time, however, twasn't the demons and nightmares or the ghosts of his da and brother that kept him from repose. Nay, this time it was a fey lass, who with every meeting and exchange, seared herself on his memory. Each day he visited her or escorted her through Hyde Park, he found himself more and more entranced.

Now, seated on a hard wooden bench in Burgess's dark, empty kitchens, with stacks of the lass's notes and a lone page with three names atop them, Hamish stared at the whiskey, a shade of light straw that put him in mind of Beatrice.

"Yer a bluidy liar," he muttered at his drink. *Everything* put him in mind of the bonnie lass. Now, he'd never taste cinnamon and honey and not think of her kiss in Lord Redbrooke's library. She kissed with the innocence of a lass who'd not had much practice, but the passion of a woman who'd longed to. And she was a chatty bird when she kissed, and it'd been as endearing as the lass herself.

Whit in hell was this?

Grimacing, Hamish tossed back the remainder of his whiskey, and then quickly poured himself another. Ruminating about the lass, when all his attention and energy should be on his plans of revenge. *That* was the sole purpose of his being here in London. *Not* to go seangan for the lass whose aid he'd enlisted. He didn't want to know about her or her likes or dislikes. Her passions.

When he'd arrived, that had been the case, anyway. What he'd not anticipated was how, in working together, their lives would become entwined in a way that made it impossible to remain detached from one another.

Hamish took another entirely too-large sip of his drink. He set the tumbler aside and, sifting past the page bearing the potential names of the one who'd wronged him, Hamish picked up a note and read.

> *I love to sing. When I do, it is as though I'm transported to another place away from this one. Not Scotland, that is. I do so love it here. Rather, away from the gilded cage I, and all ladies, find themselves trapped.*
>
> *And I resent so very much that I cannot simply find joy in singing. Even that is taken from me and made instead to be one more thing with which to raise my value as a bride.*

Hamish stared at that deeply intimate revelation. When he'd first acquired the stack of notes from Angus, Hamish had made quick work of skimming through the missives that would prove beneficial and separating out details about the lass that had no bearing or value to him.

Now, he looked at Beatrice's notes in a new way, in a new light. Each flourishing stroke of Beatrice's pen offered him a window into her thoughts and fears and wishes. They were no longer just words to be used to aid Hamish in his goals. They'd always been more. At first, he'd been so blinded by his thirst for revenge that he'd not allowed himself to see the lass as anything more than a means to an end.

That is what she is. Jeysus, he was a horse's—

"Unable ta sleep, laddie?"

Hamish jerked his head up so quickly, the muscles of his neck wrenched, and he welcomed that discomfort. Caught woolgathering? What was next? Reciting sonnets and penning verses to the lass's beauty?

Picking up the short glass, Hamish tossed back the rest of his drink. He made to rise, but Ole Angus waved him down.

"We Campbells dinnae stand on ceremony," his uncle said, as he limped over. "Aside from yer ma who delighted in all things fancy."

Angus joined Hamish on the opposite side of the table. Bemused, the older man eyed the piles of papers. His gaze lingered on the one still clutched in Hamish's fingers.

Hastily turning the letter over, Hamish returned it to the pile, and, leaning back, he fetched another tumbler from the counter behind him.

"A wee dram?" he asked, already splashing whiskey into a glass.

Angus snorted. "Amen't a scots or nah?"

Uncle and nephew shared a smile, and then, touched glasses in a toast, and shared a drink.

They sat in a heartening silence, sipping their whiskey, and it harkened Hamish back to another time, in a different kitchen, when he and Finlay had sat at the same stone table that had dated back to the first Earl of Brewster, and listened while their da and his brother had traded stories of past greatness.

Hamish anticipated the surge of anguish…that this time, did not come. This time, Hamish sat in a fond remembrance of those times past.

Angus tossed back his whiskey, poured himself another, and then refilled Hamish's half-empty tumbler. His glass in one hand, Angus reached with his other for one of the pages.

Hamish tensed, but it wasn't Beatrice's letters his uncle helped himself to. The old Scot moved his gaze over the three names.

Angus grunted. "Thae ur th' men."

It wasn't a question. His uncle well knew what Hamish himself did about the names Burgess's aunt had provided Hamish back when he was still serving time for a crime he'd not committed, and had little hope of returning to Scotland, let alone having justice on behalf of his family.

Angus turned the page over in his hand, and then set it aside. "We've bin 'ere 'ow many days now?"

Far longer than Hamish ever intended to be.

" 'N' how mony o' thae households hae ye visited?" he asked with a casualness Hamish didn't believe for a minute.

At Hamish's silence, Angus continued. " 'N' how many times have ye paid call to the lassie?"

He'd lost count. He called daily. There were trips to the park and museums. He'd even endured a dinner party and a trip to the theatre to be close to her.

"Ah've had to bide my time," Hamish groused, "and wait for certain events."

Angus lifted a bushy orange eyebrow. " 'N' *Scarborough* dinnae host a dinner party just last week?"

His uncle knew that.

"Ah considered it," Hamish mumbled. "It seemed wiser to wait for an affair where ah could more easily escape notice."

His godfather shifted on the bench and the old oak slab groaned under that movement. "Do ye ken what ah think, laddie?"

Hamish shook his head. He didn't know what to think anymore.

"Ah think ye'r heid isnae on revenge, bit rather on thoughts o' th' lassie."

Hamish opened his mouth, but the denial didn't come.

His uncle pressed his point. " 'An' mayhap, Hamish, that is fur th' best. Mayhap that is why she wis meant ta write they letters, 'n' why ye were meant ta return an fin' them."

Sweat slicked Hamish's palms. It couldn't be. He wouldn't do something so foolhardy as to go losing his head for the bonny Beatrice. He didn't have a future to offer, and for that matter, he didn't want a future beyond exacting his retribution.

That'd been the case anyway.

It still was.

Wasn't it?

His mouth suddenly dry, Hamish tossed back his whiskey, and this time forsook a refill for the whole damned bottle.

"Ah thought ye hated all things English," Hamish said after he'd taken a long swig.

Angus's eyes sparkled with the jovial mirth that had always been as much a part of him as the Campbell plaid. "Ah'd be willing ta mak' an exception if it's a guid lassie that mak's ye happy 'n' helps ye let go o' th' past." Lifting his drink, Angus toasted him.

How could the other man talk of Hamish simply forgetting what had happened? How had he managed to do it? Hamish felt himself equally awed by and frustrated with Angus for that feat.

Hamish dropped his elbows on the table, and that movement sent Beatrice's letters fluttering.

"Ye'd have me just forget everything, Angus?" he implored. "What was taken? What was done? My brother. My mother's suffering. My father. *Your* brother."

Grief twisted Angus's wrinkled face, and he stood. "Ah should be finding my bed."

Hamish dusted a hand across his mouth. He didn't want to raise old hurts for his uncle. The Lord knew he'd suffered just the same.

"Forgive me. A'm not judging ye. A'm just…trying to ken."

Perhaps so that Hamish too could find even a sliver of the grace his uncle had retained in the face of the darkest evil.

"Tis aboot finding peace, laddie." With that Angus took his leave.

Hamish sat there in the kitchen long after his uncle had shuffled off to find his bed.

He considered Angus's words—*all* of them.

Ole Angus may have managed to achieve peace after the Campbell's suffering, and Hamish was grateful he had. But Hamish? He'd a responsibility to his late father and brother, to avenge their names, and right past wrongs done to them. And his mother. The countess had suffered so very much, too, only to then die without any kin but Ole Angus about her.

Hamish's godfather wasn't wrong—Hamish *had* been preoccupied with the bonny Beatrice. He'd allowed himself to become so distracted, for a moment, he'd lost sight of his sole reason for being here.

He flexed his jaw.

It was a mistake he'd not allow himself to make again.

CHAPTER 10

My dearest Hamish,

Among the gentlemen who've paid me calls through the years, I was never driven to daydreams and distraction—until you. Each visit is never enough. I want all my moments to be spent with you, and I long for the day when nothing keeps us apart.

With Love and Longing,
Beatrice

HE'LL BE HERE. HE HAS *to. He'll be here.*

Later that week, standing on the sidelines of Lord and Lady Shaftesbury's crowded ballroom, sandwiched between Robert and Helena, Beatrice replayed that mantra over and over in her head. He'd come. If for no other reason than because Lady Shaftesbury's ball afforded Hamish an opportunity to venture inside the household of one of Hamish's three suspects.

In a terse letter he'd sent days ago, he'd requested entry to Lord and Lady Shaftesbury's ball. In the scheme of time they'd spent together, a handful of days wasn't much.

And although he'd not visited, as promised in the conditions she'd laid out for their arrangement, he faithfully sent flowers, and a letter for each day he did not visit, and in so doing, he effectively perpetuated the myth of their *grand love.*

But…Beatrice didn't care about keeping up the pretenses…she bloody missed him. She'd come to enjoy his company, sparring with him, and his teasing her.

Out the corner of her eye, Beatrice caught movement at the rapidly dwindling receiving line, as a new guest arrived.

Do not look. Society expects you will be searching for him and are just waiting for you to look for Hamish.

In the past, it'd been all too easy to make it a point of not looking for the respective gentleman courting her that year. This time proved different. This time, she *longed* to see the current suitor in her life.

This is also why you don't let a man too close, that silent voice lambasted her.

Where gentlemen were concerned, their unreliability proved the only thing reliable about them. Ultimately, they were singular in their interest, fickle with their regard, all of them, every single one of them left.

Beatrice stared out at the dance partners moving through the sweeping steps of the waltz. Her gaze landed on the deliriously in love Earl and Countess of Sinclair. The gentleman had been the first in a long line of Beatrice's suitors.

The strains of the orchestra's melody drowned out her sigh. The thing of it was, from the onset, Hamish's eventual departure had never been in dispute. He'd been set to leave before she and he had even met.

Stop. You are being illogical. Hamish wouldn't leave until he had the information he'd set out in search of.

A thought slipped in—what if he'd already attained the proof he'd sought? Then, there'd be no reason for him to remain. He'd already said he'd vanish after he accomplished what he'd set out to do.

Panicky dread left a knot in her stomach. And all the past humiliations and hurts from suitors past came rushing over her, like a slow-building tidal wave, encompassing Beatrice, swallowing her.

Only, this time it was different.

This time, it *felt* different. Because it was. This wasn't about wishing to save face in front of the *ton*. For the first time ever, she'd allowed her feelings to become entangled. She'd not shared a single part of her soul or thoughts with one of those men who'd courted her. Hamish had been the first. She'd shared her regrets and frustrations with her lot as a woman, as well as the dreams she carried. She'd shared all that with Hamish.

No! He wouldn't leave. He'd vowed to see he fulfilled the end of the bargain he'd struck with Beatrice, and she trusted him. Right or wrong, prudent or foolish, somewhere deep inside she knew Hamish was a man of his word.

He'll be here. He'll be here…

A dark-haired gentleman appeared at the top of the receiving line, and Beatrice arched on the balls of her feet, and craned towards…

A shorter, more wiry, dark-haired Lord Brantley.

Tamping down her disappointment, Beatrice sank back on her heels.

"He'll be here," Helena said quietly at her side.

"I know," Beatrice replied automatically, not even bothering to pretend Helena had misunderstood the reason for her fretfulness. She silently prayed her perceptive sister-in-law attributed Beatrice's desire to see Hamish to what Beatrice had already revealed in terms of her arrangement with the surly Scot.

"Are we *sure* he'll be here?" Robert weighed in—unhelpfully—from the corner of his mouth.

Sister and sister-in-law spoke as one.

—"Shut your bone-box."

—"Hold your tongue."

Helena rapped her husband on the arm for good measure and then turned a smile on Beatrice. "Though I'll say, I do far prefer your more *incisive* choice of words."

"Thank you for that devotion, dear wife," Robert muttered, as he rescued a glass of champagne from the tray of a passing servant.

Both women ignored him.

"Thank you," Beatrice said, inclining her head. "Though, I confess, shut up, you great big goosecap, tends to be my more favored one at home. Given our current surroundings, I thought the former was more polite."

"Oh, yes," Robert drawled, from around the rim of his champagne flute. "Because telling someone to shut his *bone-box* is the very height of proper."

Helena laughed, and Beatrice made herself join in. She knew what Helena and Robert were trying to do, and she appreciated their efforts. Until Hamish arrived, however, they'd be in vain.

Why wasn't he here? Why—

Beatrice went motionless, as she had a taste of knowing what those intuitive creatures in the wild sensed before a storm. An electric charge passed over the ballroom, and she felt him. She *felt him* before she saw him. She sensed his arrival even before the low murmur overtook the ballroom and became a roar of sound.

Hamish.

Her eyes found him at the entry of the ballroom. The receiving line had long since faded, and the host and hostess of the evening's festivities found themselves trapped amidst the crowd of their guests, straining to get a look at Beatrice's suitor.

Not did she believe for a single moment the crowd's fascination had anything to do with his status as Beatrice's latest beau. Nay, darkly handsome, from his sinfully dark hair drawn back at his nape, to his broad, muscle-hewn frame attired in the finest black wool, he'd command a kingdom with ease.

Hamish peered around the room; his gaze that touched the tops of the heads of various guests radiated annoyance…and then his eyes landed and locked on her. And the way he looked at her… like she was the only woman in the world, robbed her of breath.

"I do not think you need me to point out that Lord Hamish has arrived," Helena said teasingly.

Beatrice knew words were expected of her, preferably light and playful in return. But God help her she couldn't manage so much as a single letter, let alone a casual utterance. She was incapable of seeing or focusing on anyone, on anything but him.

Then, Hamish started down the stairs, and, as the crowd of lesser men and women parted, Beatrice thought this was what it would have been when those legendary waters once opened.

She followed his every step; the way he plainly evaded their host, Lord and Lady Shaftesbury, continuing past the most influential peers whose wives craved a connection and information about the enigmatic Scot. He moved with confident, bold strides down the steps, the crowd allowing him passage like the king among mere mortals that he was.

Beatrice's breath hitched and then came quickly as she, riveted as every other lord and lady present, watched his approach.

And then, he was there, before her.

Rather, *them*.

"Lord Hamish," Helena greeted, with the grace and aplomb she'd exuded from the moment Beatrice had first met her sister-in-law. "It is a pleasure."

Hamish dropped a deep, deferential bow the queen herself would have been hard-pressed to find fault with. "Yer Grace," he said in that deep, lyrical, lilting brogue that Beatrice knew she'd hear play in her mind, long after he'd gone.

While her faux suitor and sister-in-law exchanged pleasantries, Beatrice, who'd had over a thousand lessons on elocution, and, who'd perfected the art of exchanging pleasantries and small discourse from her days in the nursery, found herself, for the first time, without a word to utter. Not a witty one. Not a flirtatious one. Not a casual mention of the fine weather they'd been enjoying. Not a *single* one.

So, this was what it was to be tongue-tied?

At last, Hamish turned his attention from Helena to Beatrice, and, even knowing the heat of his eyes was all pretend, her heart still jumped.

"Will ye honor me with the next set?"

"You dance?" she blurted.

"Aye."

It was a reminder of just how little she knew about the man before her…and more dangerously, how much she *wanted* to know.

She felt Helena's astute eyes on them, taking in the exchange as she always took in everything. This time, Beatrice couldn't care. She could only care about Hamish being here, beside her. For when he was near, the loneliness she'd felt these many years…

faded away. With a breathlessness she prayed he took as feigned, she allowed him to lead her onto the dance floor.

"Surprised ah can dance, are ye?" There was a teasing quality that slipped into his speech as rare as a shooting star, and she longed to catch one of those flying celestial bodies so she might wish for more of that lightness from him.

Beatrice placed her fingertips on his sleeve. "Surprised you'd *want* to," she said under her breath. Given the fact he'd stopped visiting, it'd become all too clear that his only interest in her stemmed from his search for his family's accusers.

"Ach," he said, as they joined hands. "But how could ah nah relish the opportunity to have ye in my arms, lass?

This is pretend. This is make-believe. Reminding herself of that didn't help. The heat of his touch coupled with his captivating words sent a lightening charge of energy burning through the fabric of her glove.

As the orchestra launched into the next set, the quiet, seductive strains of the waltz, couples hurried to take their positions around them. Beatrice rested one palm on Hamish's shoulder and twined her other hand with his.

That radiant heat that always sparked when their fingers touched flared to life and muddled her senses. Her legs went weak, and Hamish instantly adjusted his hold, gathering her more closely, and helping her find her feet.

"That's braw. Ah expect goin' weak in th' knees is a surefire sign o' an enchanted lassie."

What was he saying? Between the sorcery of his touch, and the rick, thickness of his brogue, everything in her mind had become all confused.

Leaning down, Hamish placed his mouth close to her ear; his breath, lightly tickled her. "How am ah doing in my part, lass?"

Then a wave of cold hit her, effectively killing the splendor.

His part.

Their arrangement.

His absence these past days.

He'd taken her dazed state for an act, and she gave thanks for small miracles. Because the alternative? That he knew she found herself falling in ways she couldn't afford to fall would be a humiliation far greater than all the others that'd come before.

This is what happens when you let yourself feel.

Dredging up the remnants of her shattered pride, she brought her shoulders back. "You haven't come to call."

"Ah've been busy conducting research."

Chastising him for not visiting when he'd been seeing to far more important business, how petty and petulant she sounded.

"Did ye nae receive my notes and flowers."

"I did."

"Did ye nae like the blooms?"

"They were lovely," she allowed. She'd loved them. The gardenia was her favorite of all the flowers. Hamish hadn't known that, of course.

"Aren't they yer favorite flowers?"

At that supposition, Beatrice missed a step, and he expertly righted her. She searched her mind for when she'd shared that particular detail with him. She'd not written it in the notes she'd left and he'd discovered. Nor when she'd gone through the terms of their pretend courtship.

"How…?"

"How did ah ken?" he finished the question for her. "Ye've worn either crystal gardenia hair combs or the flower itself tucked in yer tresses, lass, each time we met. It didn't take long to gather as much."

But he'd been the only one who had. He'd been the only one to look so closely at her that he'd not even needed to ask because the answer had been right there.

A ball of emotion filled her throat.

"Did ye ken, the flower was named after a Scots fellow?"

"I…didn't."

Blast it all. Why must he come here knowing her favorite flower, and also its origins? He was making it impossible for her to remain indifferent to him.

"Still cross?"

And he knew her well enough to gather when she was cross.

"You *are* late," she felt inclined to point out.

"Aye."

Oh, the laconic lummox. That was all he'd say to her admonishment? *Aye?*

Hamish led them through another sweeping turn.

"Someone once told me that a truly devoted suitor cannot stay away, Lord Hamish."—She'd once longed for that. She'd also let that dream go.—"That when a man is truly in love, he'll defy all social conventions and rules, just to be with her."

"Tha' someone sounds like a moost clever someone," he said, his features deadpan.

"A most *arrogant* someone, more like," she said under her breath.

His firm lips twitched.

How easily his smiles now came. How different he was than the man who'd first barged into her family's gathering, and maneuvered Beatrice into helping him. And how much harder it would be to let him go.

Her chest hitched painfully.

"Yer right, and ah would have preferred it that ah could have been here earlier with ye, and yet meeting our host face to face in the receiving line, didn't seem wise."

"Of course," she said. "That makes complete sense."

And what accounted for his absence the days prior? Only the death-grip she had upon her pride kept her from asking him that question. Surely he'd only been away because he'd been setting into motion whatever he planned for Lord Shaftesbury this night.

Why did that realization make her feel somehow worse?

"What will you do?" she made herself ask.

He flexed his jaw. "Ah cannot answer that here, lassie." His lips barely moved as he spoke.

"Tell me how I can hel—"

"Absolutely nae," Hamish cut in before she could complete that thought. "Ye have done enough to secure my entry. Ah'll nae involve ye further."

"I'm already involved," she protested.

"Nae more than ah'll have ye be."

Too soon the strains of the orchestra's waltz came to a finish and the moment it did, she felt the change overtake Hamish. Driven by the very quest for revenge that had brought him into her life, he'd already moved on from both Beatrice and her request. The moment he turned her over to Helena, he exchanged brief pleasantries, before cutting a path along the perimeter of the ballroom.

"Your brother went to fetch refreshments," Helena said after Hamish had gone.

Not taking her gaze from Hamish, Beatrice continued to follow his movements.

"Hmm?" For one so broadly muscular, the handsome Scot moved with surprising stealth. The moment he reached a doorway at the far left corner of the ballroom, she turned to Helena.

"If you'll excuse me?" she said to Helena. "I see Cousin Abigail motioning to me."

Frowning, Helena glanced about. "Where is she?"

"Over beside Lord Redbrooke." Beatrice motioned to a large crush of guests.

It was a lie. She didn't even know for certain whether Abigail had received an invitation or whether she was present. Not allowing Helena an opportunity to offer to accompany her on a fictitious meeting, Beatrice bussed her sister-in-law on the cheek and rushed off in pursuit of Hamish.

She let herself out the same oak door he'd exited through. Her ears still ringing from the din of the ballroom, Beatrice bustled down the hall, making quick work of entering room after room, in search of Hamish.

Where in blazes had he gone?

Irate, she let herself in the last one in this corridor, when suddenly, a shadow moved. She gasped, and even as she made to scream, a large, gloved hand covered her mouth, burying that cry for help.

Beatrice thrashed, bucking against the enormous stranger.

"Will ye calm doon, bonny Bea, afore ye bring us an audience."

That lilting Scottish brogue punctured through her terror, and she stilled. "Hamiff," she whispered against his hand.

"Aye." Hamish removed his palm, pushed the door closed quietly behind them. "What are ye doing, lass?"

"What are *you* doing?" she whispered.

"Locking the door," he answered and turned that little latch with a *click*.

"Not that. I meant…" His sapphire blue eyes glimmered. "You're making jests?" she whispered furiously. "Now, of all times?"

Not breaking his stride, Hamish gave his broad shoulders a lopsided shrug. "It seems as guid a time as any."

Gawking, Beatrice followed him as he made his way across Lord Shaftesbury's dimly lit office and headed for the Chippendale pedestal desk.

Hamish dropped into the folds of the walnut and leather carved armchair and set to work pulling out the drawers; he methodically sifted through them. Systematically, opening book after book. Some he set discarded after a quick scan of the contents. Others, he perused for longer, but was still brisk in his examination.

Beatrice joined him at the desk. Engrossed in his search, he didn't so much as look up. "What are you searching for?" she asked quietly.

"Transactions." He directed his response to the ledger in his hand. "Deals struck, arrangements made, anything sizeable and significant around th' time my brother and ah were carted off."

"Let me help."

Frowning, Hamish paused, and glanced up. "It isna safe—"

Beatrice headed off his protestations. "I'm already involved," she beckoned with a hand. "We can make far quicker work of this if we both read through the information here."

Hamish hesitated a moment, and then with a grunt, he passed a leather ledger emblazoned with Lord Shaftesbury's initials.

Beatrice accepted the book and her arms sagged under the unexpected weight of the tome.

"The first week of April 1820, is when it began," Hamish said. His eyes darkened, and her heart seized at the pain reflected back in his gaze.

Adjusting her hold on the ledger, Beatrice freed a hand, and laid it upon Hamish's, in a show of silent support. She'd come to know him so well. A man of Hamish's pride would take any apology or words of sympathy as pity, and proud as he was, he'd only reject that offering.

He stared at the top of her hand a moment and then lifted his gaze to hers. "Thank ye, lassie," he said gruffly. "For helping."

She understood. Even though he hadn't spoken the words, his meaning was clear—he appreciated her being here for him in this moment.

Popping the heavy ledger open, Beatrice scanned the dates. "What information might be helpful?" she asked.

"Search for anythin' just prior…any noticeable differences in Shaftebury's finances afore the radical rising and then after the unrest was crushed. Search for any transactions he had with Scottish gentlemen."

Beatrice looked up briefly at him. "Is that something you think may have happened? That Scottish men betrayed their fellow Scots?"

Together they searched, and, working in tandem, Beatrice and Hamish efficiently searched every sheet of paper and every book or ledger.

Hamish cursed. "Nothing."

"Yes, but is it still not helpful? Doesn't it now allow you to focus your attention on the other two gentlemen on your list?"

He dragged a hand through his hair. "That it is, unless information implicating Shaftesbury is hidden elsewhere."

Beatrice looked about. "We can do another search. Perhaps of—"

"Tis enough for tonight, Beatrice. As it is, we risk people noting our conspicuously timed absence."

She waggled her eyebrows. "Ah, yes, but then that is the perfect cover, is it not?"

A black scowl darkened his face. "Ah'll not let yer reputation be ruined in my investigation. Ye need to get back to yer family, lass."

He was trying to be rid of her. No, correction. He *was* getting rid of her. If there'd been any doubt—which there hadn't—Hamish took her gently by the arm and guided her to the door.

"Ah'll wait long enough to not rouse any suspicions." With that, he drew the panel open a fraction and ducked his head outside. He looked back and forth, and then, with a pride-crushing alacrity, he guided her out into the hall.

She took the corridor quickly.

Do not be offended. It was silly to be offended. After all, Hamish had but a short window to conduct a search of Lord Shaftesbury. She wasn't so much a birdbrain as to think he could spend all evening speaking with her about flowers and—

A tall, willowy figure stepped into Beatrice's path.

"Helena," she rasped, her breathing coming fast from a different, but no less damning or awful, discovery. "I was…"

Her sister-in-law lifted an eyebrow. "*Yes*?"

Beatrice glanced about.

"Your brother is still on the seemingly futile quest of locating your cousin and her husband," Helena said with more of that drollness.

"Indeed?" she asked sheepishly. "I'm certain I saw them."

With the poise befitting the owner of this residence, and not an errant guest wandering the halls, Helena opened the door beside her and motioned Beatrice inside.

"You were saying?" Helena asked when they were alone.

Had she been saying anything? Beatrice still found herself so caught off-guard she couldn't get her thoughts together to formulate so much as one plausible reason she'd been sneaking around the earl's residence.

"I was…looking for you," she said on a rush.

"In Lord Shaftesbury's office?" A faint thread of amusement underscored Helena's question.

Heat suffused Beatrice's cheeks. *Stop. You aren't a girl of eighteen who just made her debut.* She was a grown woman…with a pretend sweetheart.

With a sweetheart! Of course.

Beatrice let her shoulders sag. "You have me. I *did* sneak about the earl's residence…and I *was* in his office."

"Yes, I believe I've already ascertained that," Helena said dryly.

Goodness, her sister-in-law was formidable. Certainly, it would have been far easier to pull the wool over Helena's eyes, had the duchess been born to the *ton*, and not first raised on the streets, then in a gaming hell, before marrying Robert and finding herself elevated to the unenviable role of duchess.

"I was meeting Hamish." And born of truth, that confession

came far easier than the stammering lies of before. "We wanted to steal time alone, and," as their time together was limited, "having been parted before, the moments we can find together are all the more precious."

Helena considered her. "You are in love with him."

No! That denial sprung to her lips, born of dread, and the need for self-preservation. She didn't love Hamish. She couldn't. Her heart belonged to her, and only her, and was safer for it. Only…for all intents and purposes, the immediate answer was: yes, she loved him desperately.

Everything was all mixed-up: pretend twisted up with that which was real, fiction twined in with fact, so much so that she couldn't make sort of anything anymore. She yearned to dig her fingertips into her temples and rub at the crushing pressure there.

"Beatrice?" Helena gently prodded her to the present.

"Of course, I love him," she made herself say for her sister-in-law's benefit. Because it couldn't be true.

"It wasn't a question, Beatrice," Helena said gently.

"Oh."

"You were meeting him," Helena continued quietly, and without recrimination, "and yet…for a couple desperate to steal an intimate moment for your own, you spent a good deal of time pillaging through our host's desk."

Beatrice recoiled. Oh, God. Helena had heard that, and if *Helena* did, then anyone else may have heard Beatrice and Hamish.

"No one else was near," her sister-in-law hurried to reassure her, "and I come with quite a bit of experience in sneaking about." As a child, Helena had been a pickpocket, and that hardship, unfortunately for Beatrice, had afforded her sister-in-law an uncanny ability to slip about while remaining undetected. "May I venture whatever you and Lord Hamish were doing in here has something to do with the three invitations you asked me to secure on behalf of you and the earl?" Helena asked quietly.

Beatrice closed her eyes. She'd really been rubbish at all this. Hamish couldn't have wound up with a more inept partner in his plan.

She sank onto the edge of a pink satin sofa. "I expect you have questions."

"Oh, I do." Helena slid onto the seat beside Beatrice. "But I'm not so domineering as to expect answers. Every woman is entitled to her secrets and stories." She paused. "Just as every woman deserves to have someone in her life she can rely on and trust."

"But Robert—"

"Is my husband," Helena gently interjected. "And if you want to talk to me about anything, you may do so with the assurance that you'll have my complete confidence." Helena laid her hand on Beatrice's. "We women must stick together."

Biting at her lower lip, Beatrice stared down at her and her sister-in-law's connected hands and warred with herself. To say anything to anyone violated Hamish's trust, and even as Helena vowed she'd not share anything revealed with Robert, the fact remained Helena might not feel so inclined to keep that confidence when she discovered the nature of Beatrice's relationship with Hamish.

Ultimately, the yearning to share her circumstances with someone won out. Beatrice made herself speak. "He was not really my suitor," she whispered. "He never really was."

She went on to explain everything: from the frustration and hurt at being continually rejected which had led her to invent a suitor, and then Hamish's subsequent discovery of her letters, and his arrival in London, to the arrangement they'd come to. All of it. When she'd finished, Helena sat with the silence of Beatrice's revelation.

And then, her sister-in-law sighed.

"I know it is madness," Beatrice said so that Helena couldn't be the one to say how foolish Beatrice had been. "I do, and I understand you and anyone must think me mad for having agreed to this, but I'm just so very tired of having no control over the suitors who've come to call. This allowed me to take control of my narrative and create an end to the pursuits of future suitors."

Restless, she surged to her feet. "Only, I'm not being completely truthful," she said, at last wanting to free herself of all the lies. "Yes, I saw how helping Lord Hamish benefitted me, but I also saw how he'd been wronged, and helping him attain justice was the right and honorable thing to do." She'd just never anticipated how far, and how fast she would have fallen for the big Scot.

The fight left her limbs, and she sank back into her seat.

"Beatrice," Helena said in heartbreakingly gentle tones, "do you truly believe that *I*, of all people…a woman engaged in a pretend courtship, for far less noble reasons, would dare pass judgment on *you*?"

That silenced Beatrice.

Helena stood, but only so that she could sink to a knee before her.

"Beatrice," her sister-in-law said, clutching her hands. "I will support you and Lord Hamish in any way."

Beatrice's heart stilled. "You will?" she whispered.

Helena rolled her eyes. "Of course, I will, you goose. And your brother will—"

Beatrice was already shaking her head.

"That is, *if* you decide to entrust Robert with this confidence, I have every faith he will lend Hamish any assistance he can. I needn't tell you that together our connections to the *ton* and underworld and everything in between are vast."

Helena's was an understatement. Helena and her found-family, who were the duchess's only family, had first owned and operated one of London's most prosperous gaming hells. Since that initial venture between Helena and her brothers, they'd acquired countless other businesses and expanded their ventures into all aspects of society, *and* the network of people with whom they worked and dealt.

Hope stirred in her breast. Hamish didn't have to live in the shadows and be alone in his quest for justice. He'd lost his family and forgot what it was to have those on which to rely.

As soon as the thought took root, logic popped it as effectively as a pin entering a soapy bubble.

"He is proud," she explained, lifting her gaze to Helena. "He will not take well to the idea of trusting his secrets with others and taking help." More like, he'd hate it.

"Beatrice, there isn't a man who was more closed up and resistant to help than my brother, Ryker." Helena flashed a wry grin. "If *he* can be convinced, then the Devil himself can."

Her sister-in-law's pretty brown eyes twinkled. "Plus, I do not think you give yourself enough credit for being able to show the gentleman that every one of us should be able to find and accept help sometimes."

Beatrice stared sightlessly across the room. Hamish expected that when he took his revenge, it would mean he'd need to leave. But if he allowed justice to play out through the proper channels, then, he'd not only be vindicated, he'd be free to live out in the open with his identity no longer secret. And mayhap, he'd even… stay. Or move between London and the Highlands, to his family's ancestral seat.

The more she thought of what the future could be for Hamish, the greater the eagerness filling her breast. Helena was right. Beatrice *could* convince Hamish to let her family help him so he needn't face this alone.

She had to.

CHAPTER 11

Bonny Bea,

Gardenias are pink. Gardenias are yellow. When I have you near, I'm the most fortunate fellow.

Lovingly Yours,
Hamish

SINCE LORD AND LADY SHAFTESBURY'S ball last evening, Beatrice had been beset by a sense of purpose. Upon her return and following her talk with Helena, Beatrice had dashed off a note to Hamish. In it, she'd requested he meet her in Hyde Park when daylight first broke.

They met at the gates just as the orange orb of the sun peaked over the horizon and inserted its place where the night sky had once been. But for the errant rider and handful of nurses and babes, the park remained quite still. Behind in the carriage, Lily, her sleepy maid, had begun snoring before Beatrice had closed the door behind her.

At that moment, she led Hamish over a slight rise and off the graveled path, to the edge of a familiar copse. As she made to enter, Hamish stopped.

She looked questioningly back. "Well?"

Wordlessly, he joined her.

The moment they walked past the pair of English oak flanking the entrance, Beatrice looked about. Even as Hamish cast a dubious glance about the wooded sanctuary, Beatrice took it all in. Overhead the leaves of the ash, chestnut, hawthorn, and poplar formed a canopy of emerald green. While at their feet, the old leaves, some crisp, some wet, remnants of the previous fall made a blanket in varying shades of brown, upon the forest floor. Pebbles and rocks of varying sizes, lay strewn about, as if Mother Nature had left pleasing trifles about with which visitors might play.

Beatrice wandered to the edge of the shore, where the lake kissed the ground of the copse. The sun shown in the water, leaving a bright glare upon the crystal depths. Enthralled, Beatrice dropped to her haunches and picked up a small, perfectly rounded rock. She stared at it for a long moment, weighing it in her palm. Then, coming to her feet, she launched the stone across the water. The small projectile skipped once-twice-three-four times, before disappearing under the surface.

Hamish whistled softly. "Ye'r good at skipping stones, lassie," he said, bringing his hands together in a slow, appreciative clap.

Catching her skirts, Beatrice sank into a flourishing curtsy. "It's among my most impressive skills. That, along with singing, embroidering, sketching, and every other dull pastime ladies are tasked with perfecting." She grimaced.

Hamish joined her at the shore, and together they stared out across the expansive waters.

"Here, one can forget they are in London. We may as well be a world away," she said wistfully, "in a land untouched by man, and the blights they leave upon nature."

"So verra beautiful," he murmured, and something in that deep, sonorous declaration brought Beatrice's gaze back to him.

From under those thick, sooty lashes, Hamish stared at her with a piercing intensity, that stole the breath from her lungs, and in this instant, with that fierce spark in his eyes, she could almost think… he'd spoken…of her.

Hamish looked away first, and the earth slowly resumed spinning.

"Ah never imagined there was a place like it in London."

You silly ninny. Of course, he was talking about this forested area. Get a hold of yourself.

"This is what drew me to your family's keep," she confessed. "Being there…it is like…it is like…"

"Aye?" he quietly urged.

She searched her mind, for fitting words, and found only one: "Magic," she whispered. "Those lands, *your* lands." Not hers. They hadn't been meant for the English. "It is as though time marched on, but the wilds of the Highlands stayed still, locked in a state of their eternal beauty and majesty."

Something flashed in his eyes; some subtle, undefinable emotion, that was gone too quick.

"Do you plan to go back?"

He stared at her.

"To Scotland," she clarified.

"Ah haven't given much thought behind making the ones guilty of betraying my family pay." Hamish did another sweep of the land around them. "Ye come 'ere often, lassie, then?"

He didn't want to talk any further about what exactly his plan and its conclusion were.

Odd, how quick she'd learned the nuances of a man who'd until just recently, been a stranger. It was how she knew how he evaded topics he'd rather not speak on. In this case, he didn't wish to talk about Scotland.

"Here?" Beatrice shook her head. "I've visited or walked *past* it. But no, I've never stepped *inside* this forest before."

Within the lake's unblemished depths, she caught the way Hamish's brow creased with consternation.

"Tis not a place ye visit. Then why come here? There's no one to see us here, together, then why come to such a secluded spot?" he asked perplexedly. "Doesn't it defeat the purpose of yer efforts?"

"It serves another purpose," she murmured, staring at a pair of pink pelicans glided across the lake. Periodically, those well-beaked birds dipped their enormous heads under the water, in search of food, always coming up empty. It was a state she could relate to, all too well.

"Everyone comes here," she said, directing her words out at the pelicans.

Hamish glanced about at the quiet surroundings of the heavily wooded shores.

Beatrice looked at him. "Couples that is," she clarified.

Understanding filled his eyes. "Ah, our comin' to this place where sweethearts gather, will lend further proof o' our romance."

"No."

"No?" he repeated.

He looked so hopelessly, so endearingly perplexed, Beatrice laughed.

"Ah don't understand."

"You don't want to."

"Ah do," he insisted.

Beatrice peered at him. "The answer has nothing to do with the information you've come to London in search of."

"A'm curious about ye all the same, lass."

Her heart fluttered. How easily that word rolled from his lips, and when spoken in that Scottish brogue, it may as well have been an endearment bestowed upon a sweetheart.

"Why?" she made herself ask. "Why does it matter to you either way."

He moved his gaze over her face. "Ye'r certainly right. It doesn't have anythin' to do with my bein' 'ere, one way or another…but for some reason, Beatrice, a'm wanting to ken about you." Hamish shrugged. "There ye have it."

"Fine, you may want to know, but *I* don't want you to."

Hamish touched a hand to his broad chest. "And here ye ken all my secrets."

"Yes, but yours are about injustices done to you and your family. This isn't…" Even as they were alone, she dropped her voice to a low whisper. "This isn't…"

He stared at her. "Aye?" he prodded when she couldn't muster the courage to finish the thought.

Exasperated, Beatrice tossed her arms up. "The same!" she exclaimed, and then promptly dropped her voice. "It's not the same."

"Ah have begged fur food 'n' water, 'n' fought other, weaker men fur th' smallest scraps. Dae ye think ah'm one to judge?"

It was the first glimpse he'd allowed her of his time as a prisoner, and her heart ached at imagining a proud, honorable Hamish locked away, with other criminals and for crimes he'd been innocent of.

"Those were crimes committed against you, Hamish," she said softly. "They were adversities you overcame, ones that left you stronger. The things *I'm* speaking of, aren't at all even struggles. Not really, in the scheme of life." In fact, she regretted having brought it up.

"Try me, lass."

"Oh, you Scots *are* tenacious," she muttered, pulling a chuckle from him.

That laugh, it came so easy, and the sound of it, though rusty, was free and light and offered a glimpse of who he might have been…and who he could be. And more…she saw a vision of what it would have been to be courted by Hamish, not as part of a ruse, but of genuine desire and—

Beatrice's heart thudded sickeningly against her ribcage.

No.

She didn't fall for suitors. It was a hard and fast rule she'd lived by years ago. Certainly not real ones, and absolutely not a fake one. Ultimately, the gentlemen who entered her life invariably chose another. As such, she protected her heart; shielded it. She never cared too deeply. And she never let those walls down.

But somehow, Hamish had slipped past those defenses and left her weak in ways she couldn't be weak. Hamish, who, unlike her other suitors who'd at least set out with intentions of courting her in the hope of marrying her, had absolutely no interest in her. That was, no interest outside of the help she could provide him on his path of retribution.

I'm going to be ill… "Oh, God. This is bad."

"How about ye let me decide for my own, lassie?" he drawled.

Beatrice jumped. "Did I s-say that ou-out loud?"

He nodded. "Ye did."

Now, I'm talking to myself.

Oh, dear, this was *worse* than bad. This was catastrophic. Fortunately, however, he'd mistaken her mutterings for her reservations in sharing with him, and as it was far more humiliating to admit she'd been dreaming of a real courtship with him, she explained her affinity for this place.

"Since I made my debut a lifetime ago, I've come near this hidden part in Hyde Park at all different hours of the day. What I've learned is that most ladies and gentlemen with intentions of marrying, *want* to be seen. But the couples who are in love? They don't need to have an audience. They don't want the world's eyes upon them." She briefly spread her arms wide. "They want the privacy that this place brings. They want only each other."

Beatrice stared off into the distance at the pelicans who'd become mere specks on the horizon. "I've been seriously courted no fewer than nine times. *Nine*. Do you know how many of those suitors were so beset by a genuine desire for me, that they squired me to this place…or *any* place, for that, matter?" Beatrice asked, unable to keep the bitterness from creeping in. She brought her thumb and forefinger up to form a perfect circle. "Zero, Hamish. *Zero*.

"All those men, they saw my bloodlines like I was some prized horseflesh. None of them wished to know anything about me." Just as he didn't. Beatrice gave herself that reminder, so as to keep from falling any more than she already had for him. "They'd visit and they'd bring flowers. Always flowers. They never asked if I had a favorite bud because it didn't matter. *I* didn't matter."

Her words came faster and faster, each rolling into the other, and filled with restive emotion, she began to pace the shore.

"They didn't care to know about my dreams and hopes, or even wonder if I had any, Hamish. They didn't care to learn about my family, or even so much as talk to my niece and nephew," she paused briefly. As Hamish had done.

Beatrice cast a look back his way. "And the thing of it is, Hamish? I cannot blame them. You were right in what you said about me not having really experienced anything. I've not seen or known the world as my sister-in-law did, and not the way you have."

He made a sound of protest.

"I admire you for your honesty," she said dryly. "Do not disappoint me now by giving me false objections. I was born into a life of privilege and luxury. I was destined to marry and marry well. And…I never questioned that path for myself. Along the way,

I realized…" She glanced down at her toes.

"Realized what?" he asked quietly.

Beatrice looked up. "I don't know *who* I am, Hamish. I don't know what my purpose in this great world is. For so long, I thought it was to be a wife…but *is* that a purpose?" she asked, and he didn't attempt to answer that rhetorical purpose.

"Those women," she continued, "the other ladies chosen by every one of my suitors had something that defined them, that made them extraordinary and interesting and admirable in ways that I'm not." And that was why she'd never attained one of those great happily-ever-afters in romantic tales she'd once so loved to read.

Beatrice took a breath.

He said nothing for a long while. Only the chirp of the birds and the faint wispy rustle of leaves met her telling.

"We've already covered this, lass."

The matter of her long stream of suitors and so much of this had been confined to her letters.

"Oh. Yes."

Mortification threatened to swallow her whole, and she just wished it'd be a swift end. She glanced down at the rocks scattered about the earthen floor. "I'd forgotten for a moment you'd…read all that." All her innermost thoughts and secret yearnings splashed on the pages she'd hidden in the broken walls of his ancestral keep.

"That isnae whit ah referred to." His low, sonorous brogue brought her eyes closed.

Coarse knuckles touched her cheek, in a roughened caress, as Hamish gently forced her eyes to his.

"Yer clever and fearless. Yer a lass who's unafraid to go toe-to-toe with any man—including, me when ah took ye by surprise that first night we met and the Sassenachs dinnae have a brain in their heads, if they fail to appreciate a woman such as ye," he murmured.

Her breath caught.

His gaze slipped to her mouth, and then back to her eyes.

Their bodies swayed toward one another like the branches of the fragrant, slender May-trees in full bloom around them.

They were in each other's arms in an instant; two people who'd fought valiantly the attraction between them, but who remained powerless to the pull that had existed from the moment they'd first met.

Since their first and last kiss, she'd lived in the memory of his embrace. She'd yearned to have his hands on her, and his lips on hers, again. Beatrice opened her mouth to him, and he swept inside, taking what she offered, and giving her far more. She wanted him. She wanted to know him in every way a woman could know a man.

Beatrice curled her fingertips into the soft wool fabric of his jacket and gripped him tightly.

He made to take her lips again, but she edged slightly back.

"Lass?" there was a question in his eyes.

"I have thought a good deal about it."

Hamish released a pained laugh. "If yer doing a guid deal of thinking while in mah arms, lass, then ah'm definitely doing it wrong."

"I want you to make love to me."

HE'D HEARD HER WRONG.

I want you to make love to me.

It'd only been because, in attempt to banish the memory of her in his arms and regain mastery of his self-control and focus, he'd spent days avoiding her. Now, he imagined her solemnly spoken request. He'd spent so many days dreaming of that very plea falling from this lass's lips, that he heard what he wanted.

"I want you to make love to me, Hamish," Beatrice repeated again.

Nay, there it was. She'd said it again; that utterance falling for a second time from her crimson red, cupid-bow lips. She wanted him to make love to her.

Hamish closed his eyes and focused on inhaling and exhaling. All his efforts to stay away from her had been in vain. The hungering to be with her, in this way…and others, overwhelmed and consumed him.

Hamish made himself open his eyes. "Ye—"

"If you tell me I don't know what I want, Hamish," impatiently, Beatrice interrupted him, "I'm going to scream this copse down."

A grin pulled at his lips. "Ah was going to say, ye know if we do this, it canna be undone."

She blinked her fathomless blue eyes slowly. "Oh." Beatrice paused. "You…*want* to make love to me, then?" She sounded so hopeful and happy, and a woman of her character, grace, and beauty should never so doubt herself.

Hamish touched his brow to hers. "Ah have wanted to make love to ye since the moment ah first drank of your lips in Redbrooke's library."

Her lips formed a lush moue. "Oh." Then a little frown furrowed that place between her eyebrows. "Not before that, though? Just—"

He laughed softly, burying that sound in the crook of her shoulder. "Ah noted yer beauty from the moment ah clapped eyes upon ye, bonny Bea, but fought mahself from feeling more."

"So, you will make love to me?" she asked. "Because I should warn you, I've never—"

Hamish gently kissed away that worry from her lips and drew her close. At the feel of her so soft and inviting against him, his body went instantly hard.

He was going to hell. Granted, he'd likely already secured a direct route to those fiery gates for the things he'd done in the name of survival. But if there'd been any doubt as to where he'd spend his final days of rest, it was confirmed in this here moment.

Hamish ran his hand down the curve of her hip, and Beatrice's legs weakened.

He caught her and pressed her against the slender trunk of the conveniently close elm. All the while, they sparred with their mouths; slanting their lips over one another in an urgency-fueled kiss.

Catching the hem of her day dress, Hamish dragged the shimmery fabric up. As he bared her long, graceful limbs to the morning air, he availed himself to that satiny softness of her thighs. Slipping a knee between her legs, he gently parted her and found her core with the palm of his hand.

A hiss exploded from Beatrice's lips. At his touch she jerked her hips, arching reflexively towards Hamish and the glide of his finger moving in and then out of her soaking wet channel.

"Th-that feels very g-good."

At her chattiness in the throes of lovemaking, through the agony of Hamish's wanting, came a grin. "Does it, lass?"

Her speech dissolved for a moment, and she gave an indistinct and unintelligible utterance. "Mm-hm."

Hamish rewarded her honesty by slipping another finger inside her.

"S-so n-iiiice," she moaned, managing to turn that one syllable into six.

He lowered his mouth close to hers, and then stopped with just a hairsbreadth away, simultaneously teasing Beatrice and tormenting himself.

"Just nice?" he whispered, and as his lips moved from that query, his mouth touched hers in an all-too fleeting accidental kiss.

Hamish teased that nub between her legs. "I like it i-immensely," she cried out softly and proceeded to run through a shopping list of her likes and dislikes. "More than chocolate and raspberries and raspberries dipped in chocolate and—"

"Ye enjoy chocolate?"

Biting at her lower lip, she rocked against his hand, her thrusting an evocative imagery that conjured thoughts of her hips moving to receive him. Beatrice forced heavy golden lashes up. A question filled their expressive blue-green depths.

"Chocolate," he said, helping her find her way back to what they'd been discussing.

"Doesn't everyone?"

"Ah dinnae have a taste for it."

"Truly? Because there is nothing sweeter than—mmmm," Beatrice moaned slow and low, as Hamish freed her breasts from the bodice of her gown and dropped a worshipful kiss atop the tops of her bosom.

"Do ye ken whit ah have a taste for, Beatrice?"

She opened her mouth to answer, just as he flickered his tongue back and forth across the pebbled peak of first one breast, and then the other.

"Ye, lassie," he breathed against her chest.

And he'd a fear that one taste of her would never be enough.

Beatrice's lips remained agape like that, wonderment and bliss frozen. Then, Hamish drew one of her pink nipples deep into his mouth, suckling her and Beatrice keened. While he continued stroking her center and worshiping her breasts with his mouth, she moved restlessly against him.

Hamish withdrew his fingers, and Beatrice let out a soft cry of protest.

"You h-hate me," she panted, lifting her hips searchingly. "There is n-no other a-accounting for your st—" The rest of her admonishment died on a long, quiet hiss as he swapped his fingers for his thigh.

"Och, ah like ye verra well." He adjusted her so that she was perfectly perched upon him. "Better than anyone else." And there'd be time enough later to panic at that dangerously true admission.

Beatrice panted. "I am honored. I like you very much, t-too," she said and gave a bold, experimental thrust of her hips.

"Like this, lassie." Gripping her hips, he helped Beatrice set a rhythm, letting her use his body for her pleasure.

Beatrice buried her head in the crook of his shoulder.

He placed a kiss on her neck. "Don't turn shy on me now, lass."

"I'm not sh-shy. I…" She bit her lip hard. "It feels so good. *T-Too* good."

"There's na such thing."

"Oh, there i-is, and this is ahhh…" Her explanation faded to a low, husky groan, when he palmed her breasts, and brought them both together, so he could flick his tongue back and forth over each swollen tip.

Beatrice's thrusting grew more frantic, her movements less fluid and jerky, indicating she was close to her climax. It'd been so long since he'd been with a woman, and holding this particularly lush, bonny lass threatened the thin thread of self-control he grasped desperately onto.

He wanted her. He hungered for her with a fierce, burning hunger, that—if he were being honest with at least himself in this instant—had little to do with the fact that she was just any woman, but rather, was *this* woman.

Beatrice's movements grew increasingly agitated. He paused and stepped back only long enough to toss his jacket as a makeshift blanket onto the earthen floor. Then lifting Beatrice in his arms, he brought her down on the soft silk interior of his jacket. He stopped just over her. Through passion-glazed eyes, she stared questioningly up at Hamish.

He stroked a palm along the curve of her cheek. "Are ye sure ye wish to do this, lassie? Because isna too late. If ye want to stop—"

Beatrice gripped Hamish hard by his nape and forced his face down for a violent kiss. He devoured her lips. He slid his tongue inside the moist, warm cavern of her mouth.

How freely shared all of herself with him. At every turn, she tossed the windows open, and let Hamish in.

Sweat beaded at his brow. He'd never wanted a woman the way he wanted this woman so unabashed and unabandoned in his embrace. He tugged his shirt free, and then after he'd tugged off his boots and trousers, he came down beside her.

A soberness overcame the haze of desire in her eyes. Hamish followed her stare to what it was that had caused that gravity and stiffened.

Beatrice brought herself slowly up onto her knees, and then with an infinite tenderness she traced the tip of her finger along the thin strips of white scarring left by the lash of a whip.

"Who did this?" she whispered.

"A warden who had a taste for inflicting pain on his prisoners, and he took a particular liking for punishing me for being too obstinate."

"How they hurt you," she whispered.

"It doesna hurt now." In fact, since her, he'd not thought of his days in that prison, once.

"But it *did*." Then, Beatrice pressed her lips to those hideous marks he'd been left with as a gift from a cruel prison warden.

As she brushed butterfly soft kisses over each scar, Hamish's eyes slid closed. The part of him that instinctively wished to shut her out from this ugly side of his past, screamed for Hamish to set her aside. But the part of his soul that longed for the light she exuded, took the gift she offered; each brush of her lips upon him felt like an absolution.

Suddenly, it was too much. With a growl, he brought her down quickly underneath him and found her again with his fingers.

Beatrice splayed her legs and lifted herself up into Hamish's fingers. He continued to work her, worship her, tease her until he'd reduced her to a keening pleading. Positioning himself at the damp, honey-colored curls shielding her womanhood, Hamish slowly entered her and was immediately gripped by the whitest, tightest, hottest heat.

He gritted his teeth. "Ye feel so good, lassie."

"You do, too." Beatrice moaned as he slid another inch deeper inside her.

All the while he entered her channel, he teased her with his fingers, preparing her for his entry.

"Ah fear ah'll hurt ye," he said hoarsely.

Beatrice reached up and framed his face between her hands. "You could never hurt me, Hamish."

Shaken by that undeserved faith in him, Hamish kissed her to silence her, and then slid all the way home.

Beatrice gasped, and he swallowed that quick exhale.

"Am I ah hurtin' ye—"

"It feels so good. Do not stop," she pleaded, her ragged breaths coming rapidly. "Please."

And when presented with that desperate entreaty, he could deny her nothing. Hamish began to move, stroking his length in and out of her with slow, steady strokes. The feel of her, so wet and tight threatened to send him climaxing too soon. And he fought that release, wanting to give Beatrice pleasure first.

Beatrice lifted her hips into each downward thrust of Hamish's hips. Their movements grew more frenzied.

"Hamish?" she cried.

Hamish trailed his lips down her neck, nipping a path along the sensitive flesh as he went. "Aye, lass," he said, his voice gruff and low. "'Tis ah. Nah other."

Beatrice's body went taut; her facial muscles froze in a mask mixed with splendor and wonderment.

Then, throwing her neck back, Beatrice cried out, coming in waves. Her channel clenched and unclenched around him, as her clever inner muscles gripped his shaft. With a shuddery gasp, she collapsed.

Hamish fought his release a moment longer, and when the pleasure built to a point that bordered on pain, with a guttural groan ripped from deep in his chest, he withdrew and spent himself in shuddery arcs onto the weathered leaves around them.

Replete, his entire body sagged. In one fluid motion, he collapsed onto the ground and brought Beatrice so that she rested atop his chest. Closing his eyes, Hamish folded his arms about her. He'd been angry for so long. Haunted by ghosts and nightmares, and only black memories, that he'd never thought to feel this light.

She was the sunshine, ushering in a rainbow after a rainstorm.

She was sanity amidst the madness that had gripped him.

She was salvation.

CHAPTER 12

Bonny Beatrice,

You deserve to have sonnets penned for the splendor of your spirit, and the brightness of your smile, and the sharpness of your wit.

You deserve romantic. You know by now, I'm not and never will be...but I wish I could be...for you. You deserve that, lass.

Lovingly Yours,
Hamish

HAMISH SMOOTHED A HAND IN slow, soothing circles over the small of Beatrice's back.

She didn't want this moment to end. She wanted to stay here in this private wooded sanctuary, folded in Hamish's warm, powerful embrace, forever. For on the shore of the Serpentine, wrapped in Hamish's arms, Beatrice at last understood.

She understood the depth of passion that had driven her past suitors to forsake all in the name of love...because she loved Hamish. She loved everything about him. The way he'd treated her as an equal from the beginning. The way he teased and also the way he blustered.

Why had she fought this? It had been futile.

That realization didn't bring with it the terror she'd thought it would. She felt…freed, and hopeful that he too might want a future with her.

Sometime later, after he'd retrieved his kerchief from the folds of his jacket and tenderly cleaned Beatrice between her legs, she lay back down atop him, and rested her chin on his chest. "I wanted to speak with you about something."

He caressed his left hand over her buttocks. "This seems serious, lass."

"Hush." Beatrice swatted at him. "It is."

Hamish rose up and leaned against the tree they rested under. "Ah good serious or a bad serious?"

"The former."

Hamish looked expectantly at her.

Funny, since speaking with Helena, she'd thought only of this meeting, and yet she'd not prepared how to tell him.

Beatrice took a deep breath and just said it. "Last evening, we—you and I—were discovered in Lord Shaftesbury's office."

Under her, Hamish's entire body tensed.

"By my sister-in-law," she hurried to reassure him.

" 'N' this is somehow *good*?" he asked his voice garbled.

"Yes. No!" she said when his dark brows shot into a single line. "I can certainly see how you'd feel it isn't good news, however, it is."

His eyes darkened, and he continued to stare in that penetrating way.

Unnerved by his silence, Beatrice cleared her throat and tried again. "I claimed we had met…" Her face warmed. "For… romantic purposes."

"And?"

"And she listened in a nearby room close enough to ascertain that wasn't the case." Not this time. She took another breath. "She heard us going through the earl's things…and I…"

His eyes narrowed into impervious slits. "Aye?"

"And I spoke to Helena," she said on a rush.

Hamish looked at her. "Aboot what, lass?"

There was a steely edge contained within that query, as all the previous excitement to speak with him about Helena using her connections to help Hamish wavered.

"I explained…it all to her."

"All?" His propensity for terseness dissolved even further, into curt one-syllable responses.

She nodded her head slightly. "Everything."

"Everything," he stated flatly.

She nodded once more.

For a long while, Hamish said nothing. The occasional plunk of a pelican's beak striking the water, filled the otherwise vacuous quiet.

Beatrice dampened her lips. She wanted him to say something. *Anything.* Anything other than this stark nothingness.

Stonily silent, Hamish stood.

She followed him as he stomped over and angrily snatched up his trousers. He stuffed his legs into them and quickly pulled them up.

His rejection stung, and yet, she should have anticipated a man so proud, one who'd relied on no one to become defensive.

Drawing her bodice into place, she shoved her skirts down and hurried over to join him. When it became apparent he'd no intention of speaking, she made herself be the one to do so.

"You are angry I spoke to Helena."

"How did ye think ah'd take it, lass?" That term, usually an endearment, emerged as a volatile hiss. "Did ye think a'd be happy ye betrayed our pact with yer sister-in-law, th' *duchess*?"

Beatrice recoiled. "I didn't…" Only, she had shared his confidences. Granted, she'd done so because Helena had come upon them. But all the same, Beatrice saw how Hamish felt betrayed. She tried a different approach. "Forgive me, Hamish. I didn't set out to betray you."

"And yet, that's just what ye did," he snapped.

He'd fixed on the wrong thing. "Hamish, it is all right to accept help," she said earnestly. "I know you've been alone since—"

"Ye think ah don't have anyone. Ah've an uncle, Angus, and a friend whom ah can rely on. A man who was with me from the start of my hell in that penal colony."

Beatrice started. In the scheme of this great unraveling between them, it was a silly detail to fix on, and yet…she didn't know he'd a friend and confidante.

And I don't even know their names…

"I…I… didn't know that," she whispered.

"Why would ye?" he scoffed. "Ye dinnae need to."

His meaning couldn't be clearer—she hadn't needed to because she meant nothing to him. Had he slapped her with the back of his hand it couldn't have hurt more than the lash of his words; harshly blunt, and so very much worse for the truth of them.

He was trying to hurt her. She understood that.

Beatrice took a deep breath and forced a calm into her voice. "Very well. You do not want to accept my family's willingness to help. What is your plan once you determine the identities of your betrayers?"

"Ye—"

"And do not say I don't need to know. Whether you like it or not, I am the woman whose help you sought. As such, I'm involved." She took a step toward him, seeking some kind of answer from him. "What will you do when you finally learn the identities of your betrayers, Hamish? What is your plan exactly? To kill them?"

Tense silence served as Hamish's only answer.

Then, it hit her.

No.

"Hamish?" she asked haltingly.

"Aye?"

"You intend to kill them." It was why his plan didn't end with his return to Scotland.

Hamish flexed his jaw. "On a field of honor," he said, at last, confirming that horrifying supposition.

"A field of honor? A duel," she said, her voice pitchy to her own ears. "Call it what it is. It is a duel."

"Fine." A muscle rippled along his cheekbone. "A duel. What did ye *think* ah was going to do? Knock on their goddamned doors, and ask for a bluidy apology?"

She hadn't allowed herself to think. Mayhap because deep down she'd already known. It was spiraling out of control. Everything was happening too quickly.

Fear licked at the edges of her mind, leaving her thoughts in tumult. "But Hamish…it is murder. Either you will be the one to d-die," Oh, God. The moment she spoke that word, it was as though the very life had been sucked from within her soul. Grief cut up ragged holes all over her heart. "Or you will commit murder."

"Ah'm nae afraid to die, Beatrice. Ah've learned there are far greater sufferings."

And heaven help her, if it were to be so, she'd want Hamish to survive, anyway she could have him.

Imploringly, Beatrice stretched out a hand. "Please, don't do this."

Hamish took an angry step forward. "They carted my brother and my father off like they were traitorous monsters, Beatrice." Her name slipped out as a sharp hiss. He wrapped a hand about his own throat. "Ah watched from a crowd of cheering, laughing Englishmen as they lowered the noose around their necks."

She proved to be the worst sort of coward because she couldn't hear more.

Beatrice clamped her hands over her ears. She didn't want to have the scene of his suffering painted out in perfect clarity as because of her ignorance, he was forced to relive his misery, and yet she wanted to know even these darkest parts of his life.

In the end, Hamish made the decision for her. He took her hands firmly but gently from her ears and forced her arms back to her side.

"Ye dinnae want to hear it, but ah have to live with those memories every single day, Beatrice. Every single day. Ah had to watch as the stools were kicked out from under my da and brother's feet, and they used the last of their life's energy to writhe and twist, fighting for just one more breath."

Tears fell down her face; they left a stark, desolate trail of grief for all Hamish had endured.

Beatrice tried to breathe through the pressure bearing down on her chest, but every inhalation proved agonizing. How had she moments ago been lamenting her many years of rejection? How very insignificant her own miseries were compared to the real suffering Hamish and others had known.

Only, he wasn't done.

"People? Thay think it's quick. That th' force o' th' body's weight comin' off that stool wull put strain on th' neck, 'n' break it," he continued relentlessly, brutal in his truthfulness. "Bit that isna th' case. Tis slow. In mah da's case 'twas nine minutes. For my brother, my big brother who'd been a hero ta me as a laddie, it took him fourteen minutes because he didna wanna die. He'd so much life to l-live." His voice broke.

It marked the first time she'd ever seen him vulnerable, and she touched his arm, aching to hold him, wanting to take his suffering her own so that he could be free of the demons that haunted him.

"Do you truly believe they'd want you to give your life for them?" When he didn't answer, she asked him another one. "Would you have wanted *them* to give their lives for you?" She touched his arm, but angrily, he shrugged off her touch.

"Do ye ken how lang nine minutes 'n' fourteen minutes realla are?" He jabbed a finger at Beatrice. "Stare at a clock one day, lass, and watch as time ticks by, and tell me how bluidy quick that death trulla is. They dinnae even let me mourn them. They brought me in that same day, tossed me 'n' a cell, and put me through a sham of a trial." Hamish's eyes glinted with sorrow. "'Twas th' twelv'f o' May when ah wis shackled 'n' dragged aboard a prison hulk in chains. My brother would hae bin twenty-four that day." His features twisted in a mask of grief. "Instead, it marked th' day ah died completely inside"

The ache in her chest made each beat of her heart painful.

Hamish sucked in a slow, steadying breath through his teeth, and when he again spoke, he did so in his measured emotionless way. "Noo, tell me if 'twas yer brother 'n' faither who'd bin sae brutally slaughtered, would ye still be sae magnanimous wi' th' ones who murdered thaim?"

She remained silent. For in truth, she couldn't say she'd not feel precisely as Hamish felt and want to exact retribution.

"Nay, ah dinnae ken so, lass."

Tiredly, he swiped up his rumpled jacket and pulled it back on.

If possible, this deflated version of the ornery Hamish proved all the more agonizing to witness.

"Hamish," she implored, taking his hands in hers. "Listen to me." When he tried to tug free, she tightened her grip and held onto him. "Your entire family was murdered, and you deserve justice, but…justice? It doesn't have to be the way you think. You don't have to conduct it in the shadows, risking your future to see justice is done."

"And who is this honorable body or person who'll do it? Hmm?" he pressed when she didn't immediately answer.

"The courts?" she ventured haltingly.

"*English* courts?"

At her hesitant nod, Hamish tossed his head back and roared with an empty and awful laugh. "Do ye want to ken about yer Sassenach *courts*, Beatrice? Provocateurs came from England and encouraged good Scots to take up arms for unions and a vote in Parliament. Many Scots were not even involved but were made to look guilty as was the case with my da 'n' brother."

His gaze grew distant, and she knew the precise moment he ceased seeing her and became lost in the memory of that time. "Lord President Hope claimed Scot laws wur not equipped tah deal with such offenses." His lip peeled back in a sneer. "Och, Och, because th' Sassenach hae only viewed Scots as savages. Hope couldnae even hide his disdain of my people through th' proceedings. That member of th' English law establishment placed in charge of conducting th' prosecution was sae belittling, sae evident in his disdain fur th' Scots, he nearly faced a duel from th' Tory Sheriff of Scotland. So dinna talk to me about having trust in th' *English* courts," he spat.

He spoke of intolerance and injustice she as a duke's daughter had never known. She'd been insulated from the ugly reality of what Hamish, his family, and so many other people had suffered. She found herself humbled and shamed by her ignorance and naivete.

"I know—"

"Ye ken wha exactly?" he barked with such mocking derision, she curled up within herself. "Ye dinna ken anaythin'!" Hamish thumped a fist hard against his chest. "My name tis all ah have, Beatrice. Tis *all* ah have."

"That isn't true, Hamish. You have something few men and no women possess—an earldom," she said, willing him to see. "You can use your power and influence to help all the other people who have been denied a voice."

"Ah've no money to m' name, Beatrice," he said flatly. "Ah man with no fortune cannot feed a family let alone command change."

"And…that isn't all. You also have…"

He stared pointedly at her.

She dampened her lips. "You…have me, Hamish."

Oh, God. How had she found the courage to say it?

The canopy of leaves swayed overhead as the only movement in the copse.

He continued to stare at her.

"Or…you could? If you wanted to," Beatrice ventured.

Hamish hooded his lashes. "Whit are ye saying, lass?"

Beatrice drew a breath in through her lips. "I love you, Hamish."

Color slapped his cheeks. "Ye'd use tha' to try and stop me from whit ah've come to do?"

And the tiny sliver of hope that he might utter those words back, cracked, and sprinkled into a million pieces inside of her.

"No," she whispered. How could he think she'd weaponize her love for him? "I love you. I want to be your partner in this and in life."

His eyes were almost pleading. "Ah never asked ye to help me find justice, Beatrice," he said hoarsely. "Ah wanted nothing more from ye than to gain my entry into th' households of th' suspects."

She drew back.

Had he shouted it from a tower, his repudiation couldn't be clearer—he didn't want her.

She could not hate him for the words he spoke, for he'd only ever given her the truth, and this was no different. In terms of what he wanted from Beatrice, Hamish had been clear from the start. Just…along the way, they'd become close, sharing parts of themselves. Apparently, those exchanges hadn't meant the same to him as they had her.

Beatrice stared sadly at him. "You are a man blinded by hate and buried in the past, and there are times I feel as if I don't even really know you." How was her voice so even? How when every part of her hurt and trembled inside?

"Ye were never supposed to." With those cold, empty words, and nothing more, Hamish strode off.

Beatrice stared blankly at his retreating form, silently imploring him to look back; pleading in her mind for him to return and apologize for words spoken in anger, and to tell her that she did mean something to him.

But he didn't.

He continued walking, out of the forested grounds, and out of her life. Just like every other suitor before him. He'd been no different. He'd wanted something, all the same…just something different than what the other gentlemen had come calling for.

Beatrice stood there, afraid to move. Afraid to exhale the shuddery breath trapped inside her lungs, for fear if she did, when she did, she'd break apart, and be unable to put herself back together.

A lone teardrop slipped down her cheek. Followed by another. And another.

They were the first tears she'd ever shed over a man's rejection, and she now knew with an even greater acuity why she'd fought falling in love.

CHAPTER 13

My Bonnie Bea,

I know you have a love for chocolate and raspberries and raspberries dipped in chocolate. I confess to more traditional Scottish favorites like Cranachan, caramel shortbread, and clootie. As a lad, I'd sneak into the kitchens at night and help myself to the treats prepared for the next day. Someday, when we are wed, you and I shall sneak into those kitchens together.

Lovingly Yours,
Hamish

THE LASS HAD SHARED HAMISH'S confidence with the duchess, and in doing so, all Hamish's plans for revenge hung in the balance. After all, the Duchess of Somerset may have been born on the streets of London, but she—along with her husband, Beatrice's brother—now rubbed elbows with England's most wealthy elite. Their loyalty would never lie with a Scot whose kin had been charged with treason.

That and only that, should be all he could think about. So why then, two nights later, did he find himself seated at the pianoforte of Burgess's music room, staring down at those ivory keys, unable to think of anything except Beatrice?

A memory slipped in, of Beatrice as she'd been when persuading him to continue their embrace.

"...Scots are bold, stubborn, and a-arrogant...I cannot be made to fall. It has never happened, and it never will..."

She'd been so confident she'd never fall in love with anyone, and after years of hurt at the hands of unworthy suitors, Hamish understood why she'd sought to protect herself.

He depressed a key.

Another memory of Beatrice surfaced—but this time with tear-filled, swollen eyes, and her pale cheeks damp from the tracks those drops had left in their wake.

"I love you, Hamish..."

In an attempt to drown out the echo of her whispery soft declaration, Hamish pressed another ivory key, hard.

It didn't help.

Nothing had and nothing would drown out her words of love—love, for *him*. She'd told him she loved him and how had he responded? He'd been so bluidy terrified out of his mind by how wonderful it had felt inside to hear Beatrice declare her love for him, he'd lashed out. He'd scorned her profession of love.

Hamish scrubbed a hand over his stubble-covered face. He'd never *not* be able to see her as she'd been at that moment—anguished, because of him.

Nay, he missed the lass. He missed sparring with her and teasing her and talking with her.

Since Hamish had lost everything, so much—nay, *all*—of his existence had become centered on retribution. It'd consumed him. Fueled him. Given him purpose, so that finding the identities of those who'd wronged him and exacting justice had been all that he was.

And then, she'd entered his life.

Or rather, he entered hers.

In being with Beatrice and in talking to her, all those darkest memories and his plan for vengeance had been brushed to the side, and oftentimes forgotten in favor of just being with her.

He missed her, and after having stormed out like the stubborn Scot he was, he found himself confronted with the future that awaited him—one without her in it.

That vicious knot in his chest grew and pulsed.

When he'd come to London, he'd had but one thing on his mind, and falling for a wee, spirited lass had not been it. And yet, there was no helping it. The lass had slipped past his defenses and landed herself a place in his once-deadened heart.

There came the low, unmistakable shuffle of familiar footfalls. Tiredly, he turned and greeted his uncle. "Angus."

"Laddie," the gruff Scot returned, as he limped slowly over to Hamish.

Heading him off to spare him further strain on his rheumatic limbs, Hamish crossed to meet him. "Ye should rest yer knees."

His uncle of old would have protested that he possessed the strength of a dozen younger men and could stand until the cows came home. This newer, aged, more wrinkled version collapsed heavily into the folds of the nearest chair. If possible, their time in London had further aged his last living relative.

Hamish followed, taking a seat at the upholstered shepherd's crook armchair nearest Ole Angus.

With a grunt, Angus fished a kerchief from his pocket and dusted at his sweaty brow. He panted slightly from the exertions it had cost him on his walk through Burgess's residence. "Thae auld limbs aren't whit thay used ta be."

How much that betrayal against the Campbells had changed them all.

His hands balled into a familiar reflexive fury. Only…the pain and rage were…muted, those sentiments dulled by the row he'd had with Beatrice.

Whit are ye thinking, letting that brawl between ye in the lassie cloud yer thoughts? Dinnae think about how her crystalline blue eyes welled with hurt at each blunt charge you leveled her way. Think about whit Ole Angus endured. That was true suffering.

"Ye shoulda been afforded a life of comfort," Hamish said quietly, that reminder as much for him as his godfather. "Ye deserved far more than…*this*."

Angus scoffed. "Bah." He gave a big wave of his hand. "Whit need does a Scot hae fur anythin' ither than th' use o' a pure tough, sturdy body, 'n' th' wilds o' th' hielands?" He uttered that familiar phrase, in that thickest of brogues Hamish recalled of his childhood.

Hamish had once possessed that romantic Scot's views on the material. Serving time in a harsh penal colony had quickly taught him the truth on that score. "We deserve to ha a home and food and security. That isna so verra much for a man to ask for in this good life."

"Aye," Ole Angus allowed. "Ye are right. That 'n' the love of a good lassie."

Hamish stiffened.

Resting his hands on his lap, Hamish's godfather leaned close and peered at Hamish. "How dae ah hae th' feeling ye ken something o' that?"

A flush climbed his neck. "I dinnae have a lassie."

But for these past weeks, he had. For a brief time, he had engaged in a game of pretend with a golden-haired enchantress, and he feared there'd be no dislodging thoughts of her from his stubborn head.

Angus peered at him overly long, and then slowly sat back in his seat. "Ye stopped calling on th' lass."

Hamish stared mutinously at the empty grate of the hearth across the room. "She told her sister-in-law the nature of our arrangement." He braced for the famed, fiery explosion of Angus's temper. His uncle, however, didn't so much as flinch.

"Ye arena surprised?" he muttered.

Angus chortled, his big shoulders heaving with his amusement. "Surprised? Laddie, th' ainlie thing as reliable as th' rising sun, is that th' sassenach wull betray a Scot."

His uncle was not wrong, and yet, that portrayal of Beatrice rankled.

Hamish frowned. "Ah thought ye favored the lass."

"Whin ah thought she cuid mak' ye forgoat th' bygane, ah did. Noo th' lassie haes shown her true colors, 'n' once a body betrays ye, a' trust in thaim is shattered."

There it was again. Hamish grunted. "The lass didn't betray me."

"Didnae she share yer secrets wi' her sister-in-law? At that, a bluidy duchess?"

"Aye, but she sought to help." Now that he'd finally gotten hold of his blustery temper, he saw that. Her efforts had come from a place of good.

'N' ah railed at th' lassie bit guid…

"Beatrice said th' duchess would help me find out who betrayed the Campbells, that she and th' duke and duchess would use their connections to investigators and peers to get just—"

"Bahh," Angus spat. "Th' sassenach hae made a guid many promises whaur th' Scots ur concerned." He rested his old, gnarled hand on Hamish's shoulder. "Partnering wi' th' sassenach, 'twas ne'er destined ta end weel. Ye hae ta ken, it's fur th' best. Th' sassenachs, thay cannae be trusted, Hamish. Tis time ta lea this place before ye fin' yersel' clapped in irons again."

"Look at me, laddie," Angus implored. "Twas risky enough comin' 'ere 'n' bribing a duke's sister, but noo anither body kens, 'n' it wilnae be lang afore that secret is freely flowing. It's over…for noo. We'll lea, 'n' then…find some ither wey ta git th' information ye seek."

"We."

Angus cocked his head.

"Dinnae ye mean, th' information *we* seek."

His uncle paled, and then all the color came flooding back to the roots of his fiery orange here.

"*O' course* ah referred to both of us, laddie," he whispered, his voice stricken. "Ah'm joost tryin' tah protect ye, lad." Pain bled from his godfather's rheumy eyes. "Ah always tried to protect ye… even then."

Hamish's chest wrenched. "Ah ken that," he said hoarsely. "Ah do."

"Promise me we'll go, afore tis ta late 'n' thay pairt us, this time forever." Tears filled Angus's eyes; great, big wells of misery that hadn't even been there when Hamish's brother and father had been hanged as traitors.

"Ah promise ah will not let that happen. Not again."

An intense and obvious relief filled Angus's eyes. "Ye wur always a clever laddie." He slapped Hamish on the back.

After his uncle took his leave, Hamish ran the back of his hand across his brow. Everything logical and reasonable within him said his uncle was unfailingly right. Although Hamish knew Beatrice had been well-meaning in her intentions and he trusted her implicitly, he couldn't say the same with absolute certainty for her kin.

Remaining now, with his intentions known by the duchess, and more than likely the lady's husband, he risked everything…all over again.

"You look like hell."

Hamish glanced up. "Burgess," he said tiredly.

"I came across your uncle. He was smiling his first smile since he learned of your efforts to flesh out your betrayers. I take it we're leaving?"

Aye, because Angus had been clear from the onset exactly what he thought about the plan Hamish concocted, and also his longing to be as far away from London, and as near the Highlands, as possible.

"Aye." Hamish went on to explain the reason for their impending flight.

"And you intend to what? Just leave the lady in the lurch knowing precisely how she will be dragged through the gossip pages and shamed for your defections."

A vise tightened about his heart. He couldn't think about that, because the thought of her, the proud, spirited lady facing down this latest humiliation, this time, as a result of Hamish, left him hollow inside.

Burgess wasn't done with him. "As it is, the gossip columns have already noted the once devoted Lord H has gone days now without sending notes or flowers or paying a visit to a certain Lady B."

Rage brought Hamish's hands curling into fists. *Ye are the one responsible for the pain she now suffers.* Being split in two by the Campbell claymore that'd once hung in the Great Hall of Hamish's familial home, wouldn't have hurt more than this.

But it didn't change anything. They still needed to be clear of this place…for now.

Hamish flexed his fingers. "The gossip pages are shite."

"Ah, yes," his friend said sardonically. "I'm sure that will bring great solace to the lady—now an object of ridicule—being splashed all over the front pages."

Proud, strong, and courageous as the lass was, she'd hold her head up high through this latest scandal. But Hamish knew Beatrice and knew that protective exterior would conceal a wealth of hurt and humiliation.

He couldn't think of her that way. It would break Hamish… and his resolve to leave.

"Do you know what I think?"

A friendship forged from a shared hell left them with the ability to say anything to the other…whether the other party wished to hear it or not.

"That appears to be th' question of th' night," he muttered. "Ah suspect ye'll tell me."

"From the start, the lady has conducted herself with honor and shown you far more generosity than any other woman would. By rights, she should have turned you over to her brother, the duke, and let him ensure your silence about those letters and put an end to your mad idea that she help you flesh out the ones who wronged you. But she didn't. She secured your entry into households of the men whose names you supplied her with."

Every statement was an arrow that struck, hitting him in various parts of the chest, with those truths.

But Burgess wasn't done. "Yes, she spoke to her sister-in-law about the things you've shared with her. She confided in her, just as you confided in me and Angus. Yet, you'd deny her a confidante in whom to discuss circumstances that are not yours alone; circumstances that, because of her arrangement with you, very much affect her, too."

The remaining remnants of his frustration and anger with Beatrice melted away, to be replaced by more of that awful guilt which, since their last meeting, had built inside, and now threatened to overwhelm him.

"But I don't believe that is why you're really leaving Lady Beatrice in the lurch. I believe you're running because you are afraid, but it isn't of being carted off to prison again you fear. Not really…but rather everything the lady makes you feel."

A denial sprung to his lips, along with a curse to tell th' other man to mind his bluidy business; to tell him pointedly he dinnae ken a damned thing.

Only…

Hamish froze.

His heart knocked against his ribcage. "Och, hell," he whispered.

Ah love her.

It was why he'd not had a sense of urgency to gain entry into those households and had, instead, relished each day where he and Beatrice would meet. It's why he'd not balked at entering ballrooms or attending formal events because doing so meant she'd be there, and when she was there, he remembered what it was to smile and laugh and live not in the misery of the past, but in the joyous present with her.

After the spring of 1820, falling in love, and enjoying a blessed union like his own ma and da had was a fate and future Hamish hadn't envisioned for himself. Ladies didn't wed convicted felons, with the sin of treason stamped upon their sullied names.

Now, Burgess had forced Hamish to confront his own cowardice, and that which had allowed Ole Angus to convince him to head for the hills—he…loved Beatrice Dennington.

Hamish briefly closed his eyes. "Damn ye, Burgess."

His friend grinned. "Finish the thought, Hamish."

"Damn ye for being right," Hamish mumbled.

Burgess swept a flourishing brow.

"It doesna, however, change anything."

Burgess quirked a brow. "This I have to hear."

"The lass is the sister of a duke. Ah've only an empty, run-down keep with abandoned lands to my name."

"Lands which can be improved and prosperous again, slowly and over time."

"A name that carries with it a disgraced legacy—"

"A legacy that is and was false," Burgess persisted relentlessly.

"Even if ah manage to clear th' Campbell name, it willnae change th' world's perception of me and any woman ah take as my wife, and bairns ah may have will wear th' same mark of shame."

"Why don't you allow the lady to decide for herself whether any of that matters?"

"And ye call me the obstinate one." Hamish gnashed his jaw. "It matters to me."

Burgess inclined his head. "I'm sure the lady will appreciate very much that her opinion matters not at all." He thumped Hamish hard between the shoulder blades. "Pride is a lonely bedfellow, my friend. Your Scottish stubbornness kept you alive in Australia, but it will kill your happiness here in England."

Nay, his sweet Bea would detest that with every fiber of her being. Beatrice who yearned for some control, and who'd asked Hamish to be her partner in life, would only feel fury at Hamish's high-handedness.

Burgess spoke in solemn tones. "In all the years I've known you, Hamish, I didn't know you to smile, not even once. Until you came here and met Lady Beatrice, and, I can say with absolute certainty, if you leave without finding out if she loves you in return, then you'll always wonder and always regret."

What a bluidy fool he'd been. Och, he was as quick-tempered and bullheaded as th' lass said.

Hamish needed to see her. Now. He dragged an uneven hand through his hair. "Ah dinnae ken where the lass is this—"

"If you were looking to see her this night, The Duke and Duchess of Bentley are hosting a ball."

Bluidy hell. Hamish didn't have connections—

"Fortunate for *you* my late Aunt Araminta was best friends with the duchess." Burgess lifted a blond eyebrow. "How soon can you be ready?"

Grabbing Burgess by the shoulders, Hamish planted a kiss on the other man's cheek, and then thundering for a horse, he bolted upstairs.

CHAPTER 14

My dearest Hamish,

As a girl, I had many governesses. Each woman believed a duke would want his daughter to be instructed by stern, unbending governesses, who didn't allow his daughter any frivolity or joy. I excelled at running each of those women off. Until eventually, a kindly, warm-hearted woman who respected me and supported and nurtured my interests and passions. So many times since I made my Come Out, I've wanted to dredge up my girlhood antics of long ago and send my fortune-hunting, power-seeking suitors off the same way.

Lovingly Yours,
Beatrice

FROM THE MOMENT BEATRICE HAD arrived that evening with Helena, at Lord and Lady Roxburghe's dinner party, every person present had stared.

All twenty-one guests gawked at Beatrice.

And she…at the clocks: first the ornate bronze Louis XV cartel clock fixed, peculiarly but conveniently above the buffet, and directly across from where Beatrice sat. And then the pretty, painted Mora clock in the parlor where all the ladies assembled after dinner adjourned.

While the eleven women present laughed and talked and whispered, Beatrice crossed the room, and stopped before the Gustavian-style clock. Her eyes went, not to the idyllic painted floral details upon the white birch but rather to the Arabic numerals.

Six minutes after ten o'clock.

Blindly, she stretched a hand up and touched her finger to the smaller minute hand of the clock.

In my da's case 'twas nine minutes…Fur my brother, my big brother who'd been a hero ta me as a laddie, it teuk him fourteen minutes because he didna wanna die. He'd so much life to l-live…

Beatrice closed her eyes.

Until she was an old, lonely aunt, who dangled her brother's grandbabies upon her knee, she'd forever recall the torment and misery that had contorted Hamish's features. And she would forever regret that she hadn't been enough for him.

Out of the corner of Beatrice's eye, she spied Helena's approach.

"I find myself counting down to the end, too," her sister-in-law whispered, teasingly. "But perhaps we might be a touch more discreet."

Beatrice smiled.

Or she tried to.

Her muscles, however, moved awkwardly in something that felt more like a grimace. She was never going to smile again.

"I confess," Helena said quietly. "I'd thought Lord Hamish would be here tonight."

Because Helena knew the names of the suspects, she'd expected that too, despite his absence these past several days, he'd come to the baron's, if for the sole reason of searching for potential evidence.

"No. I…suspected he'd not be," she said softly. She'd, however, hoped.

Even though she'd laid her very heart and soul bare before him, and he'd rejected those parts she'd so once closely protected, Beatrice had wanted him to attend. Not because of her, but because she knew how important it was for Hamish to have the answers he'd come to London in search of.

Beatrice felt Helena's eyes on her. She knew her sister-in-law wouldn't be content with just those handful of words to her earlier statement. It was best to simply say it, so Helena didn't ask questions, and in telling Helena here, Beatrice would be spared from detailed probing.

"We…Hamish and I ended our relationship." *How is my voice so steady?* And how did just speaking that into existence make her want to curl up in a corner and weep like a hurt babe?

"I take it he was not receptive to what you and I previously spoke about."

"…Ah never asked ye to help me find justice, Beatrice, Ah wanted nothing more from ye than tah gain m' entry into th' households of th' suspects…"

"No. He was decidedly not."—Beatrice cursed the tears that welled in her eyes.—"He qu-quite despises me."

Funny, to be seen crying at a *ton* event would lend fodder for the gossips for Seasons to come, and yet, Beatrice couldn't even summon the energy to care.

Helena scoffed. "I do not believe that. That man is in love with you."

Beatrice laughed. She couldn't help it. Nor was that startled expression of mirth filled with bitterness, but rather surprise.

Helena looped her arm through Beatrice's. "Good," her sister-in-law murmured. "More of that." She gave Beatrice a little squeeze and quietly continued. "Beatrice, I've lived on the streets and worked in a gaming hell. I've taken part in more *ton* events, than I care to think of. I've rubbed elbows with lords of every rank. I've witnessed all manner of men. Most bad. Many greedy. Some good," she allowed. "A few great. I'd be hard-pressed to name a single one amongst the hundreds and hundreds who'd have taken your place at the front of Lady Redbrooke's music room and sing in your stead."

Beatrice started.

"The tale of that romantic gesture was all anyone at any event would speak of."

"That was the plan," she said, that bitterness creeping back in, after all. "It was a perfect part of the ruse." They'd convinced Polite Society of their love. "The only reason he sang was—

"He didn't *have* to play that instrument and sing to further perpetuate your ruse, and I think, somewhere inside, you know as much."

Beatrice's heart quickened, flaring on a desperate wave of hope. "Perhaps," Beatrice said non-committal.

Helena's eyes twinkled. "The truth is, Beatrice, it is usually hardest for those whose hearts are engaged. It is everyone around us who tend to see first, that which is right in front of our eyes." Her sister-in-law again hugged her arm. "I know this has been a lot. Perhaps it would be best if we took our leave before Baroness Roxburghe's daughters begin their recital."

"I...do not wish to leave." She couldn't. Hamish might not have taken advantage of the opportunity to get inside the baron's residence, but that didn't mean Beatrice intended to let it slip from her grasp.

"Are you certain?" Helena leaned in and whispered in her ear. "Because I trust it would be a good deal easier to *slip off* while the rest of the guests gather for the performance."

Beatrice went still. Was her sister-in-law suggesting—?

"I know why we are here," Helena spoke in such hushed tones, Beatrice barely detected.

"You do?"

Helena gave her a wry look. "Beatrice," she admonished. "Of course, I do." A mischievous glimmer twinkled in her sister-in-law's eyes. "Why do you think I insisted Robert remain home while I accompany you?"

And the fact Robert hadn't joined them at the baron's indicated Helena had kept the promise she'd made Beatrice.

For the first time since Hamish's rejection, Beatrice's lips formed a slow, wide smile.

They made their excuses, with Helena pleading a megrim. The moment they took their leave of the other women in the parlor, Beatrice and Helena continued arm and arm down the baron's wide, high-ceilinged, and brightly lit corridors.

"The baron's office is located on the next floor. We'll use the servant's entrance to access it."

Beatrice stitched her eyebrows into a line.

"I made sure to put out inquiries about the layout of the baron's household," Helena explained.

Admiration for the other woman's skill and foresight filled Beatrice. "You are *vastly* better at this than me," she breathed.

Helena patted the top of Beatrice's hand, still looped through her arm. "Again, I've had entirely too much experience."

As they walked, Helena gestured to one of the bronze hunting horns wall lamps lining the corridor. Anyone who may have observed them in that moment would have taken Beatrice and Helena as two ladies admiring their hostess's décor.

"Less lighting is always better," her voice muted, Helena imparted that guidance the way a governess might instruct a lady on the proper way to hold a fork. "However, one is left to do the best one can with the given circumstances."

They reached a small, less conspicuous door, and Helena hastily opened the panel. "When we climb the stairs, we must do so slowly and carefully so as to not cause the wood to groan."

Beatrice hurried in, with her sister-in-law following behind her. The moment Helena brought the panel silently shut, the cramped space was instantly doused in darkness. In a bid to bring her vision back into focus, Beatrice blinked furiously.

Helena touched a fingertip to her lips. "This way," she mouthed.

With her sister-in-law's instructions fresh in her mind, Beatrice climbed the narrow, unimposing steps with infinite slowness. When they reached the next landing, Helena cracked the door a fraction and ducked her head out. She glanced up and down the second-floor hall, then silently motioned for Beatrice to follow.

"That is it," Helena murmured while pointing to the door in question. "The baron's office. I'll remain here while you conduct your search. If at any point, anyone is coming, and we face discovery, I'll knock once if you're to exit left when you leave the room, and twice if you are to go right."

"Where will you be?"

Helena pointed, and Beatrice followed the tip of her sister-in-law's finger.

"Should I be discovered, coming out of the closet with a commode offers a perfect, if embarrassing explanation as to my presence. If at any point, I hear anyone approaching, I will be sure to loudly exit the closet, and engage whomever it is that comes upon us."

Helena had truly thought of everything.

Emotion threatened to overwhelm her. "Helena," she said, her voice thick. "I cannot—"

"If you say 'thank me', I shall never forgive you." She gave Beatrice a gentle push. "Now, go. Getting in quickly and getting out even faster is another very important skill."

With that guidance fresh in her mind, Beatrice let herself inside. Unlike the corridors which had been bathed in candlelight, the baron's office was pitched black, without a single, lit, wax taper. As she hurried over to Baron Roxburghe's mahogany kneehole desk, she recalled her and Hamish's search of Lord Shaftesbury's.

…Search for anythin' just prior…any noticeable differences in Shaftebury's finances afore the radical rising and then after the unrest was crushed. Search for any transactions he had with Scottish gentlemen…

She reached for the center drawer and then stopped.

Some ten years ago, it was more likely the ledgers she sought, ones that might have the information she searched for, wouldn't be closest in reach to where the desk's occupant sat.

Dropping onto her knees, she tugged out the left bottom drawer. The instant it opened, papers—some wrinkled, some not—spilled over the side like the pages had been constrained so long, they now surged for freedom.

Beatrice wrinkled her nose. Sloppy, and filled to overflowing, the baron could have learned a thing or two from Lord Shaftesbury's meticulous storage and filing system.

With a sigh, she set to work pulling out page after page and combing through them for dates and any other information that might put them in the timeframe of the rebellion.

"Getting in quickly and getting out even faster is another very important skill."

How much more efficient it'd been when she and Hamish worked side-by-side together, at Lord Shaftesbury's office.

At last, Beatrice finished rummaging through all the contents, she sat back on her heels.

Nothing.

Crawling over to the other bottom drawer, she made to tug it out…and stopped. Her heart thumped in anticipation. When she'd done her cursory assessment of the kneehole desk, she'd failed to note the small lock which had been affixed to this particular panel.

Her heart thumped wildly.

Immediately removing one of the gardenia hair combs from her hair, Beatrice bent the tooth on the end so it jutted out from the rest.

Then, as Helena had taught Beatrice to do some years ago when she'd shown her how to pick a lock, Beatrice inserted the sharp, pointed end into the small keyhole.

Click.

Hurriedly setting aside her favorite piece, Beatrice pulled the drawer open. Though disarrayed like the other one she'd just scoured, there was more of a measured sloppiness to this particular drawer. It was as if the top layer of pages and papers strewn over the others had been done with deliberateness.

Beatrice sifted past those notes and reached inside deeper. Her fingers collided with a book. She pulled the small leather ledger free and proceeded to leaf through the pages. All the while, she skimmed the columns for any identifying information about the timeframe.

"The first week of April, 1820 is when it began…" Hamish's voice rose up from the past to remind her.

Giving up the slow, page-by-page examination, Beatrice fanned through the ledger. Names and dates whirred past.

Beatrice stopped. Heart hammering, she hastily flipped back through the book.

And then she found it.

Beatrice stared at the inked dates; her gaze locked in one column.

> *"… 'Twas th' twelv'f o' May when ah wis shackled 'n' dragged aboard a prison hulk in chains. My brother would hae bin twenty-four that day… Instead, it marked th' day ah died completely inside…"*

12th of May, 1820.

Transfer of Leith Hall in the village of Stonehaven, and one thousand pounds paid to…

Beatrice sucked in a breath.

Oh, God.

It was here, inked in pen; the betrayal that had shattered Hamish and his family.

Her hands trembling, Beatrice touched a fingertip to the transaction which had forever changed the course of Hamish's life. Whom would he have been had men that day not valued greed more than human life?

How much time he'd lost.

How much *everything* he'd lost.

She wanted to toss her head back and rail at the unjustness of it all. From the moment she'd learned Hamish intended to duel the ones who'd wronged him, she'd wanted to stop him. She'd wanted him to find another way, *any* other way so that he wouldn't risk his life, either dying by a bullet or by hanging for killing a man in a duel.

But this information? He needed to see. He deserved to, at last, have answers to the questions that haunted him…even if he'd be haunted all the more for knowing.

"Tell me, my dear, have you found what it was you were looking for?"

Startled by that cheer-filled query, Beatrice gasped, and the force of its fall sent the pages tearing.

She peaked her head over the top of the desk.

Her heart and belly both somersaulted in opposite directions.

Her host, Baron Roxburghe, small and rotund, with cherry-red cheeks and a confusingly generous smile stared back.

Curling her hands, she did what any lady in her position would do—she sailed to her feet and opted for flattery and feigned flightiness.

"Lord Roxburghe!" she greeted him like he was an old friend, and not the one who'd perpetrated the crimes against Hamish and his kin. "I heard you have the most wondrous poetry collection," she hastened over. "And," she said in a noisy whisper, "that you're skilled in penning verse, too."

Clutching at his lapels, the baron preened under her praise. "My reputation does precede me."

Fortunately, it did, and she gave silent thanks for having the foresight to find out whatever she could about the three suspects on Hamish's list.

"If you'd wished to see my work, my dear, you needn't have gone picking my lock and rummaging through my desk drawer."

Beatrice stilled.

The baron's smile remained affixed to his plump face.

"See, I *may* have been inclined to believe you had it not been for the warning I received about your intentions, my dear."

A hulking figure stepped out of the shadows. Only, there was something almost jovial about the bright-haired stranger. In fact, had she not herself read the crimes spelled out in the baron's books, Beatrice would have taken *both* smiling fellows for kindly ones.

Instead, she took a reflexive step away from both.

Only, there was nowhere to go. She knew it. *They* knew it.

"You see, Lady Beatrice, I've established quite a comfortable life for myself here in London. I'm respected and influential. I've power in Parliament. I'd not have you upsetting any of that."

Giving up all earlier pretenses, Beatrice glared at the baron, making no further attempt to hide the hatred she felt for this man.

"You have your comfortable life because you lied, stole, and murdered for it," she said coldly.

As if she'd dealt him the greatest affront, the baron drew back. "I didn't murder anyone, my dear," he said, pressing a hand to his heart as if appalled she'd so much as accuse him of such a heinous charge. "I merely gave them suspects, and judgments were made by English courts."

This is why Hamish laughed over her faith in the English legal system. "Those courts were corrupt."

Baron Roxburghe dusted his immaculate white evening gloves together. "Perhaps," he allowed. "But they are the foundation of our legal system, and no one, absolutely *no one* will question the rulings against those men, without proof."

Reflexively, Beatrice balled her hands more tightly.

"It really is unfortunate it must be this way," he continued. "Though, with the humiliation you've endured, and this latest rejection?" He made a clucking sound with his tongue. "Perhaps it is for the best."

The baron didn't explicitly say what fate awaited her…but he didn't need to. She heard it in the finality of his cryptic musings. Dread spiraling through her, Beatrice stared past her host, and to the doorway out. Silently, desperately she willed Helena to enter.

Unless… they'd found Helena and even now Beatrice's sister-in-law, Robert's wife lay somewhere…

This is my fault. I put her in this situation. Helena could even now be dead, and Robert a widower, and her children motherless…

Beatrice struggled to breathe.

Stop!

Panic would help neither Helena nor Beatrice. "What will you do with me?" she managed to ask.

How did that question come out so evenly?

The baron's gleaming, white-toothed smile widened. "Do not make me say it, dear. I think you know how this must end for my sake. As a poet, I don't like speaking about icky business. Now, I believe we've said all there is to say. Mr. Campbell will…escort you." The man gestured, and his right-hand accomplice strode with smooth, quick strides for someone of his sheer size.

He reached for her, and she jerked away from his touch. "Do not," she said, glaring at him.

"The world will know what you did. Eventually, the truth will win out. It always does."

"Ah, how refreshingly innocent of you, but, my dear, that isn't ever the case. Not truly. Greed wins out. Greed and power, and with you gone, why there's no one capable of learning anything about that day."

"It wasn't a day," she spat. "Men," Hamish and his kin, "spent time in prison, and were put through false trials, and hanged, and then others tried and shipped off, suffering *years* because of you!" Beatrice turned her hate-filled stare on Lord Roxburghe's still-silent partner. "And because of you."

And because she'd gone and gotten herself caught, Hamish would never know, and she'd never again see him. She loved him and she knew he didn't love her in return but loving someone wasn't about reciprocity.

Tears formed in her eyes, and she blinked angrily.

His other betrayer grabbed Beatrice by her upper arm and, in a punishing hold, steered her toward the same side door they'd used to surprise her, and ushered her through a winding series of dark corridors to meet whatever dark fate they'd planned for her.

She hardened her jaw.

The hell they would. Resolve filled her. She'd not have her life cut short by the same men who'd brought so much suffering to Hamish.

A short while later, she was shuttled into one of the baron's black lacquer carriages…and plotting her escape.

CHAPTER 15

My dearest Bea,

When I was a lad, I hated dance lessons. My mum would laugh and insist there'd come a time I fell so in love, I'd long for the opportunities to dance just so that I could hold my sweetheart close. I didn't believe her…until I met you.

Lovingly Yours,
Hamish

HAMISH AND BURGESS STRODE SWIFTLY down the halls of their host's residence.

The lass wasn't in attendance at the Duke and Duchess of Bentley's ball.

As Burgess had promised, Beatrice was supposed to be a guest, but the lady had never arrived, and had instead, along with her sister-in-law, sent their regrets last minute.

Could anyone blame Beatrice for not showing? She'd found herself the object of ridicule and scorn…

Because of me.

The muscles of his stomach seized viciously, and he welcomed that slight, but deserved pain. From the onset, she should have by all rights, had her brother haul Hamish off, for having dared to enlist her in his scheme of revenge. But she hadn't. She'd not doubted the veracity of his claims nor his and his family's innocence. And how had he repaid her faith? By spurning her love and throwing her to the lions of English High Society.

Brushing past the butler hurrying to open the door for Hamish and Burgess, Hamish threw the door open, and took the steps sideways, by twos.

"I spoke to the Duchess of Bentley," Burgess said, the moment they were outside. "I inquired about other events being hosted this evening where the lady might be.

"The lass willnae be at any event," Hamish said, as they went to collect their reins from the two lads watching after their mounts. Beatrice despised *ton* events and would hate them all the more now that she was the talk of them.

With a word of thanks to the lads, Burgess handed them several coins.

Hamish made to swing up onto his mount.

"Lord Roxburghe and his wife are of a sudden, hosting a dinner party this evening."

Hamish froze.

There. The lass *would* go there. His heart thudded dully against the walls of his chest.

Fear left an acrid taste in his mouth, bitter like vinegar, hot like fire.

Nay. The last he'd been with Beatrice, he'd been a bluidy bastard. He'd said all number of hateful, hurtful things to the lass. Why would she go despite all that, and put herself in danger fur him?

Of their own volition, Hamish's eyes slid shut.

Because it is Bea. That tis why. She'd go because the lass was loyal and daring, courageous, and honorable.

Cursing, Hamish climbed into his seat, and kicked his horse into a break-neck gallop, taking the mount up onto the pavement to pass too-slow moving carriages.

Burgess followed in close pursuit.

Shouts from angry drivers and footmen followed in their wake. Those cries, however, combined with the pounding of his horse's hooves, came muffled in his ears.

She'd be all right. She had to be. And when he had her in his arms and saw with his own eyes that she was unharmed, he'd beg her forgiveness, and tell her he'd been the biggest fool, and tell her he loved her, and that if she was willing to take a poor Scot with little more than a keep falling down around his ears, then he was hers. And he'd spend the rest of his days attempting to make himself worthy of her love.

Emotion threatened to consume him; it formed a ball in his throat and choked him with a misery of his own making. He'd thought there was nothing more the world could take from him. He'd believed he'd already lost it all.

But he'd been wrong.

He'd manage to climb back from the grief and despair of losing his da and brother and find a way to make it through each day. But if something happened to Beatrice, if she—

His mind balked, and he didn't allow himself to complete that silent thought. Hamish couldn't go on living in a world that she wasn't in.

I love you. I love you. I love you…

To keep from going mad, he repeated that vow over and over in his mind.

Why was it taking so long to reach her? Why?

Hamish came out of his saddle and tilted forward to urge greater speed from Domino, and the glorious stallion reveled in that freedom.

The baron's Mayfair residence appeared just in the distance. The crystal panes of the majestic brick townhouse, covered in ivy and erected behind a gleaming iron fence, were awash in candlelight. The carriages of the baron's guests lined the way.

Hamish dismounted, and even as Burgess collected his reins from him, Hamish was searching those rows of empty conveyances for a familiar seal.

And then he saw it. The Duke of Somerset's seal, etched upon the door.

She *was* here.

Hamish took off running.

Logic said a gentleman wouldn't commit murder, and certainly not in the midst of a formal gathering he hosted. Life's lessons he'd received, however, had taught him there was no limit to man's evil.

His chest ached and his breath came ragged.

A hand caught him by the shoulder and gripped Hamish hard enough to slow him.

Half-mad, crazed as he'd been when he'd watched hopelessly while his da and Finlay were dragged from the Campbell keep, he fought to free his arm.

"Hamish. *Hamish*," Burgess repeated more firmly, and the sound of his friend's voice managed to pull him back from the precipice of dread. "What are you thinking to do? Storm inside?"

"Yes." That was precisely what he intended to do.

Burgess blocked his path.

"Get th' bluidy hell out of my way."

"On the unlikely chance the lady has found herself in trouble, do you truly believe giving yourself away like this, is the way to help her?"

They'd both relied on stealth and clear heads enough in prison that the lesson had been ingrained into them. That'd been before, however. When the only threat had been beatings and isolation and being starved of rations.

This was Beatrice's life.

"Listen, I am not saying *not* to enter," his friend said, as one of Baron Roxburghe's guests took their leave and the slow clip-clop of the team's hooves echoed in the night. "I am merely saying you need to have your wits about you."

His wits about him? When Beatrice was inside, and knowing the lass as he did, certainly sneaking off and going through her host's private papers? His friend charged him with an impossible feat.

Hamish looked away…when his gaze snagged on the passing conveyance.

He froze.

Upon his return from Australia, he'd used every opportunity to discover what he could about the three suspects given him by the late Lady Araminta. He knew the clubs they belonged to. The spirits they preferred. The vices they possessed.

And the seals to their revered, noble names.

As that carriage continued along, Hamish followed it with his gaze.

"Roxburghe's seal," he whispered.

His friend stared at him questioningly. "Campbell?"

"Tis Roxburghe's carriage," he said, and Burgess followed Hamish's fixed gaze to that conveyance in question. "Why would Roxburghe be departing from an event hosted in his own home?"

They looked at one another, and then, as one, Hamish and Burgess scrambled onto their horses. Back long, eyes forward, and knees close, Hamish galloped after the carriage. He and Burgess overtook the team in a moment; both men drew their mounts in front of the carriage, heading it off.

Roxburghe's driver drew on the reins. "What is the meaning of this?" the liveried servant shouted.

Ignoring him, Hamish jumped down from his horse and sprinted the remaining way to the carriage. Fishing the pistol out from under his jacket, with his other hand, Hamish yanked the door open…and froze.

"Beatrice?" He lowered his gun.

"Hamish," Beatrice whispered.

She is safe. She is here. She is with me. The voice inside his mind reminded Hamish of that, over and over.

Relief so great threatened to bring him to his knees.

"Aye, lass," he said hoarsely. "'Tis ah."

The shock and relief at finding her here faded, and he shifted the head of his pistol to the man seated opposite her.

Confusion knocked Hamish briefly off balance. The gun wavered in his hand.

"*Angus*?"

His uncle smiled as if they met at Campbell keep restored to its former glory, and not the carriage of a man suspected of destroying their family.

"Hullo, laddie! Mah timing is great isnae? Ah ken ye had nah managed to search the baron's 'n' came to see to it myself. Ah dinnae find the information we sought but did manage tah come tah the lass's rescue. Hid 'n' the baron's carriage, ah did, 'n' waited until one of the Sassenach's servants stuffed her inside. None too gentle they were with her, either." Angus turned that big smile on

Beatrice. "Isnae that right, lassie?"

Still flummoxed at finding Angus here, Hamish returned his gaze to Beatrice.

Wan, she sat there, motionless.

Hamish sharpened his gaze on her. Never, in all the time he'd known Beatrice, not even when he'd taken her by surprise at her sister-in-law's gathering, had she demonstrated the fear she did now.

Hamish lowered his weapon. "Lass?"

She hesitated and then gave a warbly nod. "Yes. The baron had a pistol trained at my chest, and *Angus*," she gestured to Angus's left hand, "intervened."

Hamish caught the flash of silver from the gun his uncle held close to his side—a weapon fixed on Beatrice.

In an instant, Angus's smile vanished.

"Stop there, lad," he said, with an icy cold Hamish had never before heard from his godfather.

But then, had he ever really known the monster before him?

"He betrayed you, Hamish," Beatrice said in a rush.

"Ah ken, lass. Ah ken."

Beatrice continued talking, the words tumbling quickly from her lips. "I have a page from the baron's records. Angus, he received property and money and—"

Angus drew back the hammer on his gun. "Shut yer mouth, lassie. Nah a wird more." He cast a glance at Hamish. "From either of ye. Drop yer weapon, lad."

"Don't do it!" Beatrice cried.

"Ah said nah another wird," Angus blustered, rage deepened the ruddy flush on his cheeks.

Dread briefly paralyzed Hamish. "Ah'm putting it down," he spoke in soothing tones. "Just dinnae hurt her." With slow, deliberate movements, he lowered his gun and lay it at his feet.

Angus grunted. "Ye always were a clever lad."

Funny, this had been the second time his godfather had directed that praise his way.

"Not so clever, as to see what ye'd done, and all the signs before me pointing to yer betrayal." God, the signs had been there all along. "Ah, my brother, my father, all were carted off, while ye remained miraculously untouched. Then ye, pressuring me to let th' past go."

At every damned turn, his uncle had sought to dissuade him from finding answers and getting justice.

"Why?" Hamish implored, needing to know. Even as no explanation his uncle gave could justify an evil this great.

"Ah always cam second tah yer da. Everything went tah him. Th' land. Th' wealth." He paused. "Yer ma, who he wooed awa' fae me. Ye wur lik' me, Hamish. Finlay came first, 'n' ye were destined tah end up juist lik' me."

The pain of betrayal ripped a hole through him. Nothing more than greed and jealousy had compelled Angus. 'Twas why, even as Beatrice had revealed, Angus received money and property, he'd chosen to live in the remnants of the Campbell keep he'd desecrated.

How was it possible to have known someone so little?

Hamish growled. "Ye best be prepared to put a bullet in me and kill me dead with it—because if ye harm a hair on th' lass's head, 'n' dinnae finish me off, ah'll snap yer neck the same way Finlay and my da's was."

The gun Angus had trained on Beatrice, wavered.

"It wasnae suppos' tah be tha' way, lad," Angus said, pleadingly. "Ye wur always like a son tah me."

"A son ye loved so much ye had sent to prison," Hamish said frostily. He shook his head in contempt. "Ye were no father to me and ah'm nothing like ye. Do it."

Angus furrowed his brow.

A shadow of movement flickered in the window, and Angus turned.

Burgess, seated astride his mount fired.

The window shattered in an explosion of glass as the blast of the gun thundered, leaving remnants of smoke.

Angus lost his hold on his weapon, and as he clutched at the gaping hole in his arm, he slumped on the bench.

With a cry, Beatrice scrambled for the door.

Hamish was already there, drawing her out, and into his arms.

Even as Burgess moved to snatch Angus from the carriage, Hamish angled his body, shielding Beatrice.

He folded her in his arms.

She is alive. She is safe. She is here. I have her. I have her.

Beatrice wept against his chest.

"Are ye hurt, lass?" he asked hoarsely.

She shook her head.

Frantic for proof of his own, he ran his trembling hands over her, searching Beatrice for injuries, and finding none, he drew her close.

She is safe. She is safe.

And with guests rushing from the baron's household—and all the surrounding homes—to find the cause of the commotion in the streets, Hamish buried a kiss into the top of Beatrice's golden curls.

It was done.

CHAPTER 16

My dearest bonny Bea,

I never in all my life knew there was a woman like you. If I was a poet, I'd tell you how your smile soothed me. How your laughter healed me. How your love saved me. You are all I never knew I wanted, and absolutely everything I ever needed.

Lovingly Yours,
Hamish

ALL THE PAPERS AND ALL the gossip at every breakfast table the following morning was about Beatrice.

Or, that was according to this particular gossip column.

At least, this time they weren't talking about her having been thrown over. Now, they were writing of Hamish's heroic rescue of Beatrice and the grand love that had sent him racing after her.

Seated alone in her family's breakfast room, Beatrice shoved aside the newspaper. But then, the gossips always got it wrong.

Oh, Hamish *had* saved her from certain peril, but he didn't love her. But she wanted him to. She wanted it so badly.

Footfalls sounded in the hall. It'd been inevitable. She'd expected she would have heard those same footfalls long before now. Heaven knew she deserved whatever lecture he'd held off on delivering.

"Beatrice."

As that deep baritone filled the breakfast room, Beatrice forced her gaze up. "Robert."

She dimly registered her brother quietly dismissing the servants. The moment the door closed with a firm click behind the last of the footmen, Robert dragged a chair close and looped his legs out in front of him. Then, clasping his hands across his flat belly, he waited.

In a bid to buy herself more time, coward that she was, Beatrice made herself take a bite of her eggs. The food sat dry and heavy on her tongue, threatening to choke her. Reaching for the small decanter of ratafia, Robert poured a glass, and wordlessly, he pushed it towards her.

Beatrice took the opaque twist glass and drank. When she'd finished, she stared into the caramel-colored contents.

"I am so sorry, Robert," she said, directing that apology at her glass.

"Is that what you think I'm here for?" Robert asked quietly. "To *lecture* you?"

Beatrice forced her gaze up. Her brother appeared wounded like he'd been physically hurt by Beatrice's assumption.

"I am deserving of it, Robert," she said on a rush. "I put Helena in harm's way."

"Helena is a grown woman, who has always made her own choices." His lips quirked in a wry grin. "And, as this case would have it, she chose to get herself locked in a watering closet… which, given I know the outcome and that my wife was completely unharmed, I shall never allow her to live down."

Beatrice managed her first smile that day.

"No, I'm not here to scold you for Helena helping you, and I'd never be so foolish as to try and dictate what my wife should or shouldn't do. Her brothers attempted to keep her shuttered away in the Hell and Sin for her own safety, and, having myself witnessed how *that* worked out for them, know better than to ever try and constrain her."

Helena had met Robert wandering the halls of the private suites and thus had begun their tumultuous, at-first, love affair.

Robert dropped a hand atop hers. "What I am here to say is that you need never feel alone. When you are in trouble, you may rely on my help. When you are sad, know you can cry on my shoulder. I am your big brother."

Tears filled her eyes. "I love you."

"And I you." He patted her hand, and made to rise, but then stopped. "Oh, and there was something else I wished to say…all those suitors who tossed you over? I'm glad they did."

She laughed wryly through her tears. "Thank you, dearest brother."

"What I am saying, Bea… is those men? They were all bloody fools for failing to see the gift you are. The man I'd *hope* you marry will be one who'll see you as the rare diamond you are and who'd see you as I see Helena…my partner in life."

When she'd made her debut, that hope her brother spoke of, had also been the one she'd carried in her heart. And for a fleeting moment, with her pretend suitor come to life in Hamish, she'd believed she might have had it.

Robert nudged her shoulder. "Mayhap Lord Hamish? Eh?"

She swatted at him. "That was a pretend courtship," she reminded him. After her abduction last evening, Beatrice had given Helena permission to share everything with Robert.

"You don't love him, then?"

Oh, God. She bit her lower lip hard. "I love him more than anything." With a love so great, she didn't have the words to fully capture and explain to her brother.

Grunting, Robert stood. "You're wanted in the music room." With that, he took his leave.

Furrowing her brow, Beatrice stared after him, and then slowly came to her feet. She wandered out into the hall and then stopped.

Dropping to a knee, she picked up the flower nearest her fingers. Beatrice looked down the corridor to the long uneven line of gardenias. Her heart beating faster, she slowly stood, and then proceeded to make her way toward the music room; all the while picking up stems of gardenias as she went until her arms were filled to overflowing.

When she reached the entryway, Helena stood in wait. "I'll take these," she whispered, relieving Beatrice of that bouquet, and then, with her eyes twinkling, she cocked her head towards the doorway.

Beatrice stepped inside, and found him in an instant, seated at the pianoforte. She faintly registered Helena closing the door behind them.

The moment Beatrice started forward, Hamish began to play, and it was that song he'd sang at Abigail's, back when they'd been pretending to be in love.

O, my luve is like a red, red rose,
That's newly sprung in June;

A pressure built in her chest. But there was no need for a ruse any longer.

"O, my luve is like a melodie
That's sweetly played in tune."

Why then had he laid a path of gardenias leading to him?

"As fair art thou, my bonnie lass,
So deep in luve am I;"

Why did he sing to her?

"And I will luve thee still, my dear,
till a' the seas gang dry.

And she was too scared to dare hope that it was because…he did.

She reached the side of the pianoforte just as Hamish finished singing.

He stood, but remained behind the oak bench, and it made a small wood barrier between them.

His gaze lingered briefly on the thistle brooch fastened to Beatrice's gown—that gift he'd given her when he'd promised he was a man of his word.

"Beatrice," he murmured, in that deep, lyrical brogue.

"Hamish," she whispered. It was the first time she'd seen him since his uncle had been carted off late last evening. She waited for him to speak.

Then they did at the same time.

"I—"

"Beatrice—"

Beatrice and Hamish stopped.

He waved for her to speak. "Ye first."

"I wanted to say how sorry I am, Hamish. I know how this betrayal has hurt you." And she'd do anything to take that from him. "I've…read," For Hamish hadn't told her the outcome himself, "about your uncle."

He grunted. "Aye, he'll be sentenced for his crimes."

"Yes, charged for theft with violence while the baron escapes with petty larceny and his life spared. These were the injustices you spoke of."

"Ah dinnae come to talk about Roxburghe or Angus," he said quietly. "He was dead to me th' moment ah saw him in that carriage with ye."

He paused, and the muscles of his throat worked. "All ah cared about in that instant, was ye. Ah needed ye to live. Ah needed to ken ye are happy. Ah needed to ask yer forgiveness."

This is why he'd come and strewn flowers and sang that song upon her pianoforte?

Deflated, Beatrice shook her head. "You do not need to—"

"Och, but ah do. From the moment ye came into my life, ye were only goodness and light, and ah didn't ken what to do with that, Beatrice. Ah didn't ken what to do with ye, and how ye made me feel. Because ah was angry and bitter for so long. Ah didn't ken ah had any lightness left within me. But it was there, and ye kindled it like a small ember and kept it alive so that it grew and grew and…and ah want to spend the rest of my days with ye, lass. Even as ah ken ah don't deserve ye. With ye, ah'm happy and ah want to make ye happy as ye make me."

"You already do," she whispered.

"Impossible." Hamish cupped her cheek. "I love ye, Beatrice."

Her heart stopped. The earth and its movement and all movement, along with it.

"What did you say?" she whispered.

"Ah love ye, lass. And ye were right. Ah'm a stubborn Scot, too obstinate for my own good, and ah dinnae deserve ye after th' way ah left ye that day, but ah'm also selfish enough to want ye anyway. My lands and my keep is in disrepair. It will take a good deal of work and time before it—and my crofters—are restored to their former greatness. But my friend who ah told ye about, Burgess, he's offered a loan."

Hamish grimaced.

She knew how difficult it would be for a man as proud as Hamish to take that.

"And ah've accepted his generosity because some clever lass once reminded me how bull-headed ah'm."

"That someone sounds like a most clever someone," Beatrice whispered.

His eyes twinkled at that shared remembrance of words he'd spoken during that beautiful waltz.

"Aye, the most clever."

Hamish held her gaze. "If ye are willing to work beside me, Beatrice, and restore Campbell Keep, ah'll nah let my own pride cost me th' only thing—th' only person—ah ever wanted."

Beatrice bit down hard on her lower lip.

He stepped out from behind the bench, and the wooden legs scraped along the floor. "Marry me, lass."

Through the tears blinding her, Beatrice struggled to see his beloved visage.

"As ye said," Hamish went on gruffly, "we can work together to try and use th' influence we were both born with to make an unjust world, better for th' bairns we one day have." He pressed his right fist to his chest. "And ah will spend my *every* moment dedicated to ye and yer happiness and—"

With a cry, Beatrice launched herself at him.

"Aye," she cried, between her laughter and tears. "Aye, I'll marry you."

Hamish grinned. "Och, that was what ah was *hoping* ye'd say."

As he took her lips in a kiss, Beatrice smiled.

All those years of being courted and passed over had been

because of this. So that fate could bring her together with this man, the most stubborn, wonderful, handsome Scot ever born.

THE END

Also, join Christi Caldwell as she returns to where it all started—the Scandalous Seasons series!

Be swept away in the passion, drama, and splendor of Regency England, where the ballrooms glitter and the dukes are sexy and brooding, and the ladies dare to love.

Enjoyed *Endlessly Courted, Finally Loved*? Be sure and check out the next books coming in the Scandalous Seasons series!

Coming September 2023

Once a Rake, Suddenly a Suitor sees London's most scandalous rogue, Phineas Lesar, the Marquess of Landon falling for the last woman he should…Miss Anwen Kearsley, his best friend's younger sister.

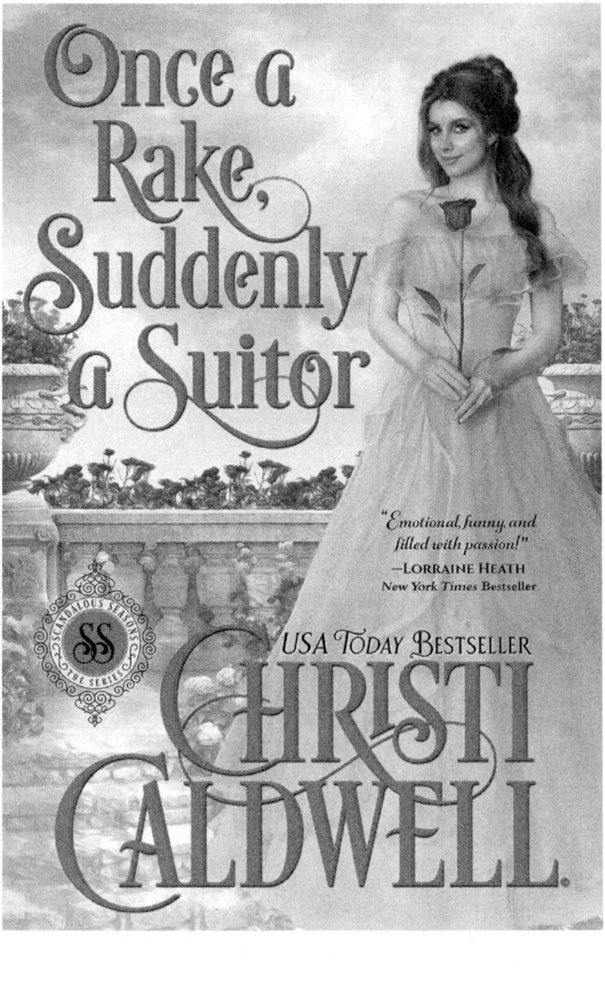

Coming November 2023

Once Upon a Betrothal, brings readers a winter-set romance between former lovers, Mr. Broden Burgess and Miss Harmony Beresford.

OTHER BOOKS IN THE HEART OF A DUKE SERIES BY CHRISTI CALDWELL

TO HOLD A LADY'S SECRET

Book 16 in the "Heart of a Duke" Series

Lady Gillian Farendale is in trouble. Her titled father has dragged her through one London Season after another, until the sheer monotony of the marriage mart and the last vestige of Gillian's once-independent spirit conspire to lead her into a single night of folly. When her adventure goes so very wrong, she has only one old friend to whom she can turn for help.

Colin Lockhart's youthful friendship with Lady Gillian cost him everything, and a duke's by-blow had little enough to start with. He's survived years on London's roughest streets to become a highly successful Bow Street Runner, and his dream of his own inquiry agency is almost within his grasp.

Then Gillian begs him to once again risk angering her powerful father. The ruthless logic of the street tells Colin that he dare not help Gillian, while his tender heart tempts him to once again risk everything for the only woman he'll ever love.

TO TEMPT A SCOUNDREL

Book 15 in the "Heart of a Duke" Series

Never trust a gentleman…

Once before, Lady Alice Winterbourne trusted her heart to an honorable, respectable man… only to be jilted in the scandal of the Season. Longing for an escape from all the whispers and humiliation, Alice eagerly accepts an invitation to her friend's house party. In the country, she hopes to find some peace from the embarrassment left in London… Unfortunately, she finds her former betrothed and his new bride in attendance.

Never love a lady…

Lord Rhys Brookfield has no interest in marriage. Ever. He's worked quite hard at building both his fortune and his reputation as a rogue—and intends to enjoy all that they can offer him. That is if his match-making mother will stop pairing him with prospective brides. When Rhys and Alice meet, sparks flare. But with every new encounter, their first impressions of one another are challenged and an unlikely friendship is forged.

Desperate, Rhys proposes a pretend courtship, one meant to spite Alice's former betrothed and prevent any matchmaking attempts toward Rhys. What neither expects is that a pretense can become so much more. Or that a burning passion can heal… and hurt.

Beguiled by a Baron

Book 14 in the "Heart of a Duke" Series

A Lady with a Secret… Partially deaf, with a birthmark marring her face, Bridget Hamilton is content with her life, even if she's been cast out of her family. But her peaceful existence—expanding her mind with her study of rare books—is threatened with an ultimatum from her evil brother—steal a valuable book or give up her son. Bridget has no choice; her son is her world.

A Lord with a Purpose… Vail Basingstoke, Baron Chilton is known throughout London as the Bastard Baron. After battling at Waterloo, he establishes himself as the foremost dealer in rare books and builds a fortune, determined to never be like the self-serving duke who sired him. He devotes his life to growing his fortune to care for his illegitimate siblings, also fathered by the duke. The chance to sell a highly coveted book for a financial windfall is his only thought.

Two Paths Collide… When Bridget masquerades as the baron's newest housekeeper, he's hopelessly intrigued by her quick wit and her skill with antique tomes. Wary from having his heart broken in the past, it should be easy enough to keep Bridget at arm's length, yet desire for her dogs his steps. As they spend time in each other's company, understanding for life grows as does love, but when Bridget's integrity is called into question, Vail's world is shattered—as is his heart again. Now Bridget and Vail will have to overcome the horrendous secrets and lies between them to grasp a love—and life—together.

To Enchant a Wicked Duke

Book 13 in the "Heart of a Duke" Series

A Devil in Disguise

Years ago, when Nick Tallings, the recent Duke of Huntly, watched his family destroyed at the hands of a merciless nobleman, he vowed revenge. But his efforts had been futile, as his enemy, Lord Rutland is without weakness.

Until now…

With his rival finally happily married, Nick is able to set his ruthless scheme into motion. His plot hinges upon Lord Rutland's innocent, empty-headed sister-in-law, Justina Barrett. Nick will ruin her, marry her, and then leave her brokenhearted.

A Lady Dreaming of Love

From the moment Justina Barrett makes her Come Out, she is labeled a Diamond. Even with her ruthless father determined to sell her off to the highest bidder, Justina never gives up on her hope for a good, honorable gentleman who values her wit more than her looks.

A Not-So-Chance Meeting

Nick's ploy to ensnare Justina falls neatly into place in the streets of London. With each carefully orchestrated encounter, he slips further and further inside the lady's heart, never anticipating that Justina, with her quick wit and strength, will break down his own defenses. As Nick's plans begins to unravel, he's left to determine which is more important—Justina's love or his vow for vengeance. But can Justina ever forgive the duke who deceived her?

One Winter with a Baron
Book 12 in the "Heart of a Duke" Series

A clever spinster:

Content with her spinster lifestyle, Miss Sybil Cunning wants to prove that a future as an unmarried woman is the only life for her. As a bluestocking who values hard, empirical data, Sybil needs help with her research. Nolan Pratt, Baron Webb, one of society's most scandalous rakes, is the perfect gentleman to help her. After all, he inspires fear in proper mothers and desire within their daughters.

A notorious rake:

Society may be aware of Nolan Pratt, Baron's Webb's wicked ways, but what he has carefully hidden is his miserable handling of his family's finances. When Sybil presents him the opportunity to earn much-needed funds, he can't refuse.

A winter to remember:

However, what begins as a business arrangement becomes something more and with every meeting, Sybil slips inside his heart. Can this clever woman look beneath the veneer of a coldhearted rake to see the man Nolan truly is?

To Redeem a Rake

Book 11 in the "Heart of a Duke" Series

He's spent years scandalizing society.

Now, this rake must change his ways.

Society's most infamous scoundrel, Daniel Winterbourne, the Earl of Montfort, has been promised a small fortune if he can relinquish his wayward, carousing lifestyle. And behaving means he must also help find a respectable companion for his youngest sister—someone who will guide her and whom she can emulate. However, Daniel knows no such woman. But when he encounters a childhood friend, Daniel believes she may just be the answer to all of his problems.

Having been secretly humiliated by an unscrupulous blackguard years earlier, Miss Daphne Smith dreams of finding work at Ladies of Hope, an institution that provides an education for disabled women. With her sordid past and a disfigured leg, few opportunities arise for a woman such as she. Knowing Daniel's history, she wishes to avoid him, but working for his sister is exactly the stepping stone she needs.

Their attraction intensifies as Daniel and Daphne grow closer, preparing his sister for the London Season. But Daniel must resist his desire for a woman tarnished by scandal while Daphne is reminded of the boy she once knew. Can society's most notorious rake redeem his reputation and become the man Daphne deserves?

To Woo a Widow

Book 10 in the "Heart of a Duke" Series

They see a brokenhearted widow.

She's far from shattered.

Lady Philippa Winston is never marrying again. After her late husband's cruelty that she kept so well hidden, she has no desire to search for love.

Years ago, Miles Brookfield, the Marquess of Guilford, made a frivolous vow he never thought would come to fruition—he promised to marry his mother's goddaughter if he was unwed by the age of thirty. Now, to his dismay, he's faced with honoring that pledge. But when he encounters the beautiful and intriguing Lady Philippa, Miles knows his true path in life. It's up to him to break down every belief Philippa carries about gentlemen, proving that not only is love real, but that he is the man deserving of her sheltered heart.

Will Philippa let down her guard and allow Miles to woo a widow in desperate need of his love?

The Lure of a Rake
Book 9 in the "Heart of a Duke" Series

A Lady Dreaming of Love

Lady Genevieve Farendale has a scandalous past. Jilted at the altar years earlier and exiled by her family, she's now returned to London to prove she can be a proper lady. Even though she's not given up on the hope of marrying for love, she's wary of trusting again. Then she meets Cedric Falcot, the Marquess of St. Albans whose seductive ways set her heart aflutter. But with her sordid history, Genevieve knows a rake can also easily destroy her.

An Unlikely Pairing

What begins as a chance encounter between Cedric and Genevieve becomes something more. As they continue to meet, passions stir. But with Genevieve's hope for true love, she fears Cedric will be unable to give up his wayward lifestyle. After all, Cedric has spent years protecting his heart, and keeping everyone out. Slowly, she chips away at all the walls he's built, but when he falters, Genevieve can't offer him redemption. Now, it's up to Cedric to prove to Genevieve that the love of a man is far more powerful than the lure of a rake.

To Trust a Rogue

Book 8 in the "Heart of a Duke" Series

A rogue

Marcus, the Viscount Wessex has carefully crafted the image of rogue and charmer for Polite Society. Under that façade, however, dwells a man whose dreams were shattered almost eight years earlier by a young lady who captured his heart, pledged her love, and then left him, with nothing more than a curt note.

A widow

Eight years earlier, faced with no other choice, Mrs. Eleanor Collins, fled London and the only man she ever loved, Marcus, Viscount Wessex. She has now returned to serve as a companion for her elderly aunt with a daughter in tow. Even though they're next door neighbors, there is little reason for her to move in the same circles as Marcus, just in case, she vows to avoid him, for he reminds her of all she lost when she left.

Reunited

As their paths continue to cross, Marcus finds his desire for Eleanor just as strong, but he learned long ago she's not to be trusted. He will offer her a place in his bed, but not anything more. Only, Eleanor has no interest in this new, roguish man. The more time they spend together, the protective wall they've constructed to keep the other out, begin to break. With all the betrayals and secrets between them, Marcus has to open his heart again. And Eleanor must decide if it's ever safe to trust a rogue.

To Wed His Christmas Lady

Book 7 in the "Heart of a Duke" Series

She's longing to be loved:

Lady Cara Falcot has only served one purpose to her loathsome father—to increase his power through a marriage to the future Duke of Billingsley. As such, she's built protective walls about her heart, and presents an icy facade to the world around her. Journeying home from her finishing school for the Christmas holidays, Cara's carriage is stranded during a winter storm. She's forced to tarry at a ramshackle inn, where she immediately antagonizes another patron—William.

He's avoiding his duty in favor of one last adventure:

William Hargrove, the Marquess of Grafton has wanted only one thing in life—to avoid the future match his parents would have him make to a cold, duke's daughter. He's returning home from a blissful eight years of traveling the world to see to his responsibilities. But when a winter storm interrupts his trip and lands him at a falling-down inn, he's forced to share company with a commanding Lady Cara who initially reminds him exactly of the woman he so desperately wants to avoid.

A Christmas snowstorm ushers in the spirit of the season:

At the holiday time, these two people who despise each other due to first perceptions are offered renewed beginnings and fresh starts. As this gruff stranger breaks down the walls she's built about herself, Cara has to determine whether she can truly open her heart to trusting that any man is capable of good and that she herself is capable of love. And William has to set aside all previous thoughts he's carried of the polished ladies like Cara, to be the man to show her that love.

The Heart of a Scoundrel

Book 6 in the "Heart of a Duke" Series

Ruthless, wicked, and dark, the Marquess of Rutland rouses terror in the breast of ladies and nobleman alike. All Edmund wants in life is power. After he was publically humiliated by his one love Lady Margaret, he vowed vengeance, using Margaret's niece, as his pawn. Except, he's thwarted by another, more enticing target—Miss Phoebe Barrett.

Miss Phoebe Barrett knows precisely the shame she's been born to. Because her father is a shocking letch she's learned to form her own opinions on a person's worth. After a chance meeting with the Marquess of Rutland, she is captivated by the mysterious man. He, too, is a victim of society's scorn, but the more encounters she has with Edmund, the more she knows there is powerful depth and emotion to the jaded marquess.

The lady wreaks havoc on Edmund's plans for revenge and he finds he wants Phoebe, at all costs. As she's drawn into the darkness of his world, Phoebe risks being destroyed by Edmund's ruthlessness. And Phoebe who desires love at all costs, has to determine if she can ever truly trust the heart of a scoundrel.

To Love a Lord

Book 5 in the "Heart of a Duke" Series

All she wants is security:

The last place finishing school instructor Mrs. Jane Munroe belongs, is in polite Society. Vowing to never wed, she's been scuttled around from post to post. Now she finds herself in the Marquess of Waverly's household. She's never met a nobleman she liked, and when she meets the pompous, arrogant marquess, she remembers why. But soon, she discovers Gabriel is unlike any gentleman she's ever known.

All he wants is a companion for his sister:

What Gabriel finds himself with instead, is a fiery spirited, bespectacled woman who entices him at every corner and challenges his age-old vow to never trust his heart to a woman. But...there is something suspicious about his sister's companion. And he is determined to find out just what it is.

All they need is each other:

As Gabriel and Jane confront the truth of their feelings, the lies and secrets between them begin to unravel. And Jane is left to decide whether or not it is ever truly safe to love a lord.

Loved By a Duke

Book 4 in the "Heart of a Duke" Series

For ten years, Lady Daisy Meadows has been in love with Auric, the Duke of Crawford. Ever since his gallant rescue years earlier, Daisy knew she was destined to be his Duchess. Unfortunately, Auric sees her as his best friend's sister and nothing more. But perhaps, if she can manage to find the fabled heart of a duke pendant, she will win over the heart of her duke.

Auric, the Duke of Crawford enjoys Daisy's company. The last thing he is interested in however, is pursuing a romance with a woman he's known since she was in leading strings. This season, Daisy is turning up in the oddest places and he cannot help but notice that she is no longer a girl. But Auric wouldn't do something as foolhardy as to fall in love with Daisy. He couldn't. Not with the guilt he carries over his past sins… Not when he has no right to her heart…But perhaps, just perhaps, she can forgive the past and trust that he'd forever cherish her heart—but will she let him?

The Love of a Rogue

Book 3 in the "Heart of a Duke" Series

Lady Imogen Moore hasn't had an easy time of it since she made her Come Out. With her betrothed, a powerful duke breaking it off to wed her sister, she's become the *tons* favorite piece of gossip. Never again wanting to experience the pain of a broken heart, she's resolved to make a match with a polite, respectable gentleman. The last thing she wants is another reckless rogue.

Lord Alex Edgerton has a problem. His brother, tired of Alex's carousing has charged him with chaperoning their remaining, unwed sister about *ton* events. Shopping? No, thank you. Attending the theatre? He'd rather be at Forbidden Pleasures with a scantily clad beauty upon his lap. The task of *chaperone* becomes even more of a bother when his sister drags along her dearest friend, Lady Imogen to social functions. The last thing he wants in his life is a young, innocent English miss.

Except, as Alex and Imogen are thrown together, passions flare and Alex comes to find he not only wants Imogen in his bed, but also in his heart. Yet now he must convince Imogen to risk all, on the heart of a rogue.

More Than a Duke

Book 2 in the "Heart of a Duke" Series

Polite Society doesn't take Lady Anne Adamson seriously. However, Anne isn't just another pretty young miss. When she discovers her father betrayed her mother's love and her family descended into poverty, Anne comes up with a plan to marry a respectable, powerful, and honorable gentleman—a man nothing like her philandering father.

Armed with the heart of a duke pendant, fabled to land the wearer a duke's heart, she decides to enlist the aid of the notorious Harry, 6th Earl of Stanhope. A scoundrel with a scandalous past, he is the last gentleman she'd ever wed…however, his reputation marks him the perfect man to school her in the art of seduction so she might ensnare the illustrious Duke of Crawford.

Harry, the Earl of Stanhope is a jaded, cynical rogue who lives for his own pleasures. Having been thrown over by the only woman he ever loved so she could wed a duke, he's not at all surprised when Lady Anne approaches him with her scheme to capture another duke's affection. He's come to appreciate that all women are in fact greedy, title-grasping, self-indulgent creatures. And with Anne's history of grating on his every last nerve, she is the last woman he'd ever agree to school in the art of seduction. Only his friendship with the lady's sister compels him to help.

What begins as a pretend courtship, born of lessons on seduction, becomes something more leaving Anne to decide if she can give her heart to a reckless rogue, and Harry must decide if he's willing to again trust in a lady's love.

For Love of the Duke

Book 1 in the "Heart of a Duke" Series

After the tragic death of his wife, Jasper, the 8th Duke of Bainbridge buried himself away in the dark cold walls of his home, Castle Blackwood. When he's coaxed out of his self-imposed exile to attend the amusements of the Frost Fair, his life is irrevocably changed by his fateful meeting with Lady Katherine Adamson.

With her tight brown ringlets and silly white-ruffled gowns, Lady Katherine Adamson has found her dance card empty for two Seasons. After her father's passing, Katherine learned the unreliability of men, and is determined to depend on no one, except herself. Until she meets Jasper...

In a desperate bid to avoid a match arranged by her family, Katherine makes the Duke of Bainbridge a shocking proposition—one that he accepts.

Only, as Katherine begins to love Jasper, she finds the arrangement agreed upon is not enough. And Jasper is left to decide if protecting his heart is more important than fighting for Katherine's love.

In Need of a Duke

A Prequel Novella to "The Heart of a Duke" Series

In Need of a Duke: (Author's Note: This is a prequel novella to "The Heart of a Duke" series by Christi Caldwell. It was originally available in "The Heart of a Duke" Collection and is now being published as an individual novella.

It features a new prologue and epilogue.

Years earlier, a gypsy woman passed to Lady Aldora Adamson and her friends a heart pendant that promised them each the heart of a duke.

Now, a young lady, with her family facing ruin and scandal, Lady Aldora doesn't have time for mythical stories about cheap baubles. She needs to save her sisters and brother by marrying a titled gentleman with wealth and power to his name. She sets her bespectacled sights upon the Marquess of St. James.

Turned out by his father after a tragic scandal, Lord Michael Knightly has grown into a powerful, but self-made man. With the whispers and stares that still follow him, he would rather be anywhere but London...

Until he meets Lady Aldora, a young woman who mistakes him for his brother, the Marquess of St. James. The connection between Aldora and Michael is immediate and as they come to know one another, Aldora's feelings for Michael war with her sisterly responsibilities. With her family's dire situation, a man of Michael's scandalous past will never do.

Ultimately, Aldora must choose between her responsibilities as a sister and her love for Michael.

BIOGRAPHY

Christi Caldwell is the *USA Today* bestselling author of the Sinful Brides series and the Heart of a Duke series. She blames novelist Judith McNaught for luring her into the world of historical romance. When Christi was at the University of Connecticut, she began writing her own tales of love—ones where even the most perfect heroes and heroines had imperfections. She learned to enjoy torturing her couples before they earned their well-deserved happily ever after. Christi lives in Charlotte, North Carolina where she spends her time writing, baking, and being a mommy to the most inspiring little boy and empathetic, spirited girls who, with their mischievous twin antics, offer an endless source of story ideas!

Visit www.christicaldwellauthor.com to learn more about what Christi is working on, or join her on Facebook at Christi Caldwell Author, and Twitter @ChristiCaldwell!

Printed in Dunstable, United Kingdom

63869986R00127